IN LIMBO

E.C. Marsh

Dear Dottie!
I hope you enjoy this
book as much as I
enjoyed writing it.
Thanks for the
wonderful support!
Erifilie C. Marsh

AmErica House
Baltimore

First printing

ISBN: 1-58851-584-2
PUBLISHED BY AMERICA HOUSE BOOK PUBLISHERS
www.publishamerica.com
Baltimore

Printed in the United States of America

This is book is dedicated to
three very special people in my life.

My son, Christopher, who never ceased to inspire and motivate me.

Beverly Jean Chamberlain, friend and mentor, who challenged me.

Jennie Wright, dear friend, who tirelessly read and re-read everything I put on paper and encouraged me to keep writing.

My appreciation to my dear friend, Beverly Jean Chamberlain. Without his belief in me, love of the English language and professional writing experience, this book would not be where it is now. He patiently critiqued, edited, made suggestions and corrections. But he also made wonderful coffee and taught me how to fix Eggs Benedict!

Beverly passed away, suddenly and unexpectedly, just a few weeks after he finished editing this book. Bev, you are sorely missed!

Prologue

Nobody should die alone.

The woman, wrapped in a sleeping bag, in the canoe, on a river in the middle of nowhere, was not alone; after all there was the man at the stern working the canoe.

The woman in the sleeping bag felt her muscles twitch. Ever so slightly, but not enough for the man behind her to notice. For a moment she became aware of her surroundings, the sloshing sounds of the water against the metal hull, the movements of the canoe and the crushing pain that seemed to be everywhere in her body.

She tried to think, but couldn't remember her own name. She tried to open her eyes, but everything remained dark. Dark and warm and humid. She felt fear building within her, becoming sheer terror. She tried to free herself from the confines of the sleeping bag, only to find she could not move at all.

The scent of the man drifted past her. She took a deep breath, taking comfort in its familiarity.

What is happening to me, she thought. The thought did not last but a moment. The sounds of her surroundings faded away, to be replaced by the pounding of her heart, then silence.

Chapter 1

I couldn't sleep. I don't know why, at least not precisely. Perhaps the humidity, most certainly the heat!

Sure, we have air conditioning. Who doesn't these days? I, for one, have never been able to figure out how our forefathers managed without AC and in those heavy clothes they wore.

It still felt sticky and hot in the house, and I felt myself adhering to the sheets. Needing to go to the bathroom and being unable to move contributed to my growing discomfort. I slowly tried to extract my leg out from under Tom. He moves in his sleep and can sleep anywhere, anytime and in any position. I don't know how he does it, but that's how he's always been. And I'm sure that's at least one of the things I love about him.

But that didn't help me tonight, right now. Right now I needed to get up and go pee, and then I would need to adjust the AC or something. I slowly pulled my leg out from under Tom and managed to get out of bed without waking him or taking the sheets with me.

Feeling better after the pit stop in the bathroom and a glass of cool water, I opened the French doors leading from the kitchen out to the deck. Glass of water with me, I sat in the porch swing. A whisper of a breeze moved strands of my hair and cooled the sweaty skin on my neck. I inhaled deeply. Aahh... around me the air smelled sweetly of cut grass and damp soil. The moon, almost full, bathed the backyard in a cool, white light. I just sat there; my legs curled up under me, letting the gentle motion slowly rock me. After a while I noticed movement among the bushes planted along the wooden privacy fence and watched a big 'possum amble along, obviously unaware of my presence. I watched as he moved toward our little tool shed and made a mental note to have Tom check and make sure we did not have a family of 'possums residing in the back of it. One year a skunk decided to have her babies in our shed. We couldn't use our backyard for weeks. Even the dogs got sprayed, and it just was a mess. We don't live all that far out of town, but obviously far enough to attract animals.

The possum had disappeared in the area of the shed, and a

whippoorwill started its loud and raucous song. Somewhere, off in the distance, I heard a train whistle and the hooting of an owl. "Never knew the night could be this noisy," I said to myself and got up to go back to bed. In the kitchen a little green fan on top of the refrigerator caught my eye. Ahh, I smiled and brought it along into the bedroom. The fan's humming and the slight breeze helped me relax and soon I felt myself drifting off to sleep.

I woke up to the delicious scent of fresh coffee drifting in from the kitchen. Tom had been up a while and had fixed breakfast. Tom is terrific. He is my husband and I must admit he spoils me rotten. Tom teaches history. He really loves his job and he loves kids. That is so obvious in our daily life. He is very much involved with our son Allen and his Cub Scout Troop. And, lately, Tom has become involved with one of the local Boy Scout Troops as well. He tells me that if we as parents don't take an active role in our children's lives, they will not take an active role in their children's lives and that will ultimately be the end of civilization as we know it. When it comes to kids, Tom gets very passionate; his blue eyes light up and, I swear, become even more intense than they already are.

They also do that when we make love. My Tom is pretty passionate about some things in life!

I felt movement on the bed and slowly opened my eyes, just as Tom handed me a steaming mug and smiled. He knows I wake up slowly, especially on weekends. I like a cup of coffee, with something sweet in it; no questions, no need for conversation, just a few minutes of quiet to make the transition from blissful sleep to everyday humdrum. And usually, right along with my cup of coffee, I take a shower. It feels good to step out of the shower, wipe the steam off the mirror, let those last sips of coffee warm my mouth, and then face the day.

Well, I wasn't about to change my routine this morning. I was still shampooing my hair when Tom stuck his head in the door.

"Sam and Marty just pulled up. We'll finish loading and we'll have some coffee until you're ready."

"Okay." I yelled over the sound of the shower, not sure if he had really said what I thought I heard. It really didn't matter. I wasn't awake enough to absorb it, and I was preoccupied trying to figure out why I would bother to shampoo my hair when in a couple of hours I would be all sweaty and on some river in the middle of nowhere. Since I couldn't answer my question, I chose to apply conditioner, rinsed and stepped out of the shower feeling gorgeous. It was still dark outside, and I opened the bathroom window to listen to the morning sounds of the world outside. I love this time of the day, even though I rarely have the opportunity to enjoy it. The air smelled sweet, clean and fresh; and the world seemed full of promise of a great day to come.

Stowing our gear was simple because we already had loaded most of it into Sam's van last night. Since this was an adults' only trip, we had taken Allen to visit Tom's parents for the weekend. He wasn't particularly happy, but Grandpa would help him get over it. I wasn't worried; I felt strangely free, a reborn kid headed out to camp. I had to laugh. This weekend would be great.

We had planned this trip for a couple of weeks, and I was really looking forward to it. Sam had known about this little river for some time, but had just recently started telling us about it. It wasn't much he had said, just a little gravel bottom river. Too shallow for speedboats, not fast enough for the whitewater crowd, but perfect for us. We could leave early Saturday morning and be back Sunday evening. Easy in, easy out. Piece of cake.

Yes, I thought, it would do us all some good to just get away from it all. I was truly looking forward to living in a swimsuit for a weekend, away from phones and beepers and everyday nonsense.

Tom and Sam had been best friends since first grade and had remained very close through marriage and children and different career paths. Tom decided in college to be a teacher. Sam had always known what he wanted to be. He works for the Conservation Department. I really do not exactly know what all he does, but he is out and about all the time and he seems to know everyone. He loves his work. I almost think he loves his work more than he loves Marty, his wife. Sam met Marty while he was in College. She used to cut his hair. Marty is a beautician, but she doesn't work full time anymore, not since the kids came. She doesn't cut hair anymore either, now she only does nails. I used to laugh about that, you know doing nails just never struck me as much of a career choice. Then Sam shared with us how much money she's made doing people's nails and I won't laugh about it anymore. Perhaps I'm the one in the wrong line of work.

While Sam is dark-haired, stocky and muscular, Marty is fair-skinned, blond and slender. In recent years Marty has gotten into the suntanned look and now works on her tan year-round. I do have to give it to her though; it looks good on her. Sam and Marty are just such opposites. Sam is down to earth, real. Marty? Well, Marty is shallow and superficial. It's probably all related to her childhood. Her parents died when she was very young and she doesn't remember them. She grew up with her aunt and uncle. I don't think she knows real happiness, but she can fake it all right.

When Sam's parents were killed in that terrible car wreck years ago, Sam inherited their little farm. Not all that little really: About 240 tillable acres and the little house on the bluff overlooking the Missouri River where he grew up. In those days it had been out in the country, but now it was on the outskirts of town. Sam and Marty were newlyweds then. Marty was thoroughly disgusted when Sam moved them into the little farmhouse. But Sam ignored her and began a restoration process that took almost two years. Along the way he sold most of the land, keeping 10 or so acres surrounding the house. The buyer developed the area into a prestigious upscale subdivision, thereby increasing the value of Sam's property. When the restoration was finished the small white frame farmhouse had become a sprawling white split-level home, the envy of the neighbors, with beautifully refinished hardwood floors, a huge stone and brick fireplace and large deck with Jacuzzi overlooking the Missouri River and the expanding city.

When Marty realized that her house was more than equal to its neighbors and in the most affluent neighborhood, she stopped nagging Sam to sell the old house and move into town. Their son was born 10 months later. Now Sam and Marty have two kids, the eight-year-old boy and a five-year-old daughter.

Sam and Tom had the last of the gear loaded up in no time. The last item was the canoe. Once it was tied down, we all got refills of coffee and took off.

I waved at Marty, she hadn't even gotten out of the van and she didn't acknowledge the greeting, just snuggling deeper into her pillow. Not that it bothered me all that much. I'm not much company that early in the morning either, but a wave would have been nice. Marty is kinda funny, she doesn't talk much, usually just sits there and smiles appropriately. I have often wondered if we overwhelm her. We are all pretty outgoing, loud and boisterous, and she is more quiet and shy. Tom thinks she has no self-esteem and is embarrassed because she has less formal education than we do, but I don't think so.

I think Marty is just a shallow, superficial person. While we are looking for substance, she is looking at appearance; it's that simple. Even though we have all been friends for years, I don't seem to be able to get close to Marty. Marty and I really do not have anything in common anyhow. She never has a hair out of place. My auburn hair is short and usually windblown. I like an easy, wash-and-wear hairstyle and do not own a can of hairspray, while Marty has "different sprays for different days." My fingernails are short and nail polish drives me crazy. Marty's nails are long and always immaculately manicured. But then, they need to be since she does it for a living. I don't understand why she comes on these outings; she doesn't enjoy them. When we embark on one of our heated debates at the campfire, she withdraws from us until Sam finally explains the topic to her, then she usually acts as if we are boring. I once mentioned that to Tom and he laughed at me and said, "Honey, Sam didn't marry her for her brains". Marty is the airhead of our group.

We made a brief stop to connect with Ralph and Sandy. They don't live far from us. Tom and Sam met Ralph at some point during their college years. Tom said that Ralph just seemed to float from one thing to another, but still managed to earn a living that paid his way through school. They sort of adopted him and introduced him to the great outdoors. Until then, he had never been fishing or out in a canoe. They tried to take him hunting, but he couldn't keep his mouth shut. So they never invited him again.

Ralph works with computers. Sam jokingly calls him a nerd, but I am not so sure that is true. At least not what I consider a nerd. I think Ralph is just a very smart guy with a very weird sense of humor. Tom doesn't take Ralph seriously. He sees him as a little boy in an adult world and says that one of these days he'll wake up, realize he's grown up and won't like it. Anyway, I'm not sure exactly what he does with computers. He describes it as taking care of a whole network. He takes care of the computers that run the prison system, that much I do know.

That's how he met Sandy.

Sandy used to be a prison guard, which is hard to believe of someone her size. She started out pushing buttons and opening doors, but one day she happened to walk in on a fight in progress and broke it up. By doing this she actually saved a fellow officer's life and, as a reward was given the opportunity to choose her assignment. She chose to become a Training Officer. She no longer wears a uniform; and despite her shortcomings, she is good at her job. I think that's because she gets to tell lots of people what to do and she really enjoys that.

Once again the men took care of the gear and Marty stayed in the van, sleeping. I helped Sandy with the last minute stuff only she can dream up. Sandy is a real bitch, always has been, always will be. I can't understand what Ralph sees in her. But then I also wonder if maybe some people say the same thing about Tom and me. I have never known anyone who can make something out of nothing the way she can. She complains, nags, whines, screams and cusses like a drunken sailor. There have been times when I have been embarrassed to be in her company and then there have been days when she was so considerate it just blows you away.

Today was not one of her better days. Apparently she had been after Ralph since last night. He had dropped off their two kids at his sister's house for the weekend. She, however, had made arrangements for them to be with her brother. Sandy doesn't care for Ralph's sister; it's kind of a mutual dislike. Ralph, not knowing of the arrangement, found himself the landfall of Hurricane Sandy. By the time we arrived the dust still had not settled, and it was quite obvious that Ralph had gotten very little sleep, if any at all.

I looked at Tom, whispered, "I love you" and squeezed his upper arm. He told me once he has noticed that I seem to do this a lot after we have been with Ralph and Sandy. I guess, after listening to all the bickering, I just want to make sure he still remembers that I love him.

Sandy's last minute crisis of the day was about how many towels everyone had taken along and did we all have dry clothes and warm stuff for the night? But it really was the towels that kept her going and she would not rest until she had packed up every towel in the house and designated those we could not use if we were muddy or in any way dirty. Wet was okay, but dirty was out of the question. I suppose you

14

could consider Sandy to be compulsive, perhaps obsessive. I'm no shrink, I just know she is a bitch and she is positively nuts.

Chapter 2

Finally we were on the way. The world seemed at peace and everything had a golden glow and smelled fresh and clean. I love to travel at dawn, and snuggled closer to Tom as I sipped my coffee. We were following Sam, with Ralph bringing up the rear. For close to an hour we stayed on the highway, and then we turned onto a narrow blacktop road. Where the highway had simply cut through the hills, the blacktop just followed the ridgeline providing us with a magnificent view.

I felt myself surrounded by an ocean of green. Not just one kind of green, but many shades of green, from light to almost black, broken up with little farmhouses, some white, some gray, with reddish brown barns, looking like islands in this ocean of green. The sky was an unbelievable array of colors. Toward the West it was a deep, dark almost black blue turning slowly into a royal blue and further to the East into a very brilliant blue with golden rays of light jutting up like arrows. The few feathery clouds shone golden against the bright blue and the chattering of the birds was loud enough to be heard even inside the truck. There was a profusion of wildflowers growing along the road in all colors, shapes and sizes. So much to look at. So much to cherish!

I took a sip of my coffee and made a face, I had gotten hold of Tom's cup. He likes his coffee black, I prefer mine sweet. It's really his only fault.

"Did you catch Sandy's crisis of the day?" I asked. Tom shook his head, " No, I guess I missed that one."

"Just be glad you did. This time it was the towels. You've seen her like that, hon. Wet is okay, but muddy is not." I made a face and made Tom laugh. "Whatever, babe, whatever. Just be grateful you're not married to her!"

Up ahead, Sam turned off the blacktop and onto a narrow gravel road. We bounced around a little at first and then settled into a comfortable speed for the road conditions.

"I'm sure glad it's still damp outside. They must have had rain here

16

last night".

"What makes you think so?"

"Well, we'd be eating Sam's dust by now."

"I was up last night, couldn't sleep. We have a 'possum setting up housekeeping in the shed."

"A 'possum? I'll check it out when we get back. Big one?"

"Yeah, pretty big. Did you remember to turn off the coffee pot?"

"Yup, I did. I got the last cup and yes, I turned it off. Don't worry."

I really wasn't worried; I was just going through my mental checklist. That's one of my peculiarities. Everybody has something and mine is making checklists. Must be the nurse in me. I really haven't given it much thought. I just make a mental list and mentally check things off and then I'm done. It helps me relax. It's me.

I started feeling good, relaxed and happy. We no longer followed the ridge, but were in the valley, driving through field corn about six feet high with black-tasseled ears and past patches of wood and pasture land.

"Watch the fields, babe," said Tom, "I wouldn't be surprised to see some deer out here."

We passed a couple of old buildings, they appeared to be abandoned barns and our passing stirred up a whole flock of big black crows. Then, as we came around a corner we suddenly found ourselves face to face with five beautiful deer. I saw one big buck, his antlered head held up proudly and cautiously. I could not count the points on him, we were too far off, moving too fast and he did not hold still. The does were not quite so shy. We stared at each other for a second or two and then they were gone. I reached over and touched Tom

"Just try to convince me that they don't know it's not hunting season yet." I said.

He nodded.

"Yup, I think I know where Sam's been going deer hunting. While we froze on that raggedy tree stand, he sat up here in one of these old barns. Probably had hot coffee too. The bum never said a word about this area, I'll have to talk to him about that."

Up ahead of us I saw Sam's brake lights come on.

"I guess that's where we'll eventually finish."

"Looks like a nice spot."

17

We rounded the corner, went down a little slope and around one more corner and there was Sam, leaning against his van, sipping his obligatory mug of coffee. It looked funny to me and so I chuckled.

"Farmer Sam looking over the day's work," I said to Tom, but I don't think he found the view as funny as I did.

We quickly unloaded our Blazer onto the other two vehicles. It amazed me that neither Sandy nor Marty got out. I was glad we would be riding with Sam and Marty the rest of the way; I couldn't deal with the fighting in Ralph's truck. Tom must have read my mind; he shifted the gear into Ralph's, leaving room for two passengers with Sam. Yes, much better!

Tom moved the Blazer out of the open field into the shade of the trees, off to one side.

I watched him, suddenly very much aware of a sadness within me, a dreading of something to come. I felt a lump in my throat and very much wanted to call out to Tom, tell him to just take me home. But the logical half of me couldn't justify my fear and so I climbed on board with Sam and Marty. We drove over to where Tom was just climbing out of the Blazer.

"Curbside service?" I could tell by Tom's facial expression that he was relaxing and enjoying himself. So I hugged him, one of these big, squeezing, bear hugs and said a silent prayer for our safe return.

Sitting in the back seat of Sam's van we headed out of the field, back onto the gravel road and back to the blacktop. It would be a little ways to the starting point of our trip. Marty finally looked awake; well, at least her eyes were open. She mumbled something to Sam and I couldn't make out his response. Then she turned to me

"Sorry I was asleep when we started, it was a long day yesterday and I just can't stand myself when I don't get enough sleep." She stretched and yawned. "Would it bother you guys if I fix my nails?" I shrugged and so did Tom. Sam said something, I don't know what. We were on the blacktop when Marty started putting on nail polish. I couldn't believe it when the smell first reached me, but then Marty has always amazed me with the inane things she does at the most inopportune moments. After the first hand she held the hand up, turned to me and asked, "What do you think of this?"

Well, I am the wrong one to ask about nail polish. I can't stand it on my nails and therefore have never really gotten into it. But, being the nice person I am, I smiled at her and said: "Looks nice."

She pulled up her T- shirt and held her hand against her swimsuit and frowned.

"But in this light it doesn't go with my bathing suit."

I peeked over her shoulder, she wore a pinkish two-piece swimsuit and the nail polish was also a shade of pink.

"Looks fine to me," I said with false conviction. "Does it really matter? The light is going to change and who's gonna see it anyway?"

Marty just looked at me in disbelief.

"Oh Chris, I don't know why I bother to ask you. No, no, no! This is all wrong." And with that she pulled out nail polish remover.

"Sam, dear, could you just slow down a little until I get my nails done? Is that too much to ask?"

Sam looked at her sideways.

"Marty, honey, can't this wait? We'll be there in just a little bit."

"No. I don't want to wait. I can't stand the looks of these bare nails."

Sam rolled his eyes and pulled over to the side. I glanced sideways at Tom. I couldn't believe Sam would pull over in the middle of nowhere so Marty could do her nails. That's Sam, though, forever giving in to Marty, forever making peace. He is such a neat guy, but the term well trained also entered my mind. Ralph and Sandy, not knowing what was going on, pulled alongside and stopped as well. Sandy rolled down her window and called out to Sam:

"What's up?"

"Give me just a sec. Marty needs to fix her nails."

"Marty needs to do what?"

"She needs to put nail polish on her nails. Can't do it while we're driving."

"Are you kidding me?"

"I'm serious."

"Tell the bitch to get a life." Leave it to Sandy to get things moving again.

Sam looked at Marty and said sweetly, "Darling, your nails are fine and they can wait until we are in the canoe or better yet until we are back at home."

He pushed the gear lever into drive, and we bounced back onto the road. Marty glared at him.

"I go on these stupid trips with you, hang out with your friends who don't like me, and you can't even do one simple little thing for me? My appearance matters a great deal to me, Sam. I will give in this time, but it's the last time. Just explain one thing to me, one little thing. Why is it that I have to give in all the time? Can you tell me that? I didn't want to come on this trip, but I gave in to you. It's always you, what you want, I guess I'm just not real important."

Marty mumbled something else, but Sam ignored her. I turned away and looked at Tom. We disagree at times, but I could not recall any outbursts like this over something so trivial as nail polish. I wanted to say, "Get a life, Marty!" But you know how it is. Sometimes it's just better to keep your mouth shut.

We traveled for about twenty minutes on this narrow blacktop, passing through simply beautiful hill country. The tension within the van was thick enough to cut with a dull knife.

Outside, everything was lush and green and overgrown. We zoomed past cornfields and fields green with crops that I could not identify. It was wonderful, and I could have gone on for an eternity. The morning was so fresh and new and everything looked so golden, so full of promises. I took a deep breath and cherished the fresh morning air and the scent of my husband next to me.

"I kinda grew up around here." Sam said it to no one in particular. He pointed to the right.

"My Grandma had a little farm over the hill there and when I was a little kid my parents would often let me spend weekends here. Grandma was really a neat lady. She was country all the way, a real old time storyteller, so full of wisdom and always willing to help me explore. I learned a lot from her. When she died and the little farm was sold, man that hurt." He took a deep breath.

"I didn't really come back down here until after my parents were in that wreck."

"Have you been down here for deer season?"

Leave it to Tom to get right down to the important stuff. Sam nodded.

"When we started to redo the house my parents left me, I started to come back down here. I wanted to keep it as authentic as possible and there is an old man over in Rawley that does fantastic custom woodwork. He helped me a lot with advice and an occasional helping hand. He also helped me find authentic pieces at sales. And yes I've been down here hunting a time or two."

Tom punched me in the side and winked at me, it didn't hurt and wasn't meant that way. He was just making a point, making sure that I caught on that he had been right earlier when he thought that Sam had been down here for deer season. I do love my husband, but one of these days I'm going to have to tell him that he does not have to poke me every time he is right about something!

A strong jolt brought me back to reality. We were once again off the blacktop and onto a gravel road, this one full of creek gravel and far more rugged than the last one. Sam was shouting at us to hang on, it would be a little rough. No kidding! More than once did I want to shout, "Just slow down;" but I didn't. Marty did that for us, but it didn't help. Sam just laughed, enjoying himself.

"We should have left your van behind and taken my Blazer." Tom had to shout to be heard.

"Aw, come on, you don't mind being rattled around a little bit. Are you getting soft from all that desk work?" Sam laughed loud and hearty.

"Soft! My ass! I just don't want to break any bones before we get to that river of ours."

The two men were shouting happily at each other, obviously looking forward to the trip. I was too, but my female counterpart had slipped on a pair of neon pink headphones and removed herself from the conversation. I was beginning to feel left out. Thank God for the beautiful surroundings!

We bounced around for what seemed like an eternity, my right hand starting to get tired from holding on to the seat for dear life. We continued to pass through fields of assorted crops interspersed with patches of dense forest. I was able to identify black walnut trees, oak, hickory, an occasional sycamore, and, of course lots of cedars. How on earth did Sam ever find this place? And, better yet, I hope he remembers how to get back out of here. I suddenly missed Allen and my house. Oh well, it's just one night and I'll be home soon enough.

There were hedges and more than once our passing stirred up a covey of quail. And there were ponds that looked like an absolute heaven for frogs. After a few more potholes, curves and bumps, we finally rounded a bend and found ourselves overlooking a large grassy meadow. Clear and green, it only needed some black and white cows to belong on a picture postcard. Sam drove on over the grass and toward some trees at the far side. And there, straight ahead of us, we finally had our first glimpse of the river Sam had talked so much about.

"There it is," Sam smiled at us. "Meet Coon River. Doesn't look like much, but just a little ways downriver it widens nicely. A little creek, Rockhouse Creek, joins what's really Coon Creek and the whole thing becomes officially Coon River."

Chapter 3

We walked over to the water's edge. I had to give it to Sam. He had done a great job finding this starting point for us. The ground sloped gently into the water, and there was a small, sandy spot which, with a little imagination, one could call a beach. For us it was perfect. We could load the canoes and push off without potentially breaking our backs or legs in the process. The water was crystal clear. When I stuck my foot in, I was amazed at how warm it felt.

Yes, I thought, this is the way I like it. A broiling hot day and a clear gravel-bottom river with pee-warm water and just enough current to keep us moving forward but not enough to turn into work.

Sam was still telling us about his river "You know, the Department of Natural Resources did a study last year to determine how clean the state's river water is, and they declared this water potable. After all, it has no industry anywhere nearby, and so there is really no pollution. I'm not so sure I want to drink it, but I thought you'd like to know.

"This could be a very interesting trip, guys. A little ways down river is a spot where last year they found a bald eagle nest. Pretty exciting! And a little further downstream, this river borders Camp Crowder and the civilian world. Most people think Crowder is a defunct military base, but they use this place for training and research. The military seems to feel that it is so isolated that the personnel have nothing to do but work. Rumor in the neighborhood has it that they are doing some testing here, top-secret stuff. Well, I doubt we'll see anything from the river, but just in case you see some little green men running around with guns: No, it's not Halloween.

"As we go down the river, watch the banks. This area is so unpopulated that many animals are not afraid of humans. These waters are also home to an assortment of turtles and lots of little fish. You'll see. Watch out for snakes. This is one of the few areas of the state where cottonmouths live and they can be very unhealthy to us humans."

I looked at Sandy; she had a look in her eyes that would kill any snake at fifty yards. Marty still had her headphones on, oblivious to us.

That left me as the only female paying any attention. I looked at Tom. He had sparkles in his eyes and was sporting a big smile. Tom loves this adventure stuff. Me, I'm not so sure. I enjoy the outdoors, but when it gets dark outside I really prefer a nice air-conditioned motel room where I can go to the bathroom and don't have to worry if I am dropping my drawers on some wildlife! Still, I go on these outings and I usually enjoy them. Knowing that we only have to spend one night really does help.

We finished loading the canoes, and the guys took off to stash Ralph's truck at the designated takeout point under some shade trees. While we waited for their return, I was reminding everyone to put sunscreen on; I am a firm believer in this stuff. As a nurse, I have seen a couple of patients with skin cancer. It is pretty shocking to see a person your own age and know that they will be dead in a year or two. I believe in sunscreen and I believe in sunglasses to protect the eyes and I believe in hats. Tom usually laughs at me. He thinks he's too macho to put on the "smelly stuff."

Sandy plopped down beside me, equally ignoring Marty and her neon pink headphones and oversized sunglasses. "Check out little Miss Priss?" She nodded toward Marty. Miss Priss, huh? Nice idea.

"Well, Sandy," I chose my words slowly "to each her own, you know. I came out here to unwind. It's been one hell of a week and I don't care what Marty's up to." Sandy hugged me.

"I knew I could count on you, kid," she said. "Me, I'm fried! Just fried! The fuckin' natives have been restless and we have a couple of new trainees that are idiots! I could just strangle them! But I can't. After all, I am a professional." She made a face. Then:

"Professionalism my ass! I just wanna fuckin' puke. I'm glad we're out here where I can let my hair hang down, scream, holler, cuss and use all the profanity I want! And one more thing, darlin', if you hear any strange noises from our canoe or our tent, don't worry! I'm just gonna fuck Ralph's brains out and unless you wanna join in, better leave us be!" With that, she leaned back until her head rested against an old piece of wood and closed her eyes.

"You know," she said kinda low, "this early morning sun against my belly makes me horny! Where the hell are the guys?"

I couldn't help myself. I burst out laughing. Sandy can be

24

impossible at times and is always unpredictable. The laughter caught Marty's attention. She lowered her headphones.

"What's so funny?"

"Sandy's feeling horny."

There was a moment of silence, and then she said, "Well good for her, just don't expect me to solve that problem." And on went the headphones. Sandy and I just looked at each other and cracked up again. There's just always such a sense of freedom when we first get started on one of our trips. And then, when we get to the end, it's such a relief to be back in civilization. Back in the world of air conditioning, running water and clean, dry clothes. I had to agree with Sandy that the freedom from everyday responsibilities, combined with the smells and vibrant colors of early morning, was a pretty erotic sensation. I may not express it as bluntly as Sandy does, but I had some plans for the night as well.

Finally the guys were back and we climbed into the canoes and pushed off. It's always such a rush when we first start. Slowly backing away from the shore, Tom always acts as if it's a major undertaking and I must admit I feed into it. I love it when he says, "Easy now, darlin', we have plenty of time." He says the same thing every time.

Chapter 4

Once out on the water, I can't help but relax; and this time was no different. The water was crystal clear. I could see all the way to the bottom and marveled at the abundance of colorful little fish zooming back and forth. There is something rather seductive about the paddle strokes and we soon found our rhythm.

From the water, the shoreline looked as if it belonged to another time. I could easily imagine being an early settler, going down to the river to fetch water. The thought of doing laundry at the river's edge briefly entered my mind, but only briefly. There is just no way I'll give up my washing machine or dryer!

Once we passed the spot where Rockhouse Creek joined Coon Creek, the current picked up some and I carefully turned around, opened the big orange cooler and got a soda out. Ahh, the cool bubbly liquid tickled my throat. And with a deep I sigh I leaned back against the cooler. The front of the canoe was wide enough to sit comfortably. Our big camping cooler fit nicely right behind the front seat and that allowed me to hang my legs over the sides and lean back. I like that! The sun felt hot on my skin. I closed my eyes and focused on inhaling deeply, the scents of nature and sound of the bugs and birds became almost overwhelming.

"Hey babe," I called out, "this is what I needed, a total get away. And you!" Up ahead I could see Sam and Marty, she had put on a wide-brimmed, yellow hat and for a moment I was delighted that she seemed to have listened to my skin cancer speeches. She even had oversized sunglasses on, but I couldn't help but wonder why she even bothered to go on these trips with the rest of us, when she so effectively shut us out. And I wondered what Sam's life with her would have to be like. Did she wear those damned headphones when they made love?

I couldn't turn around to look for Ralph and Sandy. The last time I tried something like that I almost flipped the canoe, and Tom didn't let me forget it for a long, long time.

I really didn't have to turn around. I could hear Sandy. I couldn't understand what she was saying, but I could hear her all right. You see, Sandy gets loud when she relaxes. One time when we were floating, she convinced Ralph to let her sit in an inner tube and be towed behind the canoe. All went well, until the rope came loose just as we went into some shoals. Sandy, with her butt stuck in the inner tube, got dragged across some gravel. She wasn't hurt; but her bathing suit had some holes it didn't need, and we never heard the end of it. That was so funny! Needless to say, Sandy doesn't stick her rear end into inner tubes anymore.

I didn't know what today's commotion was all about and I really didn't care. I was relaxing, my feet in the warm water, sipping a cold soda and working on a little suntan. Yes, life was good. Somewhere along the way I must have dozed off, the gentle rocking on a hot day does this to me.

When I looked up again, we were just coming around a bend in the river and directly ahead were some cattle, big black and white Holsteins up to their bellies in the water. What a sight! Tom said something about some lukewarm milkshakes up ahead. That got me laughing and the laughing was a release. Yes, life really was good.

The scenery had changed around us, and no longer were there just trees. On the left side were steep, cream-colored bluffs studded with little cedar trees growing in impossible places.

Tom splashed some water on me to get my attention. " Look," he said pointing up the bluff, "see the little dark areas? Those are cave entrances. Wanna play cave man?" At the base of the cliffs sat chunks of limestone that had broken off. I laughed at Tom's proposition. "I don't think so, I'd rather be the cave woman. You know, be in a cave with you and ravage your body." I winked at him. In response Tom aimed the canoe straight for the bluff, paddling furiously, almost ramming one of the big chunks of limestone. Fortunately, he regained his senses just barely in time.

On the right we were still looking at trees, but through the trees we could see fields. And there were pastures and more big black and white cows. I enjoyed watching the little turtles sitting on the dead logs. They were sunning themselves, at least until we came by. Then they would plop-plop-plop hop into the water and watch us with just their little heads showing. A couple of times we were buzzed by big colorful dragonflies. I don't like them up close. I always imagine what it would feel like to be stung by one of them. Tom laughs about it and keeps telling me that they won't sting, but I don't like them. As we rounded another bend, we saw Sam up ahead on the left bank, holding on to some bushes.

"What's he up to?" I asked.

"I have no idea. Knowing Sam, he probably has a surprise stashed away for us. Probably something ecologically sound, of historical value and just barely edible." Tom chuckled. I can recall times when Sam would have us tasting some wild growing things I would never have considered and certainly have not considered since. He did get me started on drinking lemon-peppermint tea, though. Pretty tasty stuff, I must say. Well, let's see what he's up to, I thought.

It didn't take long and we pulled up alongside, holding on to some bushes. Sam was smiling broadly.

"You guys ready for a little lunch?"

Oh boy, I thought, lunch time already? And Sam all smiles? What has he set up for us this time? I hadn't noticed time passing, but couldn't ignore the empty feeling in the pit of my stomach any longer. Lunch, no matter what, sounded wonderful.

"Hey Sam," I yelled. "Are you going to cook or did you arrange for takeout from fauna and flora?"

Sam laughed. "Neither, I just found the spot."

I looked over at Marty and was amazed. For the first time today, she actually looked at us – acknowledged that we were there. Who knows, I thought, maybe she'll socialize just a little bit.

Sam showed us a little sandy spot between the bushes where we could beach the canoes and get out.

"There is this cave here," Sam went on, "But let's wait for Ralph and Sandy. I know you guys will love it. I found it by accident when I came out here with my cousin late last Fall. Once the leaves are gone you can see the entrance quite well."

Ralph and Sandy arrived. "Hiiiiii guuyyes," screamed Sandy, "life is great!"

I looked at Ralph, but he just rolled his eyes; he knows Sandy. We beached the canoes and Sam guided us through the narrow strip of brush to the cliff's base. A narrow opening appeared before us.

I looked at Tom. His blue eyes sparkled, yes; my husband was

28

having a great time. Me, I could have settled for sandwiches or the like and stayed on the water.

The entrance to the cave was high and quite narrow, but we squeezed in. Sam, always prepared, had brought along a flashlight. Its beam revealed a huge room. It didn't reach the ceiling or back wall, but it showed us the remains of a campfire, complete with empty beer cans and dark-colored wrappers.

Sam shook his head.

"What a shame that some people can't clean up after themselves." He looked disappointed, but not too much. Today nothing could dampen Sam's spirit. "Guys," he said, "You ain't seen nothing yet. There are several rooms to this thing. I bet these assholes didn't find the back area. Come on."

He started to turn, but Marty surprised us all.

"Sam," she said in her tiny, squeaky voice, "Sam, I really don't care much for exploring this stupid cave. It's so boring. I'd rather work on my tan. Let me know when you get done in here, ok?"

Sam stared at her for a moment, a little disappointed, but he just swallowed.

He led the way to the far end of the cave. At the base of the wall was what looked like a dent. Sam got down on his knees and told us to get down and follow him into the next room, and then he proceeded to crawl through.

Sandy and I looked at each other. She may be a bitch most of the time, but there are times when I can't help but agree with her. With one cocked eyebrow, she looked at Ralph.

"Does he have a lot of free time on his hands?" She asked, pointing to Sam. "Any normal human being would have missed the opening to the cave. He found it and he found this hole. If you guys want to crawl through some hole in the rocks, fine. Me, I'm going to gather some wood and build a fire, and when you cavemen return, maybe we'll have coffee and hot dogs. Just watch out for little crawly things that might mistake you for the local McDonalds and try to take some bites out of your hides."

She looked at me, and I quickly agreed with her. No way would I crawl through a hole in the rocks not knowing what was ahead, below, and, for that matter, next to me.

"Yup," I said with false bravado, "we be cave women, gather wood, make fire, get meat for meal, skins for clothes."

Sandy giggled and for once had nothing to add.

Gathering wood for the fire wasn't an easy task. In the narrow strip between the cliff and the river, we found only thin sticks. It took us a while to gather enough together for a decent fire. Sandy even cleared away all the old beer cans and burned the odd dark green wrappers. We had the old coffeepot on the fire and the water boiling when the "cavemen" returned. In no time we had coffee and wieners roasting on long sticks. Sandy can be bad, but then again she also can be very good.

I stepped out to get Marty, but she didn't hear me calling. She had allowed the canoe to drift downstream a little ways, so I just tugged the rope it was tethered with. But Marty just waved at me and so I let her be. We had a lovely lunch, totally unhealthy I am sure! Then we cleaned up, burned the trash and concealed any evidence of a campfire. When we resurfaced outside, I was surprised to realize that it was already well past two o'clock. We had been here more than three hours.

Marty was sleeping so soundly we had to pull her canoe in. I made a mental note to talk to her about sunscreen once we were back home again. Of course she woke up while we were pulling her in and looked totally surprised. Must have been a pretty good dream.

We continued on downriver. I inhaled deeply; the sweet scents of nature were almost overwhelming.

"Hon, just take a deep breath. The air smells so sweet, it's almost too much."

I could hear Tom inhaling deeply. "Yeah. Incredible. Either the air is real sweet or the air in the cave was real bad." He laughed.

The pale limestone bluffs continued on the left, looming and majestic, while on the right was dense forest. Then we saw the burned out remains of some vehicle, the black carcass in stark contrast with the surrounding lush green vegetation.

"What happened here?" I whispered to Tom.

"I don't know," he whispered back, "Why are we whispering?" With a couple of paddle strokes he brought us closer to Sam.

"Sam, what do you make of that?" Sam did not seem bewildered.

"Well, this bank belongs to Camp Crowder. Remember, I told you guys we would be passing through this old military reservation? Well, this must have been the result of some test they conducted. It's old, it was here last year when I was down here."

I looked at Marty; her face was flushed looking. No, on second thought her face was red, bright red.

"Hey Marty did you put on sunscreen?" I had to repeat myself three times.

She looked at me and finally lifted those damned headphones.

"Did you put on sunscreen?" I repeated.

"Oh sure, I got that SPF 8 stuff. I do want to get a little tan this weekend. Why?"

"Well, you look awfully puffy and red. You want to try some of mine? It has a higher SPF."

"Red? Puffy? Please, say you don't mean that."

She searched through one of the bags in their canoe and produced a small mirror. Leave it to Marty never to leave home without one.

"Oh no! Do you think I've got a sunburn already? My face feels so tight. Are you sure I can use some of your sunscreen? Damn this stupid trip."

"Gladly." I handed her the bottle and even helped her rub some on her shoulders and her back. I couldn't believe that she had been this careless. We all learned a long time ago never to get on the river with minimal sun protection. On the water the sun just gets too intense.

The skin on her back felt hot and leathery. Tough, like an old glove. Must be from all those sessions in the tanning salon, I thought.

"Marty, honey, are you drinking enough?" I asked her and she nodded.

"Well I think so, I brought some of that flavored water along and I must have had three bottles so far. I just really don't feel so good, Chris."

She sounded funny, not quite right. Her voice was different, trembling, sort of. Sam was still talking. "Like I said, the official story is just some training for some special troops, but the scuttlebutt in town is that it's top secret stuff. There have been some local fishermen who have been out here during the week and then were escorted back by MPs. Course, they swore they never entered the military reservation, but nonetheless they were still booted out. They mean what they say with their "No Trespassing" signs. And then there was this little piece in the paper about agricultural research and testing being done out here.

"Well, ahead of us, I think around the next bend, is another little creek. I can't remember the name, but at that point we are more than halfway done with Camp Crowder. After that, be on the lookout for a big flat-topped rock in the middle of the river. It should still be a little ways ahead of us. Locally it used to be called the 'auction rock', and supposedly slaves were taken there for secret auctions well after slavery was outlawed. I don't know if it's true or not, but I always thought it sounded interesting. And that's where I thought we might spend the night."

"That's good. I think Marty and I are ready to call it a day," I said.

"Don't get too excited. It's still at least another hour or so. I just think we will be better off if we can get a campsite set up before dark. The bluffs block out the sunset and it will get dark rather quickly. Besides, we can find more firewood that way."

A vision of snakes entered my mind as I thought of gathering firewood after dark; and I had to agree with Sam that it was probably better to stop before it got dark. But why hadn't I thought of that? I rummaged through my camping first aid bag and found some aspirin. I passed two tablets to Marty.

"Take these, it might make you feel a little better."

"I really don't feel good at all. My left shoulder is sore and so is my neck. I think I must have pulled something. And I'm achy all over. Do you think I could have sun poisoning?"

I had to think a moment. What did she consider sun poisoning? Was she talking of heat or sunstroke? Well, she certainly was a candidate for that.

"Weelll, could be a possibility. Keep on drinking as much as you can and cool off. There's plenty of water around us, just splash some on. That will help."

I turned to Sam. "Hey, pal, your wife is getting too much sun. Let's get moving so we can get her cooled off."

He looked surprised at me, as if he had not even noticed Marty. "Honey, are you okay?" Marty nodded and swallowed. "Oh, I think I'll be fine. Chris just gave me a couple of aspirin and I'll drink some more and I think I'll be ok with that."

She may have thought so, but I had my doubts, I've seen a couple of cases of sunstroke. If that's what we were dealing with here, then Marty was in big trouble. I couldn't figure out how to explain my concerns to the others. The only answer was to keep an eye on her, keep her drinking, and remind her to splash river water on to cool off. It would be better to just get her off the river, fast.

The trees on the right shore got taller and the underbrush denser. I kept thinking about what Sam had said about top secret testing, and I wondered what was going on behind that dense vegetation. My colorful imagination was in overdrive. But I couldn't see anything unusual or mysterious, just lots of brush and big trees. It did strike me as odd, though, that we didn't see any more animals. There were no more little turtles sunbathing on the logs and it was quiet around us.

Chapter 5

Once again Tom and I were in the middle between the other canoes. Sam had pulled well ahead of us. I suppose it's part of his entertainment on these trips to be the one to yell, "We're here". He can have his fun. I like to go slower and so do Ralph and Sandy.

I turned slightly to the right, wanting to ask Tom how far back Ralph and Sandy were, when movement on the shore caught my eye. For one brief moment I saw a person in camouflage fatigues holding what seemed like a gun of some sort. But, when I raised my hand to wave, the figure was gone. I was baffled.

"Hey honey, I think I just saw one of the little green men Sam talked about this morning."

But Tom was unimpressed, "Babydoll, the river and the heat are playing tricks on you, probably was just an ugly tree stump."

"A tree stump with a gun and wearing a helmet?"

Tom just laughed in response. "Oh, come on now, babe. You probably did see one of those guys, and now he's all distraught because his camouflage did not work. You, a mere mortal spotted him and waved at him. His life won't be the same!"

Oh well, I thought, I like it when my husband is impressed with my observations. I was still certain that what I saw had been a person. Maybe Tom was right and the military didn't like it when a mere mortal could see them in camouflage? I couldn't answer that, and it really didn't matter to me anyway. I was relaxing and I was not about to let some snob in a green suit ruin this weekend for me.

I started looking for the dragonflies. I may not like them, but they are impressive to watch. This afternoon there were none. Strange, I thought. Did they all siesta at the same time?

We must have passed some tributaries, as the river had gotten wider. Behind me, Tom was humming some tune I did not recognize, and it sounded way off key. Tom can't carry a tune, you know. But humming is always an indicator that he is content with life at the moment. So I pulled my hat down over my ears, leaned back, and closed my eyes for a while

I must have dozed off a little because I suddenly realized that the rocking motion of the canoe had changed. I opened my eyes and looked around. We were in a section of shallow, fast moving water. Not white water, just fast moving shallow stuff, sometimes so shallow the bottom of the canoe scraped across the gravel. I sat upright and almost tipped us over.

"What happened?"

"Whoa," Tom shouted, "Just sit tight; we'll be through this stuff in a minute."

I didn't dare turn to ask him if he needed help, I didn't dare do anything, I just held on to the sides of the canoe and hoped he was doing as good a job as he thought. Well, Tom had been right, of course. A few minutes later the river widened and once again became the gentle, slow-moving body of water I had gotten used to. Up ahead I could see Sam. He was against the left bank.

"What's Sam doing?"

"I don't know. Probably just waiting for us. Maybe he had to pee."

"He wouldn't stop for that; he'd just pee in the water."

Tom was cracking up. "While he's paddling? He isn't that well endowed."

I grabbed a paddle and was just beginning to dip it into the water, when I heard Sandy's shrill laughter from behind.

"Out of my way slowpokes."

That's all it took! We paddled furiously. There is no way I would let Sandy and Ralph beat us. We reached Sam's canoe first, but just barely, and all of us were laughing breathlessly when we got there.

Sam had tied up to a thick branch, leaned back against, it and had his pipe in his hand. Marty had her oversized sunglasses on and the big yellow hat. She seemed to be awake, but when I looked closer I could clearly see that her face was badly sunburned. She looked puffy and red and uncomfortable.

"Our big rock is just up ahead, around the next bend," Sam smiled. "And I want you to know I have a little surprise for all of you." He chuckled, "I was down here a couple of weeks ago. Thinking we would be back this way, I stashed a bunch of good firewood. So, my friends, please don't be bashful. Grab these here pieces of wood yours truly has left, so that we may have us a good fire tonight."

We were only glad to oblige, dry wood already cut up and ready to go is a gift from heaven on one of these trips. As I looked around though, the vegetation baffled me. The undergrowth was really dense, more so than it had been earlier. Everything looked bigger, oversized, and abnormal. I tried to get Tom's attention to tell him about it, but he was so preoccupied he didn't listen and so I let it go. Probably just my imagination anyway.

Grass and weeds could not possibly be the size of bushes, and leaves on the trees could not yet begin to turn color. Much too early for it. No. I wrote it all off to optical illusions after a long day on the river.

Well, we loaded up on firewood, all the while teasing Sam about having too much free time on his hands and we'd be happy to share with him a few suggestions on what to do with his free time! He took it as it was intended. Sam is good people. I did ask Marty if she felt any better, just to get a conversation going with her. She took off her Christian Dior sunglasses and looked at me strangely.

"I'm just sooo tired. I'm sure its just being out in the sun too much today. Could be the medication, too. My doctor has me on something new." She was slurring some words.

"Oh." I couldn't think of anything more intelligent to say. " What are you taking?"

"Well, I've been a bit depressed lately, and you know how that is. When you feel down, you tend to eat too much. Well, I didn't want to put on any more weight than I already have with this pregnancy. So, I talked to the doctor and he gave me some pills to take, and they have really helped. He said it was okay; it wouldn't hurt the baby."

"Marty, you're pregnant?" I was stunned. I couldn't believe my ears. Marty pregnant? She had gained a ton of weight with her first pregnancy, had been really distraught about it, and then had worked hard to loose it. Bless her vanity! And then she got pregnant again and again she gained weight. I don't know how much she gained. I doubt it was a lot. But to her it was a ton, and before the baby was born she had Sam go for a vasectomy threatening no sex unless he got fixed. Never again did she want to get fat. I had to repeat my question:

"Marty, are you pregnant?"

She looked at me startled. "Why yes, can't you tell? This baby is due in 3 weeks and I am absolutely hideous. I can't believe Jack is making me go on this trip."

There was no way on this earth that Marty was nine months pregnant. No way! She was sitting in front of me in a skimpy hot pink bikini. And who the hell is Jack?

"You're looking gorgeous! But tell me about this new medication. You know me, I'm always curious about things like that."

I wanted to ask her who Jack is, but I didn't dare.

"Oh, it's nothing special, I can't remember the name. It's a mood elevator and it also suppresses your appetite. I like it and I think it's helping me. Of course you can't talk to Sam about anything like that. His cure for feeling down is going out and chopping wood. And that's just not my way. I've been working too much in the shop lately too. You know, taking care of all those little blue haired old ladies that seem to wander in, and they all have to have bright red nails. If I see one more head of blue hair and red nails I am going to puke."

"What about your pregnancy?"

"What pregnancy?"

"You just said you're pregnant, didn't you?"

"Me? Chris, really, you should know better. No way, I'm done having babies. Let somebody else get fat, not this body. How did you come up with that?"

I was confused; I knew I had clearly heard her say that she was pregnant. Hmm, weird. "Marty, who is Jack?"

"Jack? I only know one Jack, Jack Brittenstein. We were in high school together and dated before I met Sam. I almost married him. Sometimes I wonder." And with that she slipped those damned headphones back on and leaned back, her eyes closed. I stared at her. Her face was bright red and swollen, blisters forming on her cheeks, lips, chest and belly. I had told her to put on a T-shirt or something, but she hadn't. I reached over and touched her upper arm. Her skin felt dry and hot and hard. Marty never reacted to my touch. I called to Sam and waved him over to us.

"Listen, Marty has had way too much sun. She's too hot and she's also badly burned. We need to find a way to cool her off. Let me have one of your T-shirts. We'll get it wet and slip it over her. Maybe that will cool her off just a little bit."

He handed me the faded blue one he had been wearing, and I dipped it in the river while Sam woke up Marty. She was giggling with him and denied feeling ill and just couldn't figure out why he would be worried. And so he left us, rejoining the others to get everyone supplied with wood and back on the way. Without so much as a fuss, Marty slipped into the wet shirt and took two more aspirin from me with a big gulp of water.

"Jack is just such a hunk," she said as she slipped her headphones over her red ears and closed her swollen eyes.

I just stood there staring at her. She is hallucinating, I finally decided and that spelled big trouble. You just don't spend time in the sun and then start hallucinating without having a heatstroke or something like that. And no matter how hard I tried, I couldn't get Tom's attention.

I was also bothered by something else. I couldn't quite put my finger on it, but everything around us looked strange. Okay, I told myself, enough of this; your imagination is now working overtime. Go take a break and regroup. And so I walked a little inland, away from the group, in hopes of being able to sort out why I felt so nervous. Normally I relax when we're out and about like this. Can't get me worked up! But this trip was different. I hadn't felt comfortable about it from the beginning. I found a quiet spot and just stood still, inhaling deeply and letting sunshine, slight breeze, scents, everything soak into my skin.

Suddenly it became much clearer. Yes, I said out loud. Yes, the vegetation was different and it was too quiet. There should be noises all around me, bugs and birds and squirrels and stuff, but there wasn't. I heard nothing. Aside from the noise we were making, there was no sign of life. Weird, I thought, as I made my way back. And, as I kept looking around, I noticed more and more clearly that what I had thought were bushes looked an awful lot like oversized weeds. And everywhere I looked were dead insects and birds. I didn't see any dead larger animals, but still, this was upsetting enough. My heart was pounding as I rushed back to our group, back to Tom.

"Where were you?" he asked when I burst through the bushes. " I was beginning to worry. I'm a little too old to take on a whole army of little green men, you know."

Before I could say anything he had me in the canoe and we were back in the water. "Tom," I finally managed turning slightly and carefully toward him. "There is something very, very wrong. I know what you're gonna say, you're gonna say that I'm reading too much science fiction, but there is something very very wrong here and I am really scared."

He stopped in mid stroke. "OK, you have my undivided attention, what has you so spooked?"

"I don't know for sure. Look at the shore, the right side, the military side."

"Honey, I'm not sure, but I think we're already past Camp Crowder."

"Oh," I couldn't think of anything more intelligent to say. "Well, look around you at least. Look at the shoreline, look closely at the weeds, the bushes, all that green stuff."

He nodded and looked. "Ok," he finally said, "What am I looking at?"

"Tom, the weeds are too big. They are the bushes. Look how high the grass is! Now look at the bushes. They look way too big, too. Look at the colors of the trees. The leaves are slowly turning brownish, like early fall. This is all wrong. It's, well... it's weird! And back there, when I went into the brush, there were dead insects and birds and stuff everywhere."

I know I had an edge in my voice, and Tom did not respond right away. He slowly looked around. Then he steered the canoe back toward the shore, beached it, and actually walked over to some of these strange plants and touched them. He returned with a puzzled look on his face.

"You know, you're right," he said quietly. "It's all off somehow. I can't explain it, but the weeds are way too big and the bushes are too. Plus, they all look out of season. And there are no insects either. I can't detect a chemical odor, but that doesn't mean that these crazy bastards at that base didn't conduct some sort of test and it affected this area. Let's talk to the others. I don't like the idea of being someone's guinea pig."

But, as we got back onto the river, they were well ahead of us moving toward the campsite. The talk would have to wait, at least for now. We hurried to catch up with them, but we didn't make it. Far

39

ahead of us we heard Sam yelling, " Here we are!"

I tried to turn to look at Tom, but he grunted at my movement, so I just paddled. Up ahead we saw the landmark Sam had talked about, the huge, flat-topped rock in the river. It sure did look strange but that didn't matter to me at this time. To me, it looked strange but beautiful because it meant that we had reached the halfway point on our trip.

And, for some reason, I just wanted to get off the river.

Chapter 6
Kansas City, Saturday, 4:30 a.m.

The three men approached the airline's customer service counter from different directions. After shaking hands and exchanging the customary greetings, they headed toward the terminal exit. Although it was still dark outside, the sky to the East was starting to be tinged in shades of red and gold. Thanks to the surrounding flat countryside of Missouri's Western Prairie land, they were presented with the beginnings of a spectacular sunrise. Expecting a limo curbside and not seeing one, they stood at the exit, for a moment perplexed. They knew each other by name, had communicated for years, but had just now, at long last, met in person.

The tallest of the trio broke the silence.

"Well, gentlemen, what do you think of all this? They drag us out here at an ungodly hour, and then the limo is late. Let's go back inside and see if the coffee shop is open. I need some caffeine and somewhere in this dump I will find some."

David Smith turned to reenter the terminal, stopping momentarily to check his reflection in the glass door. He was tall, well over six feet, with ebony skin many female models would kill for. He wore a stylish dark gray pinstripe suit with matching, obviously imported, leather shoes. His shirt was a soft creamy beige, complemented by a red paisley tie. He ran his hand over his short hair, squared his shoulders and reentered the terminal.

The other two men looked at each other and shrugged. The older of the two, a man of medium height, bordering on chubby, was comfortably dressed in well-worn jeans, an equally aged tweed sports jacket and obviously broken in leather loafers. He carefully set down his bulging briefcase and brushed his unruly hair with his hand. Kenneth Messer had just arrived from Seattle, and although his eyes told him the day was beginning, his body still was on Pacific Time and wanted more sleep. He made a mental note to himself not to accept any future special assignments that involved sudden travel east of the Rockies. I'm getting too old for this nonsense, he thought.

41

The third man of the trio seemed unconcerned. He had arrived at the airport well ahead of his travel companions and spent his time on the phone making last minute arrangements. Jeffrey Craft was only in his early thirties, of average height, with short brown hair and a bushy red mustache. He was the 'boy wonder' of the group, had graduated early from high school and equally early from college. Although money had always mattered to him, prestige mattered more. He enjoyed his six-figure income, but cherished his title, expense account and the big office at the corporate headquarters.

Together, the three walked through the terminal building. They followed their noses to the food court.

"I wonder when SERPAC's driver will finally show up?" said David Smith, known for his impatience.

"Relax, Dave," said Jeffrey Craft. "I talked with the man earlier, he was already on his way. It does take a couple of hours to drive up here. I'm sure he'll be here any minute now. You guys arrived about thirty minutes early, so be grateful. Airlines are so famous for running late that we all count on it, and then we get irritated when we're actually on time. Ken, how was your flight from Seattle?"

"Too long, but otherwise not all that bad. I just hate to fly, passionately! When they called me yesterday and confirmed that we were really on, I had to leave on the spot to make my flight out of SeaTac and then I had to change planes in Denver. So, with the delays and time zones, I've been on the go for more than twelve hours. Couldn't say goodbye to the family because they were at the movies when the call came. I had a chance to call from Denver, so at least they know I've not been kidnapped by aliens."

"You didn't tell your family where you're going or why, did you? You know what Jonathon told us," said David Smith.

"I told my wife I had to go to a big shot, emergency corporate meeting in Chicago. When you have a family, my friend, you can't just up and disappear! Families have a tendency to report you as a missing person. If Jonathon can't understand that, well, that's just too bad."

"He understands, I'm sure." Jeffrey Craft sounded calm. "He just didn't want details leaking out and I think your excuse sounds great and believable. Dave, how come you're so uptight?"

"I'm tired and I want to get this show on the road. This waiting for the damn limo is for the birds. Why can't we just get a rental car, drive out there ourselves, something like that?"

"Two reasons. First of all, we are being picked up by the chauffeur because that's policy and that's the way Jonathan wants it done. Second, there are no rental cars at this airport. If you want a rental, you notify the airline counter, they notify the agency, they come and pick you up, you go into town and then you may rent your car. The agencies do not open until eight-thirty a.m. We knew that when we planned this little adventure. It's now almost five-thirty a.m. Accept the fact that the people here roll up the sidewalks at ten p.m. and do not unroll them until eight o'clock in the morning. Accept that and relax. Trust me, you'll live longer."

"What a crock! They knew when we would arrive. Don't they have clocks? Why do we have to sit and wait?"

"Because, because, because."

They sat down on concrete benches in front of the terminal doors, just as a dark green, four-wheel drive vehicle pulled up in front of them. The driver jumped out.

"Are you the gentlemen with SERPAC?"

"Yes, we are."

"Good Morning and welcome to God's country. My name is Ron. I'm your chauffeur, your guide, and your jack-of-all-trades during your stay. Officially, I'm an administrative assistant to Jonathon Brooks, but in reality I'm just his local gopher." He laughed. "Like in go for this and go for that. Do you gentlemen have any luggage I might get?"

They shook their heads.

"Well, in that case, hop in and let's get going. We'll need to stop for gas before long. I suggest you make that your comfort stop, because once we're back on the road there will be nothing worth stopping at."

They made it out of town well ahead of rush hour traffic. Ron slipped a tape of Chopin etudes into the stereo and the three men sipped their coffee and munched on their donuts in without speaking.

Brushing crumbs off his shirt, Ken Messer turned to his travel companions.

"If you don't mind, I'd like to review a couple of things."

"Come on, Ken! Get some rest, enjoy the scenery. I know you get

43

off on all that nature stuff. Save the business for later." David Smith
had a whine in his voice. "I'm tired and I wanted to get some rest."

"I have concerns. I just want to see if your data supports these
concerns, because if it does, then we need to get hold of the SPC team
ASAP."

"Oh come on! What do you have? We've covered every possible
scenario. SPC's been over it all, you've seen the reports."

"Of course I've seen the reports, but I've done some refiguring on
my own. And I am beginning to think that we are not allowing a wide
enough range for the contaminant filters. And I've found inaccuracies
in the calibration of the targeting program. I think that's enough for us
to run a diagnostic program and rethink our strategies! Plus, I'm not
satisfied with the environmental analyses. And for heaven's sake, let's
make sure we're hitting the right area, at the right time."

"Ken! We've done all that in the lab. What's your point?"

"We've done it in the lab! That's precisely my point. We are using
data from the lab and just modifying it to account for the different
distances and the size of the target area. But we did not take
atmospheric conditions into consideration. We've not run any tests to
cover that, for example. And I'm just not at all convinced that our
security measures are adequate."

"Define!"

"It seems to me, we are operating on the assumption that the area is
unpopulated. But people are in the area, rural people, and farmers.
That's an unpredictability that did not get factored in. I've read and re-
read the whole thing and I'm telling you that we are not ready,
regardless of what Jonathon seems to think."

David Smith had pulled out a thick folder and started reviewing
document after document as they traveled the interstate. He looked at
Jeff Craft and sighed. Jeff, fighting carsickness, had folded his coat
neatly and placed it under his head. His eyes were closed and he
appeared to be sound asleep.

"See," David said to Ken, pointing at their travel companion. "He
is not concerned with the contaminant filters and quality controls of the
targeting program. That ought to tell you something, 'cause that man
worries about everything twenty-four hours a day. It's his job. He is
satisfied and so I'm satisfied. They don't pay me enough to worry

along with him. I've done my share!"

"As far as environmental impact is concerned, now you're treading on my turf. I've done the homework! The demographics and surveys clearly show we have the appropriate time frame. Yes, we'll have changes, but they'll be at the cellular level and could not possibly be visualized! We are programmed for that! Definitely no human effect! We've ruled that out conclusively. Even if those filters fail, we still have enough redundancies built into the system that we are virtually fail-proof. We've been through all possible scenarios in the lab, in real-nature conditions, Ken. We've covered it all. Argue the security with Craft, I'm taking a nap."

'There are some travel pillows behind the back seat," offered the driver. Ken tried to focus on the music and on the lovely scenery around them. Try to relax, he told himself as he inhaled deeply several times. Just try to relax.

"This road is following the same route wagon trains used to take in the old days", said Ron the driver. "I've often wondered what that must have been like. What we're traveling now in a matter of hours, they did in days, maybe weeks."

"Are you from around here?" asked Ken.

"Oh, no." Ron shook his head. "I'm a city boy, from Kansas City. When SERPAC started to develop the corporate retreat, I got involved and I suppose Mr. Brooks was satisfied and so he pretty much lets me run the show here. 'Course that means I have to live here, but once you get over the initial shock – you know city versus country – it's really quite lovely."

"Have you heard of the AMAG system?"

"I know what AMAG is supposed to do and I know what the success of AMAG will do to my bank account. Plus I've been a little involved with the security issues of this thing. Maybe I can help out?"

"I don't know. Do you have clearance?"

"I have the same clearance you all have. That's why I'm picking you guys up instead of the regular chauffeur. We were concerned you would be talking shop on the way and that's not part of the regular driver's clearance."

"I'm just concerned about a negative environmental impact. We just did not do nearly enough lab simulations to satisfy me. And if something goes wrong and we start an environmental nightmare, my ass will be way out on the line. Did we look at the utilization of the area for recreational purposes? I can just envision a Boy Scout Camp!"

"Hey, relax! That's all covered. SERPAC has leased a couple hundred acres from the feds; significantly more than is really needed. All roads in will be blocked by sunrise and reopened by sundown. But really, the area is so remote, it really is the pits!" He laughed. "I talked with some local people and the area is even too remote for the average poacher. I don't have my data with me, but when we get there, you're welcome to all my stuff and I'll even run you over there, so relax."

Ken Messer took another sip of his now cold coffee. Relax, my ass, he thought. That's probably what the Vietnam Vets were told about Agent Orange. Not that this would be anywhere close to that, but he just wasn't satisfied. I've been working on this for several years, he thought and there are still too many variables remaining. They passed through a small town, never slowing down.

"Hey," he said, grabbing the door handle. "The speed limit's twenty-five and you're doing sixty!" The driver had turned off the interstate highway and was now southbound on a two-lane state route.

"Sure am." Ron did not seem overly bothered. "These little towns don't have any cops and nobody really cares. Are you one of those law and order people?"

"Not particularly. I just think that we have rules and we need to abide by them for the good of society."

"Yeah, right."

But he did slow down some as they entered the next small town. Ken enjoyed looking at the picturesque old white frame houses with their wraparound porches and bright-colored flowerbeds. He was surprised to see the number of people up and about at this early hour and equally surprised that Ron seemed to wave at everyone.

"You seem to know everyone."

"Not really. But if you don't wave, folks around here think you're some stuck up city slicker. So you wave and blend right in. See, it's all part of the PR we do routinely."

At the far end of town he slowed down and turned to the left. A small green street sign gave the name of the narrow unpaved road as "Possum Squat Road".

"What a name!" he said to Ron. "How would anybody come up with a street name like that?"

Ron laughed. "I have no idea. But they have some real winners in this town; most of the names go back to the pioneer days and are related to the first settlers in this area. But 'Possum Squat' takes the cake."

Chapter 7
8:45 a.m.

They had been given free time to unpack, with the promise from Ron to meet them in time for brunch.

Jeff Craft almost did not hear the soft buzzing. He wasn't used to the sound and did not recognize it as a phone call. His gruff "What?" was answered by a very sweet female voice that reminded him of the time, the date and that he had a scheduled meeting with Mr. Jonathon Brooks in fifteen minutes in the executive dining room in building A. Jeff just grunted in response. He stretched and yawned. Time to find building A for his meeting with SERPAC's CEO.

Jonathon Brooks was a large man in his fifties. His salt-and-pepper hair was neatly trimmed and his clothing was a carefully selected casual that probably cost more than most people paid for formal attire. He was larger than Jeff remembered from previous meetings, but it had been a while and when he stood to greet him, Jeff was awed. He must be at least six feet, six inches and tipped the scales at three hundred pounds if not more. He now sported a double chin and an expanding middle. Jonathon Brooks believed in a hardy meal and to Jeff Craft's relief also believed in healthy things. There were bowls of fresh fruit in the center of the big dining room table, next to a platter with assorted donuts and pastries.

A young oriental woman discreetly poured coffee and ice water. Jonathon Brooks quietly said, "Thank you Maria, we won't need anything else." She disappeared without a word. Jeff Craft looked around, expecting the others, surprised to find himself alone with the big man.

They sat in silence, and then Jonathon Brooks reached for a donut. "Jeffrey," he said. "You have been with this corporation for a number of years. You may not realize it, but I have been following your progress for quite a while. I'm in need of a reliable assistant. I'm looking for a man I can trust, completely! A man who will have the good of SERPAC in mind, at all times. A man who shares my vision for the future. I believe you are that man, Jeffrey. Of course your salary would reflect your new responsibilities and so will the profit sharing. With AMAG, that could be substantial! I believe you would be quite satisfied. Interested?"

The question caught Jeff off guard. He swallowed the hot coffee, searing his throat. Ever the company man, he did not dare keep his boss waiting for an answer.

"I'm honored by your faith in my abilities, Sir. I'll strive not to disappoint you."

"I take it, you are accepting my proposition?"

"Yes, I do."

"Wonderful, wonderful."

As they ate, Jonathon talked about the corporate retreat.

"When we embarked on the AMAG project many years ago, I knew we would need a base away from the corporate offices. The competition must be considered when you plan such a major undertaking as AMAG. So I decided that we would move the project headquarters closer to where we would finally do the real testing. We had a military base in mind, close to here. When the Federal Government went on a base-closing spree, we spent a fortune to keep it from happening here. We just couldn't allow the base to be closed. It's ideal for us, ideal for AMAG. It's remote, actually quite isolated, and has very little permanent staff.

"Well, sure it costs us, but Camp Crowder is no longer on the list of bases even considered for closure. One of our local operatives located the three farms that make up the heart of this retreat. We spared no expense, bought the land and paid a very healthy price. Then we hired a West Coast firm, a very discreet firm, mind you. They converted the whole thing into our retreat. From the outside, it still looks like a couple of old buildings being used for some executive R & R. That's the image we want to present to the local population. But we have labs in the barns and tunnels connecting everything. You will be amazed! We spared no expense! We spared no expense, because we believe in AMAG. We believe that AMAG will be such a success, that it will validate any expense. Our latest venture is our computer network. It's located in one of those big old barns. It links us directly to anything and anywhere in the world, including the satellites we work with. It made AMAG a reality."

Impressed, Jeff nodded. "But where do I fit in?"

"You are witnessing history in the making. Right here! Our first real test of AMAG. I believe you have already met the key players. Keep in mind, your role is different from theirs! You are to represent me. I can't be here much. The industry monitors my whereabouts and if I should spend more than just a day or so here, it would be noticed. And that's not what we need right now. This needs to remain a corporate retreat, one of SERPAC's little perks, a place for executives to come for high-level meetings and a little R & R.

I come here to fish. You didn't know I love to fish, did you? Well, I really don't, but it's a good image and it keeps nosy competitors off my back. Anyhow, I need you to be here and watch over every step of this project. You have plenty of people to do all the work, so don't get wrapped up in micromanaging this project. That's not what I had in mind. You are to be me, be visible and be accessible. If problems arise, deal with them and report to me. The others are each managing a portion of this project and they will fill you in. I'll be on my way now. I believe the chauffeur is waiting. This is my cell phone number. I can be reached at any hour. Good luck."

Saturday 12:55 p.m.
Jeff nervously clung to his empty coffee mug. David Smith had long ago draped the coat of his Armani suit over the back of a chair; his red tie was in a heap on a desk in the corner, his shirtsleeves rolled up. He too clung to his coffee mug. Ken Messer, comfortable in faded jeans and a ClubMed T-shirt, sat in front of a computer nervously watching the screen and listening to a voice on the speakerphone.

"Okay, folks, we're coming up. Looking good so far. Ten, nine, eight, seven, six, five, four, three, two, one and go." After a sixty-second pause, the voice continued. "Gentlemen, we have had a successful thirty-second pulse of the AMAG system. The rest is up to you. Good luck."

Ken turned and high five'd with everyone in the room except Jeff Craft, who interrupted the commotion.

"Okay, people, we need to get over to the area and videotape the test field. Then repeat the taping every four hours for the next forty-eight hours. Dave, Ken, let's go. The rest of you, return all your recorded

50

data, make sure we have no inconsistencies, no errors in targeting. That program has given us far too many headaches! If you find something off, give me a buzz on the cell phone, here's the number. I'll be with Smith and Messer in the chopper."

They met Ron the chauffeur, now the pilot, and in just minutes were airborne. Ron signaled for them to plug in their headphones. "We'll be over Camp Crowder in a few minutes. SERPAC leased some land from a farmer, adjacent to Camp Crowder. It's situated in a manner, that severely limits access and, when combined with the federal land, allows for a point five percent margin of error in targeting. The test field itself is on the leased land, we're using the federal land of the base as a safety buffer."

Below them a blacktop highway wound its way through hills and valleys, running almost parallel to a small river. They saw several dirt roads branching off the blacktop road and counted a couple of small farms. There were meadows with grazing cattle and huge cornfields, but mostly it was all wooded. Then they swerved to the left, crossed the river and slightly curved back.

"You can start rolling the tape now," the pilot said to Ken Messer. With one push of a button on the console beneath his forearm, Ken activated the mounted cameras on the underside of the helicopter. They descended, almost low enough to touch the treetops and swept across the rectangular field of neat rows of corn. Then they turned away and back toward the compound.

"It sure is beautiful out here," said Ken Messer.

"Say, Ron," Jeff Craft could be heard. "What can you tell me about the precautions taken on the ground here. You know, like keeping people out of the area for at least a little while today. What has been done about that?"

"That's easy. Mr. Brooks is good friends with the Base Commander. Well, it appears that the Base Commander has some training exercises going on this weekend for several local Reserve Units. Involves spending the night out in the woods. One unit handles guard duty and as a part of its training simply sealed off all roads leading into the base in this sector for the next twenty-four hours, along with all roads accessing the river just above our test site, as of this morning. The only other way in would be on horseback, across the

51

fields. We can't seal that off, it's just not possible. Would you like to see the base and some of the surrounding area? It's really pretty out here, especially if you're into wilderness camping and that sort of thing."

"Yeah, sure."

"Let's do it."

They turned back toward the river, temporarily following its winding course upriver back toward the base.

"Wow, look at those bluffs! Beautiful."

"That water looks crystal clear."

" I can't believe that nobody lives here."

"Someone needs to build a resort out here, they'd make a fortune."

"Dave, do you ever not think of money?"

"Yeah, when I'm in bed with a hot chick."

"This is awesome. I had no idea SERPAC owned this place out here! I've been with the company for years, never heard about it. When I was told to come out here, I never made the connection with AMAG."

"Hey fellas, check out the blonde down there, on that boat."

They swept a little lower and watched a young blond woman in a hot pink bikini floating in a canoe in the clear water of a little river. They forgot that the aircraft's automatic cameras were still running.

"They do grow nice looking women here."

"Well gents, let's get back. We need to set up the equipment for tonight. Jonathon wants only key personnel to be involved. That's us. Thank God for automation."

Chapter 8

I didn't have an opportunity to speak with Tom for a while after we landed because we were all was busy setting up camp. After a while I felt pretty foolish to have been so upset over some oversized weeds. Must be fertile soil here, I said to myself, or the military has played around with some chemicals. Then I put the whole thing out of my mind, at least for the moment.

Sam had chosen a nice spot for our campsite. I didn't care for the fact that it was gravel, though. Gravel gets rough on your feet and can be hazardous after dark when you try to walk around on it. But we were close to the water and the ground was level. I thought of a night under the stars in my husband's arms and couldn't help but smile. With the pads and the air mattress I would not feel a thing.

Supper was simple: steaks and barbecued beans. All of us wives enjoyed the paper plates and plastic utensils, which left no dishes to wash! Sam had been right. The sun was setting and it quickly got cooler. No one complained. We were all getting slightly sunburned, and the cooler air felt heavenly. The wet swimsuits did get a bit uncomfortable, and after a while, we changed into dry clothing and gathered around the well-established fire.

Tom and Ralph had set up a tripod and had brewed some 'hillbilly coffee', using cold water letting it boil twice. The aroma drifted through our campsite. I was blowing on my steaming mug when I realized that Marty was nowhere in sight. I couldn't recall her joining us for supper and felt pretty awful that I had not noticed her absence sooner. As concerned as I had been over her sunburn, I should have checked on her. That's when Sam sat down beside me

"Chris," he said quietly "I need a favor."

"Sure, what's up?"

"Come with me and check on Marty, I think she's pretty sick. I think she's been out in the sun way too long today."

"Do you think she's burned?" My mind raced ahead and focused on the fact that I only had a couple of things in my First Aid pack that could be used for sunburn.

"No, I don't think it's a burn. It seems more like a medication reaction. You know the, doctor put her on some antidepressants recently and it's done some strange things to her."

Marty has always been strange, I thought, even without antidepressants. But I got up.

"Sam, is there any possibility that Marty could be pregnant?"

He stopped and turned, a questioning look in his eyes. "No, none. Why?"

"Well," I tried to be careful. I did not want to get into their private business. "Well, earlier Marty said something about being pregnant."

Sam's facial expression remained unchanged. "No, I don't think there is any possibility short of divine intervention. To get pregnant one must first have sex. I had a vasectomy several years ago and we haven't had sex for almost that long."

I didn't know what to say, so I sipped on my coffee as we stood there in front of the tent staring at each other, feeling thoroughly embarrassed.

"Chris is there something you are trying to tell me? Just say it."

My coffee tasted bitter and I felt my throat closing.

"Sam I really don't know what I am getting at. Come and walk with me over to the water." I nodded toward the tent and put a finger to my lips. I really didn't want to talk in front of Marty. We walked to the water's edge and sat down. I dared another sip from my mug.

"I have been really worried about Marty," I began, "She was all puffy, with her eyelids and lips swollen. Plus, she was all red and hot to the touch, and then she was trying to convince me that she is term pregnant." I stopped, but Sam didn't say anything.

"Sam, I am not very experienced with heat or sunstroke, and it's just very obvious that Marty also a bit confused. I don't know why. Maybe it's that new medication you mentioned, in combination with the sun and the heat. Either way, I think we have a problem, and I have this feeling in my gut that we had best get off the river fast. And who is Jack?"

"Jack?"

"Yes, Marty was referring to you as Jack. Jack the hunk, I might add."

"Jack was an old boyfriend of hers, well before my time. She was pretty serious about him. He was a superficial, pretentious jackass. She almost married him, but he left town and married some east coast socialite. She was pretty bitter about that for years. I'm surprised you didn't know that."

"You know Marty and I haven't been that close."

"What do we do now?"

"Well, let's check on her, first of all; then we'll see."

Coffee in hand, we walked back to the tent. Before Sam could open the flap, Marty came out. She had changed into a large tee shirt that went almost to her knees – probably one of Sam's, I thought. She had combed her hair back, and I was finally able to see her without sunglasses or headphones on.

Her face was no longer as swollen as it had been earlier in the day, but there were some puffy areas below her eyes. The earlier redness had been replaced with a pale yellowish color and when I looked closer the skin on her face just hung loosely off her cheekbones.

"Marty how are you feeling," I asked. She stretched and twisted her torso.

"I'm so sore! I think I can feel every bone in my body and then some that I didn't even know I had. Sam, be a dear and get me something to drink please."

Sam left and I reached up and felt Marty's forehead. Without a thermometer I had to rely on Dr. Mom. Marty's skin felt hot, and dry like old leather – like an old worn out glove. I let my hand slip to her upper arms and hugged her.

"We've been worried about you, honey."

Marty smiled at me, "That's sweet, but I think I just have a flu bug or something. I just don't feel real well."

"Like what?"

"Well, dizzy, nauseated, lightheaded. You know that sort of stuff. My shoulder hurts. Actually my whole left side hurts. My throat's sore and I have a terrible taste in my mouth. Chris, I really do not feel well, but what a lousy time this is to get sick!"

"Its gonna be ok, Marty. You'll refill on fluids tonight and you'll feel better in the morning."

She looked at me kinda funny with tears in her eyes.

"I'm soooo scared, Chris. I really am afraid I won't be around in the

55

morning."

I could hear my heartbeats in my ears. I felt the hairs on my neck rise and goose bumps form on my arms. I hugged Marty.

"Why do you think so?"

"I don't know; I just feel so miserable. My left shoulder hurts, even my jaws hurt. I probably just lay wrong in the canoe. And the heartburn! It's probably nothing, but I'm short of breath, and when I stand up or just take a few steps, I'm dizzy. Chris, what's wrong with me? You're a nurse, can you figure this out?"

I couldn't, I didn't know what to think of Marty's symptoms. I was pretty sure that it was just the sun and the heat, getting a bit dehydrated, something like that. And that should improve with all the fluids we were giving her to drink.

She did not look well and I thought that if she were an older person and complaining of these symptoms, we'd be concerned about something cardiac. But Marty was in her thirties. I helped her back into the tent and got her comfortable with her drinks close by.

"I'm ruining y'all's weekend. "

"You're not ruining anyone's weekend. Close your eyes and rest while I figure out what is going on."

"I'm so scared, promise me you won't let me die."

"Marty, get real. You are not going to die."

"Promise it"

"Okay, I promise."

But I couldn't settle her down; she started to cry and held on to my hand. She kept on telling me over and over how scared she was and how miserable she felt and I didn't know what to say to her or how to comfort her, let alone what to do.

I know I sounded firm and confident, but I didn't feel that way. As she held on to my hand and closed her eyes, I sat thinking. I have never been close enough to Marty to know of her medical problems. What could be going on with her? Just when I thought that she was finally asleep and I tried to peel her fingers off my hand, she gripped tighter.

"This is going to be the best day of my life," she whispered. "Don't tell anyone, especially Jack, I want it to be special for him." I nodded. Her eyes were glazed and her face looked flushed. I couldn't think of anything to do.

"We've been going together for such a long time, I just know that he'll ask me to be his wife tonight. I just know it. And I'll say yes. I'll make him wonder for a few minutes, but then I'll say yes. Do you like my dress? It's my special dress. My Mom went and found it in Kansas City for me. She had to go there on business, and she said she saw it in a store window and she bought it for me. You can't borrow it until after the wedding."

She closed her eyes. Her breathing was shallow and fast. When she was lying down, her face and neck were full of wrinkles where the sunburned areas had been. I just sat there, stroking her hair. Her forehead was covered with big drops of perspiration and she felt very hot, but at least she finally appeared to be asleep.

"Sam," I called out, "get in here!"

He was there in an instant. Our eyes met and he followed my look to Marty's face. I raised an eyebrow.

"What happened?" I asked him quietly. " Did she sunbathe in the nude?"

I didn't remember seeing her nude, not that it would be the first time. We all had a penchant for skinny-dipping after midnight on moonlit nights and had lost what modesty we may have had a long time ago, at least within this group.

But Sam just shook his head.

"No," he said. "We were just ahead of all of you. Marty did what all of us did: Nothing different."

"Except when she decided to work on her tan while we were having lunch?"

"Well yeah. She did spend a couple of hours in the sun then. So, do you still think this is a sunburn?"

"No I don't. I haven't a clue what's going on with her. Just when I think it's sun and heat related she acts just fine and then turns around and does something completely goofy."

"Goofy?"

"Yeah, she's talking to me, but it doesn't make much sense. And look at her now; she is sound asleep. Completely out of it."

"Why is her skin all wrinkled?"

"I don't know, maybe she was all puffy and swollen from the sun and the heat or whatever and now it's much cooler and the swelling is reducing and the skin is still stretched. I'm guessing, Sam. I'm guessing."

Tom stuck his head in the tent. "What's up with Marty?"

I looked up to him, I wanted so much for him to hold me, take me away from here.

"This is so weird," I said softly. " There's something really wrong."

"Sunburn?"

"No, I think it's something else. Sam said she's on some new medication, but somehow it just doesn't fit either."

I felt her forehead again, it was hot and dry, her heart rate was up too, and I counted 120 and irregular.

Sam told us he was planning on staying in the tent with Marty for a little while and I thought that would be a good idea. She felt so hot to touch, I was sure that she was really dehydrated, and so I encouraged Sam to give her lots of fluids to drink, even if it meant waking her up.

Tom pulverized a couple of aspirin for her and dissolved that in some soda, and Sam was spoon-feeding the mixture to Marty as we were crawling out of the tent.

When three hours passed, I fed her two more dissolved aspirin and then joined the others in front of the tent. For a while, nobody said anything. Then I spoke up: "Marty is pretty sick, we need to get her off this river as fast as possible. Sam, if we push, really push, how fast can we be at the takeout point?"

"Daylight?"

I nodded.

"Oh, four or five hours."

"That's not too bad, but we need to do it faster. Sandy, did you bring your famous cell phone?"

"But of course," she said with a fake British accent. I could have kissed her. I had counted on her vanity, on her need to show off, and she did not let me down. Quickly I dialed the number to our ER. There would be a doctor on duty and I wanted help. But I never ever got a dial tone. Ralph, who is more into this stuff, told me that we were probably out of range and, in this river valley, were surrounded by too many obstacles. Now we were back to square one.

"Well, guys, for now she is holding her own, but we can't let her just lie there until morning. I think we should just take turns checking on her."

"I will be sleeping in that tent," Sam said. "I'll handle the checking"

I nodded. We sat there in silence. This wasn't what any of us had envisioned and I was pretty scared. I didn't know what was wrong with Marty and I could only hope that what I was doing was actually helping her.

Chapter 9
Saturday 5:35 p.m.

Ken Messer, Jeff Craft and Dave Smith carried a large canvas bag each. Neither had any additional clothing. Each pack contained electronic equipment they would be mounting on trees. The equipment would obtain readings during the night and make sure everything was working. This was supposed to be confirmed by the computer center. Once confirmation was received, the men were free to return to the retreat and continue the remote monitoring. Their reaction to hiking into the backwoods area with military reservists was mixed. Ken Messer enjoyed the young peoples' vigor and energy and was interested in their stories. Dave Smith and Jeff Craft wanted as little as possible to do with their temporary companions. When they realized that one of them would need to spend the night in the wild, it was only logical that Ken stay behind. He didn't mind. He rather enjoyed the company, and having always been a camper he enjoyed the reprieve from the more formal corporate life.

Chapter 10

We helped Sam move his tent closer to the fire. That way, he could check on Marty and still be a part of the group conversation. The coffee was replaced by hot chocolate and we settled down and got comfortable.

"It's a shame Marty isn't feeling well" said Ralph. "I was just thinking about that one trip we took, just the guys, and we took a bunch of beer along."

He chuckled and punched Tom on the shoulder.

"Well anyway, we were fishing all day long and drinking beer. Didn't think anything about it until it started getting dark outside. We had no place to camp, but we had a bunch of fish. Mr. Conservation here came to the rescue. He found a spot. It was just big enough for us to tie up the canoes. We couldn't cook, make coffee, nothing. Not that we cared; if we got worried about it, we just had another beer. Anyway, we spent the night in the canoes. It was wild! I'll never complain about my waterbed again! But that's not all of it: The next morning we finally realized that we did not have water with us to brush our teeth, so we brushed with toothpaste and beer. It was absolutely gross." He laughed.

"Yeah," Sandy stood up and stretched. " You guys came home so fucking hung over, it took you three days to recover. Some weekend that was. One for the books, for sure."

Tom looked over and winked at me. "Oh, it wasn't that bad now was it?"

"Don't look at me, pal!" I said. "Allen was at my parents that memorable weekend and I had to work. I came home after a weekend of puking people in the ER and there at home is this man - whom I used to love so dearly - and he is puking his guts out. Yes, Dear, it was that bad."

I took a sip of my Hot Chocolate and almost burned my tongue.

Sam crawled out of his tent and I turned to him.

"How is she?" I said between puffing air onto my too Hot Chocolate.

He sighed.

"Well, she is sleeping and she doesn't feel quite as hot to the touch as she did earlier. I've been getting some fluids into her, actually quite a bit."

"That's great! Maybe she just had too much sun? Besides, she's on some new medication, which may have had something to do with it. I'm sure she'll feel better after some sleep."

"I think so too. What was all the laughing about?"

We cracked up again and told him. He produced a bag of little tiny marshmallows and passed it around, I love little marshmallows in hot chocolate. I leaned back in my seat and looked up at the sky. The stars were so clear and bright, I wished I had binoculars. The others were also enjoying the evening, even Sandy, who seldom relaxes until all the dishes are done. And it was Sandy who surprised me.

"This is a night for a moonlight swim," she said. "As soon as the moon is overhead I'm in the water, I don't care what you all do or say."

"I may just join you," I said to my own surprise. "I just don't want to slip into that wet swimsuit."

Sandy just laughed lustily, "Who said anything about a swimsuit, anyway?"

I looked at Tom. "Go ahead, Babe," he said. "You don't need my permission. Besides, I may join you. This place is about as private as it gets."

What else can you do when you are on the edge of a river, away from everything else, on a clear, starry, moonlit night? I could think of a few more things. But I spread my swimsuit out by the fire hoping it would dry just a little bit. Before too long the topic of the campfire conversation turned toward the friendship we were sharing. I looked at the river bathed in the pale moonlight, the ripples shimmering like liquid silver, and felt drawn to it. I closed my eyes and imagined slowly slipping into the warm, black depth, with each step shutting out more of the world around me.

I looked at Tom, momentarily at a loss for words. My wonderful husband read my thoughts, took my outstretched hand, winked at Ralph and Sandy and followed me to the water.

About three or four feet from the water's edge was an old weather beaten tree trunk. Although almost half submerged in the gravel and

62

sand, it still provided us with a dry spot for towels and clothes. We undressed, clasped hands and walked into the now considerably cooler water.

I had to hold my breath for these first few steps when my body, hot from the long day out in the sun, entered the cool darkness of the river. I felt my nipples getting hard making my breasts ache, and as the water embraced me I found it difficult to breathe. Once we were fully submerged it was easier and I actually started to feel warmer again. Tom snuggled up to me and whispered into my ear, "I love the way your nipples are sticking out, baby. Makes me horny. You better watch out, I might just ravage your body right here and now."

I reached for him and with a big grin he guided my hand to his erection. Yes, it would be a memorable night. I pointed to a huge fallen tree on the opposite bank. "Let's go over there, Tarzan and see what we can stir up."

Tom loves it when I get right down to business. Just a few strokes brought us to the other side, and when Tom climbed onto the fallen log he found the remains of an old boat dock hidden behind it. The tree had actually landed on a flat section of concrete that now was just barely above the water and maybe 20 feet offshore. Giggling, I sat on the edge of it letting my legs dangle, my back turned toward our camp. Tom did not waste any time. With his hands, he urged me forward until I had to lean back to keep from slipping off the dock. By the time my upper body rested on my bent arms, his mouth was on me and I didn't care if there were birds, bees, or turtles watching. I love making love with Tom. We share the same passion for sex, and over the years we have turned pleasuring each other into an art form. Tom is gentle, firm and passionate, and he knows just where and how to touch me.

I really don't remember how long we were on this concrete platform. I didn't keep track of time. I didn't care.

Then we rested in each other's arms, breathless, warm and satisfied. I couldn't think of anything but my love for Tom, and felt almost overwhelmed by the stars, the moonlight, and the shimmering current of the river flowing past us.

The rhythm of the water splashing against the concrete was hypnotic, and I turned on my side snuggling up to Tom. Suddenly, out of the corner of my eye, I noticed movement on the bank. For a split second I saw a man standing there. He lit a match or a lighter and was gone again. Startled, I sat up, at the same time bumping my elbow on the concrete and scraping an ankle.

"Tom," I whispered. "Tom, there's somebody watching us."

"Mmmmm, its just our guy's babe."

"No, on the other shore. I'm serious. I just saw a man there, he lit a cigarette or something."

Tom turned toward the bank. "Where?"

"Right over there." I pointed to the bank, to a spot where a large sycamore was leaning precariously over the water. I couldn't see the person any longer, but I felt very uneasy. Tom scanned the opposite bank, then finally said, "OK, let's just go back, babe." He helped me off the concrete, but not without scraping his knees.

In the water and out of sight of the bank, he quietly said, "You know, it could have been a military patrol just passing by, checking on their perimeter. It's really okay. I doubt that either two-legged or four-legged animals care about what we were doing tonight."

I let myself slip into the cool waters, deep, well over my head, until I could no longer hold my breath.

"I thought you said we were past Camp Crowder?" I reached down and carefully massaged my sore ankle.

"I just hope the creep enjoyed the show." I said when I came back up, spitting out river water. "And next time we decide to fuck on concrete, let's at least bring along a boat cushion or two."

We returned to the camp. Sandy and Ralph were still sitting by the fire sipping beer.

"You two have fun?" Sandy said, raising the can of beer in greeting.

We both laughed. "You ought to give that a try sometime."

But Sandy just shook her head.

"No, I think I'll pass. You two look too beat up. Just look at your legs. You're lucky they don't have piranhas in this river."

I had to admit we did look a little rough in the light of the fire, but considering what we had been doing... I caught myself smiling.

We dried off and I cleaned the abrasions with some antiseptic wash and put on some antibiotic ointment.

When the fire finally died down, we crawled into our tents for the night. It was quiet around us. I remember thinking that we didn't tell

64

the others of our encounter with the stranger and probably should have, but I fell asleep before I could worry about it.

Chapter 11
10:50 p.m.

Ken Messer found it difficult to feel comfortable surrounded by these 10 young strangers, although they seemed to enjoy his company. They had been warned that no open fires were permitted down range because of the current drought. So much for a weenie roast, he thought. The young men did not appear upset by the news at all. When it started to get dark, they all gathered in the center of their little camp. Out of nowhere, coolers appeared filled with soft drinks and assorted munchies.

Before long, he found himself involved in a conversation with a young soldier named Randy. A skinny, awkward young man with incredibly long legs, he was fascinated with the fact that this corporate big shot from far away Seattle was out here in the woods with him. Randy had grown up not too far from here, the fourth child in a family with ten kids.

"My childhood would have made a good country song," he said with a smile. "We was dirt poor. We ate what we grew in the backyard, shot in the woods and pulled out of the water. I laugh when I see them tourists coming into the area with their fancy fishing gear. They fish for fun – we fished for food. It's different when your belly's empty.

"Pa didn't do much, he was a logger in his younger days. Then he hurt his back real bad and that put an end to the loggin'. Ain't nobody wanna hire a logger with a bum back. My Momma, she was always so busy either havin' babies or takin' care of us, she didn't hardly have no time for nothin' else. Rarely even went to church on Sundays. You know, I wonder sometimes. My Pa, his back it was always hurtin' him too much to work for a livin', but it sure didn't keep him from gettin' Momma pregnant. I left home when I was 15. I just dropped out of school; I had no more time for that nonsense. I went to St. Louis and I found me a job. Wasn't much at first, but I got better. Last year I got me my GED, and I moved over to Holsum. You know, just up the road, just ten miles or so. That's where I joined the Reserves and got me a job fixin' diesel trucks. That's my job in the Reserves too, fixin'

66

the big rigs. This weekend, I'm doing something else – for fun. I told my first sergeant that I didn't wanna be a grease monkey this drill weekend, I just wanted to do something different." He laughed. "I shoulda kept my big mouth shut. Look at me, huffin' it with these grunts, pulling guard duty." He made a face.

"Have you thought any further about going on with school? May be on to College?" Messer asked.

"Me, College?" Randy laughed and slapped his thigh. "My Momma would like that one. No, I don't see myself as college material. I don't need it anyhow. Besides, my Pa says all them college boys are just a bunch of fagots anyway. Nope, I don't wanna have anything to do with that."

Sunday

Ken Messer was wide awake at the crack of dawn. Actually he had not slept at all. He had not been prepared to spend the night in the woods, and did not bring a sleeping bag or bedroll with him. Not wanting to impose on the young soldiers, he selected a fairly smooth tree and sat leaning against it. Although he did doze off and on, he did not sleep and subsequently was not in a very good mood by daybreak. But that did not deter Randy. He came over with a stainless steel mug full of steaming coffee.

"Brought you some coffee, Mr. Messer."

"Hi there, Randy; I asked you to call me Ken."

"Oops. Sorry, Ken. I wanted to tell you something last night, but you was already asleep."

"What's up?"

"Well, you said we's the only people out in these woods, on account of your company doing some testing, right?" Messer nodded. "Well, I did see some other folks out here last night. Was pretty interesting, you might say." He blushed.

"Where did you see these people?"

"Well, I went on down to the river. You know we're not supposed to smoke around this electronic equipment. I wanted to have me a smoke. Well, I was just lighting up, you know. Then I hear some voices, somebody talking. And I see this man and this woman in the moonlight. They was on this old boat dock, and they was, you know,"

67

he blushed, "they was gettin' it on."

Messer looked at him, startled.

"You mean to tell me there were people on the river, and you watched them make love?"

It was Randy's turn to blush again.

"Yes, Sir. I sure did see that. I didn't mean to, it just happened. And when I realized what they was doing, I couldn't just leave. I'd have made noise and disturbed them. So I just waited until they was finished and then I left."

"Did they see you?"

"Naw, I don't think so. Pretty cool though."

"I'm sure of that."

Messer didn't mean to sound sarcastic, but all he could think about was their final instructions. If people were on the river, could they have been in their testing area? They knew nothing about its effect on humans. Oh shit, he thought. Finally he pulled out his cellular 'phone and dialed. Jeff answered: "What's up?"

"You are not going to believe this. We have civilians out here."

"What?"

"You heard me. One of the guys, spotted civilians last night. He didn't want to trouble me, but he told me this morning. Now what?"

"I don't know. I think we need to find them, find out how much they know, what they saw, that sort of thing. I'll let Jonathon know. Come on back to the lab. Shit."

Chapter 12

Sam must have been the first one up.

I felt as if I had only slept moments when I heard him calling our names. When I opened the tent flap the golden light of dawn and the scent of fresh coffee greeted me. Although I am not a big coffee drinker, I do like my cup of coffee in the morning and the aroma gets me going.

There was a mist rising from the river, and the leaves on the bushes next to our tent were glistening with fresh dew. I stretched and poked Tom in the ribs. "Come on sweetie, coffee's ready," I said.

I heard Sam rummaging through the supplies and listened to the clatter of pots and pans. I crawled out of the tent, slipping into my shower shoes I had stashed outside. My bladder was signaling me that it was high time to pee and nodding a still sleepy greeting to Sam I stomped off into the direction of our designated latrine.

When I returned, Sam had a mug of steaming coffee already poured for me, and Tom was just crawling out. We were hearing signs of life from Ralph and Sandy as well.

"How's Marty?" I asked Sam.

"Well, she was still sleeping when I got up a little while ago. I didn't want to wake her up. I think she's better. She sure slept soundly, all night."

But when I checked on her, Marty looked obviously worse than the night before. I had considerable difficulty turning her on her back and barely managed to get a response from her. When I finally did, it was all incoherent babbling. Her pulse was very irregular and very fast. Most of the swelling and redness was gone, leaving her skin loose, wrinkled and looking very old. She didn't respond to anything I did, and when I tried to spoon-feed some fluids into her, she did not swallow but let the fluids run out again.

Outside the tent I heard bacon sizzling and Tom taking egg orders from everyone. He loves to cook breakfast on these trips. But this morning my heart just wasn't in it. I couldn't believe what was happening with Marty and I couldn't understand it. I had never seen

69

anything like that before. Not knowing what else to do, I held her hand and stroked her now wrinkled up face and whispered, "It's gonna be ok, Marty, we'll take good care of you. Just rest and relax, we'll get you home in no time."

When I finally felt that she had settled down again, I joined the group by the fire.

"Marty is in big trouble, guys."

They looked at me.

"I can't figure out what it is. But I know we have to get her off the river and to a hospital pretty fast. I think she's had maybe some kind of wild, bizarre reaction to meds. Who knows, actually she's pretty unresponsive now. We need to get her out of here, fast. We've got to get some help and we need to get fluids into her. And we need to do this fast."

I didn't need to say more. Gone was yesterday's carefree float. We were packed up in no time and back on the river, fiercely paddling with the current, not saying much.

Although I was worried about Marty, I still was fascinated with our surroundings. Everything looked different, the trees were covered with brownish orange leaves, looking like early fall and the vegetation as a whole was strange to me. I was looking for my dragonflies, but there were none. And that bothered me for some reason.

I don't really like those bugs, I just think they are ugly yet fascinating, but I didn't see any. Nor did I see anymore little turtles sunbathing on the fallen logs along the shoreline. To me it felt as if we were in a different world. Very strange and very silent. Ralph and Sandy were up ahead, holding on to something on the shore, signaling and pointing. We paddled faster and pulled along side of them well ahead of Sam. Ralph was waving his arm.

"Look at this" he said. " This isn't supposed to be here. I reviewed Sam's map and there is no mention of this mess."

We all sat there and looked at the rippling water, I could see several large tree trunks half submerged and thought that this could become dangerous. I'm not a very confident canoeist. But Tom, my rock, said it would be ok.

"Just get speed and be on the look out for those logs in the water and we should be ok."

We agreed that Tom and I would go on ahead and Ralph would wait for Sam. Then Sam would follow, and Ralph and Sandy would bring up the rear. Tom repeatedly told them to be sure and keep a good distance between each other.

And off we went. It was a pretty wild ride. At least from my point of view, we barely missed a couple of logs and only missed them because Tom and I were both paying attention to what we were doing. Next was Sam with Marty. I was very concerned about them. Tom and I had enough trouble and it was two of us, but Sam was alone. Should their canoe flip Sam would be ok, the water wasn't very deep, but Marty could be in real trouble.

Sam had just started when I watched Sandy push their canoe into the current as well. Behind me Tom was swearing. I was holding my breath. Although I couldn't hear what Ralph was saying, based on his gestures I doubt it was friendly.

Of course the inevitable happened. Sam, not knowing that someone was following closely, slowed to move around a log. Ralph was yelling something at Sandy and she turned around. In a split second they flipped and the upside down canoe hit Sam broadside and flipped his canoe. There was nothing we could do but sit and watch.

The water was only thigh deep and they all had their lifejackets on, but Marty was in obvious trouble. While everyone came up sputtering and screaming, she floated without a sign of struggle face down toward us. By the time I realized that, Tom was already racing toward her. I had more trouble going against the current; after all I am a lot shorter than he is. Tom reached her and pulled her up. She hung in his arms limp, a wet rag doll. Sam watched, but was still too far away to get to her. Tom signaled me to just stay and headed back toward the shore and me.

Together we worked on Marty. We opened her airway, she still wasn't breathing but I could feel a faint pulse. Finally, after what seemed like an eternity, she coughed and coughed and was breathing again. Not real deep, but better than what she had been doing.

Sam arrived, towing his upside down canoe followed by Sandy and Ralph. They didn't talk to each other. Oh shit, I thought, that's all we need right now, a major blow up. We have flipped canoes before, have lost stuff before and have learned little tricks from it. Above all, pay attention.

Once we were assured that Marty was breathing, we helped Sam turn the canoe over and get all the stuff out. Then we turned Ralph and Sandy's over, but it was empty except for the cooler.

No one spoke at first. Ralph and Sandy had carried most of the foodstuff and cookware, while Tom and I had the tents, sleeping bags and clothing. Sam had carried only his cooler and our air mattresses, which he used to make a bed for Marty. Finally I couldn't stand the silence any longer.

"What the hell did you two do? What the hell were you thinking?"

We all turned to Sandy. She just shrugged.

"Come on, nothing ever happens, I just didn't want to be bothered with tying all that stuff down. What's the big deal anyway? Marty is obviously ok and the rest was just food, we won't starve, we'll be home in a couple of hours. Let's not make a big deal out of nothing, ok."

"It is a big deal!"

I was very angry.

"Marty is not ok, she almost drowned and she is still out of it. She needs medical attention and she needs it fast. And although we will be home in a little while, thanks to your stupidity we can't even boil water for a lousy cup of coffee."

I walked off to look after Marty. No way am I ever going on another outing with Sandy, I thought, no way. She is so inconsiderate, so oblivious to her surroundings she will get someone hurt. Ralph is married to her, he has to go places with her, and he has no choice, but not me. Nope, no more.

Marty looked peaceful, she was breathing more regular now, but still shallow and way too fast. I grabbed the sleeping bags but found only one that was dry. What a way to find out that your waterproof bags leak! I removed Marty's clothing and wrapped her in the sleeping bag. Even in 90-degree weather you should preserve body heat and besides it made me feel better. Then I walked away for a little solitude, therapy.

Tom saw me walking away and when I turned he nodded. He understands me and my way of dealing with life's frustrations. I need a few moments of solitude and letting things come back into focus.

Cutting through some bushes I found myself on the other side of what seemed to be a small island. This side had a nice sandy beach; the river had almost no current, seemed dark and deep and must have been about 100 feet wide. Really more like a little lake. I thought about the group fighting on the other side and Marty.

I was very worried about Marty, I couldn't figure out what was wrong with her. At first she seemed to have been sunburned, but by this morning she didn't look sunburned at all anymore. She looked wrinkled, dried out and leathery. She looked very old. Maybe its the combination of antidepressant and sunbathing I thought. They do put warnings on these medications to stay out of the sun, but if that's what happens, they should really emphasize the warning more.

I started pitching little pebbles into the water, but my mind wandered back to my earlier observations. The vegetation was different. The trees looked wrong for the season, their leaves with touches of brown, red and orange, the bushes I had walked through looked more like oversized weeds than any bush I had ever seen and there still weren't any bugs anywhere. Although I was troubled by my observations, I felt calmer and more in control of myself and decided to return to the group when I heard shouting from their direction. I couldn't make out what was being said, but the tone was very angry.

I hurried through the brush, furious at everyone by now, here we are knee-deep in trouble and these guys can't keep from fighting with each other.

Chapter 13

"Hello, Ken? It's Jeffrey; we've had a radio transmission from one of the military perimeter patrols. They have spotted the civilians you talked about earlier. We've requested that Base Command detain them until one of us can get there and talk to them. Where exactly are you right now?"

Ken Messer scratched his head and consulted his map. "I'm in U as in Uniform. Where are they at?"

"Weeellll, they are not really on our turf, take a look at your map. Just above E - Echo, is this little river, about 1/2 mile down river and on the other shore is our perimeter patrol. The river splits at that spot, our guests are on the island in the middle of the river. The patrol is on the shore. How fast can you get there?"

"You have got to be joking! Tell me you are joking? We're talking damn near one mile cross-country and how am I going to cross the river? It's gonna be awhile. Tell them to be cool. Don't do anything until I get there." Ken Messer hung up the phone swearing loudly.

Chapter 14

Tom grabbed me as I walked up to them. "Thank god you're back. These assholes say we're trespassing on the military reservation. They're pointing guns at us and want us to stay put until somebody else gets here. We've told them that's a crock and that we're leaving, but..."

The two young men in camouflage uniforms seemed quite sure of themselves despite the fact that at least 75 yards of fast moving water separated us.

"Let's just get out of here," I said to Tom. "They wouldn't shoot us, would they?"

He shrugged and whispered to Sam and Ralph. The men on the other shore kept on yelling at us to sit down and remain seated, that someone was coming and after our clearance had been confirmed we would be allowed to continue.

Ralph shouted back. "We're not on the military reservation, assholes! We're not trespassing! We're leaving, okay, there's no trouble."

They yelled back, but I couldn't make it out. And so we moved Marty into Sam's canoe and climbed into the other canoes. Tom yelled at the two men in uniform again.

"Fellas, we're leaving. Just be cool. This is just a big misunderstanding. No need for anyone to get hurt."

"You ain't leaving, asshole. You were told to sit down, now - sit down."

The taller of the men raised his rifle.

"They wouldn't, would they?" I whispered into Tom's ear.

"I wouldn't count on any anger control over there, babe. The faster we're outta here the better."

They were shouting obscenities as we pushed off. Out of the corner of my eyes I saw movement in Ralph and Sandy's canoe. Turning slightly I watched in horror as Sandy raised her right arm, extending her right middle finger in a classic gesture. This was answered by several shots and loud swearing from Ralph.

I couldn't turn around and look, we were back in fast water and I had to concentrate on what I was doing. We paddled furiously and yet careful, but we still bumped into obstacle after obstacle. There were just too many.

I expected to get shot from behind at any moment and wondered what that would feel like. Would there be a lot of pain? I wanted to tell Tom that I love him but I didn't dare turn around and if I said it out loud it would be doubtful that he would hear it. But I said it anyway, thinking that it would be better to die knowing that I said it than not. I paddled furiously, after all convinced that I was paddling for our lives.

Ever so often I would hear Tom say something encouraging or urging me to ease off. Still, we hit obstacles and came close to tipping over many times.

I know, I will never forget this river.

Finally we were through, and I was grateful when Tom steered us toward the shore. We found a small strip of sand underneath a couple of large trees and beached the canoe and just sat there for a moment. That's when my tears came. I always cry when I am under stress or very angry. It doesn't really solve anything, but seems to put me back on track once the tears stop.

"Tom," I finally said. "What on earth is happening? This was supposed to be such a smooth little trip and then Marty gets sick, we get shot at. It's a nightmare. Forgive me, but I think it will be awhile before I do this again."

He nodded. "I don't know what to say, babe. I certainly didn't expect that. None of us even thought of running into trouble, but I think we are in big trouble. As soon as the others get here, we need to sit down and figure out how we will get the hell off this rotten, miserable excuse of a river.

"Back there," he pointed upriver, " back there I had a chance to look at the map and we still have at least 6 hours of river ahead of us. This baby winds mercilessly. We are only a couple of miles from the road and only a couple of miles from the cars, but on the river it's an eternity. I don't know what Sam was thinking, but I believe he miscalculated the distance. I think we need to leave everything here and walk out, it will be faster."

"What about Marty?"

"I haven't forgotten about that. Marty is pretty little, between Sam and Ralph and me we should be able to carry her."

I sat in silence. I was not convinced that this was such a hot plan. There was this nagging pain in my gut and I just couldn't believe that all would be well now, just like that.

The first one to arrive was Sam. He beached next to us, I watched him as he bend over the canoe and adjusted the sleeping bag with Marty. His face looked old and drawn, and I felt sorry for him. This trip had been his idea and I'm sure he had to talk Marty into coming. He had probably assured her that it would be a nice trip, change of wallpaper; you can just relax and let me take care of everything. I could almost hear him. And then look what happened.

He walked over to us and sat down. He was pale and there were traces of tears in the dirt on his stubbled cheeks.

"Marty is dead," he said quietly.

The three of us sat there, stunned. The sounds of the river getting louder and louder.

"Oh no, this isn't happening!" I jumped up and ran over to his canoe.

She was all bundled into the sleeping bag, her face was a yellowish pale, full of wrinkles, looking like an old dried out leather glove, but she seemed peaceful. I unzipped the bag and felt for a pulse. There was none, there was no breathing, there was nothing. I turned and stared in disbelief at Sam.

"Come on, guys, we need to do something. We can't just leave her like this."

But Sam just stood up, came over and hugged me.

"No," he said firmly. "We will not do anything. This has been the most horrible 24 hours of my life. I've lost the person I've loved all my adult life and I don't know why or even how. But she's gone now and I fear that if we're not real careful, we won't make it home either. We can't let that happen, we have kids to think of. I don't know what we have gotten into or what we are up against. Something is obviously not quite right. I just don't understand it and I am not so sure that I even want to. I'm having a real hard time clinging to sanity at this moment, but I have to; and I would like for you to respect my decision. There is nothing we can do for Marty now, it's not even my Marty anymore."

Tears streamed down his cheeks, leaving more traces in the dirt on his face. And so we stood there, holding each other. I felt terrible when I thought back to those thoughts I had had about Marty just 24 hours ago.

Chapter 15

"Jeff? Ken here. I found the patrol. This is the biggest fucked up mess I've ever seen. These idiots took potshots at the civilians! And wouldn't you know it, they hit one. We not only have civilians on the river, we have shot civilians on the river. This is getting way too big for me. Get ahold of Jonathon, see if he'll give the ok to pull out of here ASAP."

"Shit! What the hell is wrong with those people? I told them to hang on to the civilians until you got there. I didn't tell them to fucking shoot them. How fast can you be out of there? Ken? Ken?" All he had on the cell phone was static. Shit!

He swore loudly. Trying to decide if he should call Jonathon Brooks now or try to get Ken Messer back. He decided to try Ken first, but could not reach him. Reluctantly he dialed the private number to his boss. It was answered after the first ring.

"Yes?"

"Mr. Brooks?"

"I'm the only person that will answer this phone, you may call me Jonathon. What's up Jeffrey?"

"Jonathon, I have bad news. We have civilians in the area. Messer is out with the perimeter patrol that spotted them. When they tried to detain them they exchanged shots and they believe that at least one of the civilians was shot. Messer wants to pull up stakes and clear out now while we can still control the damage, I tend to agree with him. We want your authorization."

There was a moment of silence.

"Absolutely not. Find those damn civilians, find out who they are, what do they know. Use your head! What the hell were they doing on that damn river on a Sunday anyway! Nobody in his or her right mind spends a Sunday on some rotten, little river. You are in bible country, Jeffrey! People there go to church on Sunday to atone for Saturday's sins! Your soldiers probably saw animals and were so hung over they thought they were people. We will not just up and walk away with our tails between our legs, don't be ridiculous! Find out if these civilians really exist, and then find those civilians! Find out if anyone actually got shot, find out what they know. We don't run at the first hint of trouble, we deal with it, Jeffrey my boy. If need be we buy them. Everybody has his price. Spend any amount of money, do whatever you have to do, just so they keep their mouths shut. You'll be surprised what money can do. Do you think you can handle that or do I have to come?"

"I can handle it."

"Keep me posted." And the line went dead.

Jeff Craft sat there for a moment in silence staring at the dead cell phone in his hand. Then he pulled out a thick, overflowing day planner and dialed a number. A female voice answered.

"Good Morning. "he said and tried to sound cheerful. "Is Colonel Stevens available? Jeffrey Craft with SERPAC calling."

"One moment please."

"Colonel Stevens? I'm very sorry to bother you on such a nice Sunday, Sir. I was wondering if I might ask a favor?"

A very deep, very obviously male voice responded, "No trouble at all. Go ahead, what can I do for you?"

"Sir, as you know, this is the weekend we are trying out our AMAG system. Well, one of the perimeter patrols has spotted civilians in the test area. When they tried to detain them, shots were fired and we have reason to believe that at least one of the civilians was shot. We need to find them. Can you help us?"

"Let me see if I got that straight. One of the base perimeter patrols has shot civilian trespassers?"

"Well, not really trespassers, Sir. They were on the river, not really on the base. The patrol was on the civilian side. The boys were trying to keep the civilians there until one of our men could get there to question them. We wanted to know why they were in the area. When they disregarded the patrol and left, shots were fired, apparently the civilians were hit."

"The Perimeter Patrol was off base? On whose authorization did they patrol off base, and who OK'd live ammo?"

"Sir, my boss, Jonathon Brooks made the arrangements with your office to utilize this remote section of the base. He was told, the reservists training this weekend would be assigned to guard duty.

80

Major Pendergast signed off on it, Sir."

"Major Pendergast is not authorized to make this kind of decision. We need to find those civilians, ASAP. I'll have one of the pilots call you back and arrange a pick up."

Jeff exhaled deeply. Yes! It's always better to go right to the top. Screw the middleman! Maybe this was still salvageable. There's still hope.

Eight miles away, Col. Stevens dialed. "Pendergast? I need to talk to you. You might want to take this call someplace private."

After a few moments he continued. "Did you authorize one of the perimeter patrols to go off base and carry live ammo?"

There was a moment of silence.

"Well, what I said may have been interpreted in that manner, Sir. May I ask why you are asking?"

"You moron. This is drill weekend for the reservists; the perimeter patrol is a bunch of reservists. You send a bunch of reservists out with loaded M-16's. They're out there playing cowboys and Indians; only this game is for keeps. You never, never, never authorize reservists to carry live ammo, let someone with a lot more rank than you'll ever see make that decision. And you most certainly do not authorize a patrol with live ammo go off base. There are not enough stars and stripes for that authorization. Do you understand me?"

"Well, this civilian contractor, SERPAC, they contacted me, let me know that they were very concerned about industrial espionage. You knew that they were testing this top-secret system this weekend; you OK'd the use of down range for their testing. It just made perfect sense. They're worried about espionage and the reservists could use a little live ammo training."

"How much did they pay you?"

"Me? Sir, I'm just doing my job!"

" And pigs fly! Pendergast, I want you in my office in 30 minutes. Be prepared to go downrange."

The line went dead.

81

Chapter 16

I don't know how long we sat there. When I saw Ralph and Sandy slowly coming downriver, I got up and started moving what was left of our stuff away from the bank and under some bushes. Their canoe was low in the water and moving sluggishly, and I was surprised to see Sandy paddling by herself. I hoped that Ralph had finally put his foot down and had found a punishment that fit. After all, it was her stupidity that had gotten us into this mess, and it would do her good to paddle alone.

I waved at Sandy to get her attention. "Come and be useful for a change." I yelled, not even trying to hide my disgust with her. The look on her face told me, she had picked up on my anger as well, but was too exhausted from her work to respond. It didn't matter any more, and I really didn't need to worry. Sensitivity is not one of Sandy's assets.

As soon as she beached the canoe, she yelled, "They shot at us."

"Yeah, not surprising after you flipped them off. Why did you do a dumb thing like that?"

She shrugged. "I don't know. I suppose they just pissed me off or something like that."

"How did you expect them to answer - by kissing your ass?"

But Sandy never thinks about the results of her actions, but just goes full speed ahead. Then, just as I started to turn away, I saw that Ralph was signaling me to come closer. I remember thinking, "Strange, why is he still sitting in the canoe?" Usually he just bounds out and tries to do too many things at once. I walked over to where he was sitting. He had his T-shirt off and draped across his lap. As I stood and looked, he removed the shirt and, to my horror, I saw that his left thigh was bloody, with more blood smeared over his left calf and foot. His face looked pale and, although he tried to hide it, he grimaced instead of smiling when our eyes met.

"What the hell happened to you?" I asked.

He put his left index finger over his lips and I nodded. Okay, I'll be quiet.

In a low voice he said, "I got shot. Can you believe that shit?" He grimaced. "I don't think it's as bad as it looks, but it hurts. Could you please look at my leg? Maybe we can patch it up, just enough for us to get out of here."

We wrapped the T-shirt over his leg and I helped him out of the canoe. He was barely able to put weight on his left leg and was moaning. With every move we made, more big beads of sweat appeared on his forehead. I found a fairly level spot on the sand and gravel and helped him slowly down.

Sandy had not even turned around, but was talking nonstop. "Can you believe those fucking assholes back there? Who do they think they are? We were nowhere near the reservation. I know; I checked the map. Taking fucking potshots at us! When we get back I will get hold of my congressman. My tax dollars at work, my ass. You just wait. I kid you not."

Finally Ralph took a deep breath and said in a surprisingly firm voice, "Sandy, just shut up."

She slowly turned. " Don't talk to me that way, you have no right to talk to me that way. It was your stupid idea to come on this stupid trip. It's your stupid friend that set up this stupid trip, and now look what has become of it? I never wanted to come in the first place. I told you that, but did you listen? No. You had to agree to go and made me come as well." She had finally fully turned and stood, mouth open looking at her husband lying on the sand, a very bloody T-shirt wrapped around a very bloody thigh.

"And now you got yourself hurt, and you're messing up your clothes, and when I wash them, that shit will never come out again and then, you'll probably blame me for that too."

She glared at him. Under more normal circumstances, that may have worked, but our circumstances were no longer normal. Ralph just closed his eyes.

"Sandy, let's not fight, not now nor later. I'm hurt, and whether or not I blame you will not change anything. Right now we've got to sit down and figure out what to do next and frankly, you and your feelings aren't real important at this moment."

I couldn't agree more, but I was still stunned. In all the years I have known them, Ralph has never stood up to Sandy. At least not openly.

I probably should have cherished this moment, but under the circumstances I didn't feel like cherishing anything. For now I had more pressing issues. I went for the first aid kit while the rest of the group came closer. While Ralph talked, I used some of our thawed ice and Betadine from the kit to wash his leg.

"I just can't believe it," said Ralph through clenched teeth. "These guys were just kids, kids in uniform. We were not even remotely close to the military reservation, we were not trespassing and still I get shot. When we get back I'll talk to an attorney, I'll talk to the media, anybody. We'll see who has the last say in this. And even if we had been trespassing, that still doesn't give anyone any right to just up and shoot us. We didn't destroy anything and we volunteered to leave right away."

He flinched while I scrubbed. Tom and Sam watched over my shoulder.

"What do you think?" Tom asked, ignoring Ralph.

"Well," I wiped my forehead with my forearm and sat back on my heels for a moment. "There's no doubt that this is a gunshot wound. I don't think there is a bullet left in his leg, because here is the entrance and there's the exit. But I am worried about infection and I don't think that Ralph will be doing any walking for a while. Oh, by the way, when was your last tetanus?"

He looked at me in disbelief. "I can't believe that you're worried about that now? We need to get out of here and we need to do it fast. I don't want to spend any more time here than I absolutely have to. My tetanus is irrelevant now. I refuse to worry about it! Just put a bandage on and let's get the hell out of this fucking place."

He caught me by surprise; I didn't know what to say, so I chose to ignore him. That seemed a better alternative than slugging him. After all, Ralph is used to being ignored.

"Listen to me," I said after a while as I was washing his leg. "I am very worried about this getting infected. That bullet wasn't sterile, you know. Neither was your T-shirt or the river water that got all over you. Just lay back and try to ease up a little. Sam and Tom are already working on a way out."

Ralph didn't respond. He just gave me a nasty look. I decided that I didn't like him any longer, but he needed my help, and the nurse in me took over. He was drenched in sweat and he worried me. I didn't have much to work with other than a few bandages, and we had no pain medication besides the Aspirin.

Sam had been standing behind me, quietly watching as I worked on Ralph's leg. He turned to Tom. "It's getting late. Whether we like it or not, we will have to spend one more night. As much as I want to get off the river myself, now is not the time for it. We cannot just run off half-cocked or we'll all get hurt. Right now we have one dead, one hurt and the US Army pissed off at us for whatever reason."

Tom nodded, but before he could respond, Ralph cut in.

"If you're suggesting that we spend the night in this fucking place you are nuts. I'm getting out of here and that's that. We're probably surrounded by a bunch of crazed lunatics in camouflage right now. No way am I spending one more night. And besides, what do you mean with one dead?"

"Marty died." Sam spoke with a matter-of-fact voice, void of emotion.

"Oh my God, Sam!" Ralph leaned back and closed his eyes, exhaling loudly. "Wow, that's a helluva reality check. What happened?"

"I really can't talk about that right now."

"Ralph, Sam is right."

I couldn't believe my ears, was that really Sandy talking?

"Sam is right. We have no plan, we have no gear, it's getting dark soon and it will be really dark down here because of the bluffs. My cell phone doesn't work because it too got shot. Ralph, we have got to get ourselves organized before we can do anything. Accept that."

"I'm telling you, I don't want to spend one moment longer here than I absolutely have to."

Ralph's voice had an edge to it, and I couldn't help but wonder if beneath all the earlier bravado was just a scared little kid. I continued to wash his leg, thinking that while I have him lying down, at least he cannot just run off and get himself into further trouble. Tom's hand had remained reassuringly on my shoulder. Now he moved away and I watched him gather firewood. Sam joined him, and in no time they built a small fire. Ralph still was not satisfied.

"Do you really believe this will do any good? A fire will just lead those bastards to us faster. You'll see, we'll all be dead by morning."

I had begun to wrap his leg and his movements were very frustrating. Finally, I had enough, "Hold still and shut up until I'm done or I'll strangle you. I can't get this bandage on as long as you're moving. I know you're scared, but so are all of us. We all want to go home! So help me God, if you don't hold still, I will deck you."

He grabbed my upper arm.

"Chris," he said, "I'm not just scared, I'm terrified."

He lowered his voice. "I'm not used to being this helpless. I'm the levelheaded one in the family. When Sandy panics, she has absolutely no sense about her. If I don't get out of here alive, who will take care of her? Who will take care of the kids?"

I hugged him. I know, I just said I didn't like him anymore, but I was scared too and I could most definitely understand how he felt.

"Listen," I tried to sound convincing. "I am just as scared as you are and I also do not like being here any longer than we have to. But we have got to look at our situation realistically. We're not going anywhere now, we don't know the terrain and with the recent drought we don't know what the river is like from here on."

"Yeah, and Sam miscalculated the distance, don't forget that." He sounded bitter.

I brushed mosquitoes off my arms and sat down beside him.

"Yes, I think so too. But that doesn't matter right now. Instead of focusing on whom to blame, we need to focus on what we can do for ourselves."

"How come you are so wise?"

I wanted to laugh, but I didn't feel like it. "I'm a Mom, Ralph. It's my job."

Chapter 17

To Jeff Craft, it seemed as if a lifetime had passed when the call finally came. The helicopter pilot, a young tall man with tense bony features and piercing blue eyes, did not sound enthusiastic. His facial expression did not belie the sound of his voice. His demeanor made it quite clear to everyone around that this was not his idea of fun, especially on his day off.

Finally, they were on the way. The pilot, still unhappy, seemed impatient, grimacing and frowning whenever Jeff Craft tried to initiate a conversation. They followed the river as it formed the boundary to the civilian world. No matter how hard they looked and how many times they circled, they were unable to spot either the perimeter patrol or the reported civilians. As dusk set in, their search was called off.

* * *

Sam and Tom had built the fire on a nice level spot and had started dragging the canoes closer, turning them on their sides, so we could use them as shelter. Sandy had scrounged up an empty coffee can, scrubbed it with sand and then proceeded to boil water. We carefully moved Ralph closer to the fire. It wasn't easy and he couldn't help. Every time he moved, his wound started to bleed again and I would end up reinforcing the bandage. I was getting worried about my meager supplies.

Tom and Sam had carried Marty's body out of the canoe to the water's edge, where Sam washed her. Although the rest of the group had turned their backs to him to give him privacy, I walked over. I couldn't believe what had happened to us. Never in my wildest dreams did I expect this – and I have had some wild dreams! I expected rigor mortis to have set in and thought he might need a helping hand. But he was doing well, at least physically. Emotionally – well, the tears in his eyes said it all.

"Sam, let me help you." I said when he finally looked up.

"Chris, why did this have to happen? Why?"

My heart was breaking. It hurt to see this grown man stand there with tears running down his face. I had no answer for him. I just hugged him and he sobbed on my shoulder.

"Oh honey, I don't know. I'm sure that somehow, somewhere there is meaning for all of this. I have no idea what it could be, though."

What do you say in a situation like this?

I helped him dress Marty in a pair of shorts and one of his tee shirts. "Try to think of all the good times you have had. What would Marty want you to do? Some things just can't be explained."

Sam started to comb her hair.

"I don't know why I bother with this. Look, her hair, her beautiful hair! It's coming out in clumps!"

"Just hang in there, Sam." What was there to be said? I felt inadequate for not being able to come up with something better.

"Chris, how much experience do you have with death?"

Well, now that's a good question. I had to think about my answer for a moment, wondering what Sam was getting at. Finally I said, "Well, I've seen my share of people die, if that's what you mean."

"I know that, but do you have any experience with taking care of the body later on?"

"Not really, I usually call the Funeral Home. Why?"

"I've mostly dealt with animals, you know. There is a length of time from death until rigor mortis sets in. That lasts for some time, and then it passes. I don't know for sure what the average is, I think maybe one to four hours, but I'm not sure." He hesitated, stopped and looked up at me.

"I know Marty died on the water. When we got here, she was already stiffening up. I noticed that when I tucked her in. That was maybe ten or fifteen minutes later. While you were taking care of Ralph's leg, I wanted to get the wet clothes off her and put something dry on her, but rigor mortis had fully set in, she was rigid. So I decided to wait it out. But then, while you were still working on Ralph, it was all gone again. That would have been the shortest four hours in history."

He stood up and stretched. I waited. Sometimes Sam can be an agonizingly slow speaker.

"That's just too fast, at least as far as I know. And now look at her

88

body. You know how particular Marty was about her appearance. That wasn't for me; it was for her. She liked herself that way and as long as Marty was happy, so was I."

He took a deep breath, exhaled slowly, and I waited. This had to be hard for him.

"She looks like a woman of eighty, Chris. Look at her! That's no bad sunburn, or dehydration. This is something else. Not only is her skin all wrinkled, but also it feels hard. Actually, her whole body feels hard and it was changing while I was bathing her. I don't know how to say it. You're a nurse, maybe you've seen this before?"

He looked searchingly at me. I knew he was desperately seeking explanations and I felt rotten because I had none for him.

"Chris, she is drying out in front of us, shriveling up and I don't understand how that is possible or how to stop it."

"Maybe if we wrap her in plastic?" was my feeble offer to help. We still had a good amount of large trash bags. Sam stood there for a moment and I wondered if he had even heard me. Then he said, "Yeah, that's an idea, that could work. At least it's worth a try. If we use some of the extra rope we can tie the plastic close to her body and have a way of holding on to her too. Yeah, let's do that."

"Let Tom and me do that. Try to keep her in your memory the way she was." But Sam just shook his head.

"When I married her it was for good times and bad times. We've had the good, now it's the worst, and this is the last good thing I'll ever be able to do for her. I have to, Chris, I have to."

We called Tom over to help, but the two men just sent me after something to drink. They obviously needed to be alone. The task had seemed straightforward and simple, but from where I was standing it looked like quite a struggle. Finally Sam just walked away and Tom waved at me to come over. They had stayed near the edge of the water, and when I got there I realized why. Even in this short period of time Marty's body had deteriorated much further than it should have, and the odor was pretty intense.

I looked at Tom. "What's happening here? I was just over here a moment ago and it wasn't like this. Oh God, this odor is bad! Is the heat doing this to her? Oh Tom, this is bad!"

"I know," Tom looked up at me. "Just keep in mind, this is my first

89

corpse. I normally deal with the living. You're the nurse, what do you make of this."

I was stunned; I didn't know what to say, or what to think of this. Too much was happening to us, and far too fast.

"I don't know. I don't deal with dead people every day either."

I knew I was stammering, but I didn't know what to say. I have been a nurse for a long time, but I had never before encountered anything like this.

"I can only guess the heat and humidity are doing this to her." I looked at Tom for support and encouragement, but he just shrugged his shoulders and signaled me to give him a hand. Together, we slowly and carefully slipped Marty's body into the huge bags and used rope from the canoes to tie the bags around her, like a package.

Handling her body felt strange. Every joint I touched seemed to give, and I was reminded of the Thanksgiving turkey I overcooked one year. It felt solid and hard on the outside, but when you touched the extremities, the bones came right out. The task was difficult, and I felt horrible. More than once did I start to say something, but held back when the stench hit me and I gagged. I may be a nurse, but I get nauseated like anyone else. I was glad when we were done. Our final act was placing Marty into Ralph and Sandy's shot up canoe. We counted on the breeze on the water to keep the smell away from the campsite and the cool water underneath to perhaps slow down the deterioration.

While we were taking care of Marty, Sam and Sandy had taken all of our supplies and spread everything out by the fire. Sam had not looked at us as Tom and I worked on Marty, but I'm sure he knew precisely what was going on. Sam and Sandy also had started to inventory our precious possessions by the flickering light. There wasn't much. Ralph and Sandy's supplies had gone downriver, and cooking gear was probably at the bottom of the Coon a little ways upstream. We still had their cooler and several half-gallon milk jugs filled with drinking water. It's something Tom had been teaching all of us. Wash the empty milk jugs out, fill them almost full of drinking water, and freeze them. If we decide to go anywhere, we not only have instant ice, but as the ice melts we also have drinking water. At the end of the trip, we throw the empty jugs away or burn them in the last campfire.

Sam doesn't like this method. He hates plastic things, and has told us many times that he would rather use river water. Well, one time we made him use river water he had purified with iodine pills for coffee. It tasted nasty and took care of Sam's feelings about plastic jugs. He couldn't drink the coffee, couldn't even get past the smell, and had to admit that maybe bringing water from home is not such a bad idea. It worked well for us in the past and now provided us with plenty of fresh water.

We also found a Baggie full of assorted hard candy and chewing gum, and another with tea bags and a couple of those individual coffee bags. That these were flavored, didn't matter. That they had caffeine did! Tom had emptied our canoe. Despite precautions, most of the clothing had gotten wet, and he now spread everything out over the canoes and near the fire. The sleeping bags were soaked, and we gave up on them.

We still had three tents, but only two sets of poles. We had one air mattress, and Marty's body was lying on that. Then Tom got to our camping box. It was nothing special, just an old plastic box that fits perfectly into the canoe and is usually packed full of goodies to take along on a trip on a moment's notice. I held my breath. I couldn't remember all that was in it. Tom pulled out an old skillet and wet paper napkins and a plastic bag with matches and plastic utensils. There was a small jar of instant coffee and a baby food jar containing sugar. He also produced a couple of cans of pork and beans. There were paper plates, cigarettes, and lots of other stuff, but it was all soaked and was useless.

I just sat down. I couldn't think any more and felt totally overwhelmed. I cried, big, silent tears as my Tom brought out his pocketknife with the can opener and started to open the cans of pork and beans. I just wanted to go home, hug my baby and feel safe again.

Night arrived just as quickly as we had anticipated, and the wood Tom and Sam gathered made a nice fire, with plenty of wood close by to keep it going. There is something comforting about a fire, and we sat there, close to each other, as we ate. Even Ralph finally seemed to settle down. I nestled closer to Tom. I needed physical contact with him to comfort me and he didn't seem to mind.

"I saw some mosquitoes a little while ago," I whispered.

"Excuse me?" He bent closer to me.

"There have been no bugs, no noises from bugs."

He stared at me. Finally he asked, "Are you alright?"

"Yes, I'm fine. I just thought I'd tell you that there haven't been any bugs around."

"But you just said that there are mosquitoes."

"Yes, but I'm talking about the big stuff that makes noise."

He laughed. "So what's the problem?"

"It's bugging me." We cracked up laughing.

"It's been bugging me for a while now that I didn't see any wildlife. No little turtles, no fish, no frogs no squirrels and no dragonflies. And the trees! Remember I said something to you earlier?"

He nodded, looking serious again.

"I told you there was something really strange about the vegetation. Look around us. It's August, but all of this looks like October, you know, fall. The grass is not only tall; it's also old. The trees, the bushes – hell anything with leaves on it – looks like it's Fall right now and it's still summer! Look at it; the leaves are starting to turn color. But it's the insects, which bother me the most. When you get away from the river, you can find lots of dead bugs. Its really gross, they crunch when you walk on them."

I made a face and took a sip from my hot tea.

"Honey, I don't know what has happened to us or around us, but something has. I've thought about this a lot. Our nation wasn't on the brink of nuclear war when we left for this trip, was it? 'Cause that thought has occurred to me."

Tom laughed and hugged me. "You've been reading too much science fiction." His hand massaged my upper back. It felt good, and I was overwhelmed with the urge to be alone with him in bed and just crawl under the covers and hide in his arms. Just be close to him, inhale his scent, and feel safe.

"What's funny?"

Sam sat down next to Tom, coffee mug in hand. I quickly wiped away a tear that had appeared from nowhere.

"Sam, my friend, what do you think of this fine mess we have gotten ourselves into?"

"You know, I've been thinking. I believe we need to rethink our strategy. With the low water, there are more obstacles to deal with than I even remotely considered. Ralph is pretty much out of circulation, and I doubt that Sandy can handle the canoe with him lying in the front. We can't walk out, because Ralph cannot walk, and we can't stay here. I really don't like the idea of sitting here and waiting for someone to pick us up. This is not a well-traveled river, and your local conservation agent is not going to come by everyday to see if there are any stranded tourists. The army would probably just as soon let us die. After all, those are the assholes who shot at us."

He drank some more coffee and unfolded the map in front of us.

"Now, let's look at the map." I looked over to Ralph and Sandy. He had his eyes closed and seemed to be sleeping. Actually, he looked pretty comfortable. She had found a nice sandy area and patiently removed any protruding objects. His head was propped against a couple of soggy sleeping bags.

Chapter 18

It was well after dark, when a tired, dirty and angry Ken Messer reconnected with Jeff Craft and David Smith. They arrived at almost the same time. Craft and Smith all crisp and clean, in stark contrast to Messer who was sweaty, wet and dirty from wading in the river.

"Well, don't stare at me. I'm not planning to pose for the cover of GQ. How come nothing is packed up? I thought we were clearing out?"

"Jonathon said no. He wants us to stay and find out who these people are and why they are on the river, and what they know about AMAG."

"Aw, come on! He's joking isn't he? It's dark out there and whoever it is, they are probably long gone and in their little homes. This is getting way out of hand. Let me tell you something, if Research and Planning had done their part correctly, we wouldn't be in the mess we are in now. What were they thinking? This is a rural area. People fish here to supplement their food dollars, and they hunt whatever is in season and they hunt stuff that doesn't have a season.

"I've had it with this fucked up mess, somebody else can go out there and be the smorgasbord for the local bugs. I'm filthy, tired and I smell bad! And let me tell you fine, well-educated young gents something else: The targeting was fucked up, just as I said all along. How do I know? I've been all over this wilderness we've decided to use. Really nice corn we have growing in our test field! The field particle resonance meters show zero, great big fat zero, nothing! Nothing happened! The IMPB never hit the test field. I checked meters all along the field perimeter and I checked the safety zone. Nothing happened.

"Something went wrong, Boys! I've been telling you airheads for a long time, when we are dealing with cellular restructuring at this particular frequency; we need to make allowances for distance, gravity and atmospheric conditions. This is not something you can do in the lab on a Saturday afternoon. You have to sit down and use your brains. and work at it. What the hell does Jonathon want to do now? Sit here and wait until some farmer in Timbuktu reports a bumper crop of hashish? Please!"

Disgusted he turned away from them and stared out the window.

Smith cleared his throat. "I want you to know, I headed Research and Planning for this project. We were very thorough. We used all sorts of databases and came up with the same thing every time. This is a very sparsely populated area in a state with a small population for its size to start with. The military recognized that, and subsequently moved their research and development centers to Camp Crowder."

"But that's my point precisely. You used assorted databases and reached conclusions that were purely theoretical. None of you clowns has any experience beyond punching keys on a keyboard. Did any of you masterminds come here and talk to the locals? Did anyone call me? I will give you the answer: 'No.' I submitted my report to Jonathon, but I guess I reported something he did not want to hear and so he did not share it."

"Well, in a way he did share it." Dave Smith looked uncomfortable. "He showed it to me and after some discussion we decided that you were just being overly-cautious. No, we did not actually go onsite in person. You know Jonathon had his plans for that. We just found a potential location and informed him, and he handled it personally from then on. We had nothing further to do with that, so don't blame us!"

"Christ, I don't blame anybody! That never solved anything. We need to find these people and make sure they are okay. We need to find out if AMAG misfired or if a totally different area was targeted. We need to find out what went wrong. I can think of all sorts of possibilities, none of which includes placing blame! We need to take fast corrective action."

Everyone looked at Jeff Craft. "Don't look at me! I have no idea where to start."

"I have a couple of thoughts," Smith said. "The main programming that directed the IMPB is set up to keep a log. That would tell us not only if an IMPB was generated, but also if AMAG fired it and when. It also will tell us the satellite's attitude and exact location in relation to our test site and the targeting coordinates used. That would give us a pretty good idea. Oh, not only would we see the programmed coordinates, but also the executed target coordinates. And it also does

95

a diagnostic in the particle emitter and the transducers."

They stood and stared at him. He tapped a young male technician on the shoulder, " Joe, take the rest of your shift off."

After Joe left the room, Smith sat down at the computer console. He pulled out a thick, well-worn day planner and started to punch in command after command. Slowly the screen filled with numbers, letters and symbols.

"Ok," he finally said. "If I've done everything right, we will have the answer now." He tapped on several keys and the screen changed.

"Wow! We are way off," he said. "The area hit by AMAG is miles from the programmed target area. Look at this; it's off the base, over the river. If you use the river as a landmark, then we treated an area at least five to eight miles upriver. And do I read this right?" he asked nobody in particular. "AMAG generated and fired the IMPB, on time, only at the wrong area and at a much larger area.

"Wow!"

"We need to develop a plan," Craft put in. "We can not approach Jonathon without a plan. You know how he is"

"I want to inspect the area we actually treated," Messer urged. "There have to be changes by now. Dave, did you do any research on that area? What do you know about it?"

"Just a sec." David Smith entered a new command and pulled up a report "Look at this: Mostly agricultural; cornfields, cattle, that sort of thing. No farmhouses, no towns, no nothing. Also no highways, just some gravel roads connecting the fields."

"I still want to go there." Ken Messer was restless. "Jeff, set up the helicopter for me at first light. I'll fly over and film the area. Then we'll regroup here and see what we are fighting. We can contact Jonathon then."

Chapter 19

I signaled Sandy to come over and join us.

"What's up?" she asked when she sat down next to us.

"We're trying to figure what we're going to do next."

"Can I help?"

Tough times really do bring out the best in people, I thought. We gathered around the map and listened as Sam talked.

"I've been thinking about this for a while now. This river really meanders. If you were to stretch it out it would reach clear across the state. But because it winds so much, it covers only a very small portion of that distance. Because it winds through the valleys, the road is actually pretty close to where we are now. We need to determine exactly where we are in relationship to the highway and then let's talk about maybe walking out of here. It would mean leaving our stuff here. But we could always come back later and get it." He looked at us.

"Ralph can't walk," I said. "And what about Marty?"

"We could split up."

I couldn't believe that Tom would even suggest such a thing. No way would I split up. We sat a moment in silence.

"Well?" Tom looked around at us. "If we all try to walk out together we could get into worse trouble than what we already have. Ralph isn't walking, that means that we," he pointed at Sam and himself, "would have to carry him or drag him. We can't leave Marty behind. We need to get her out, and someone needs to figure out what killed her. Sandy and Chris can't carry her. We need help. And if we stay together on the river it will be God knows how late tomorrow before we reach our takeout point. From there to the nearest phone will still be quite a distance. And that's assuming nothing has happened to the vehicles." He paused and looked at us.

"No, I think we need to split up. One group keeps going as fast as it can on the river; the other group goes overland to the blacktop. There's bound to be a farmer going by. Tomorrow is Monday, there has got to be traffic."

I didn't like his idea, but I had to admit it made sense. Sam agreed to that much.

"I just don't like the idea of splitting up," he said. "How would we do that? Keep Ralph and Marty with the canoes while one walks out? That's awfully risky."

We fell silent. None of us liked the idea of splitting up, but it did make sense. Sandy finally broke the silence.

"Okay, okay I have the answer." She whispered, "Ralph, Marty, Tom and I stay with the canoes. We use one canoe, leave everything else behind and make our way down river starting at the break of dawn. Sam and Chris leave on foot just as soon as possible. Sam, you grew up around here and you're a conservation agent, you should be able to find your way even in the dark. Besides, I figure that once you are out of this valley and your eyes have adjusted it won't be all that dark.

"You guys hitch a ride with the first farmer that crosses your path, and we all meet at the takeout. If you get there first, I have a fifth of Vodka under the passenger seat, leave it alone."

Sam shook his head. "No, no, no, I don't think this will work at all. You can't fit that many adults into one canoe and still maneuver it safely. And as low as the river is, Tom will have to get around an awful lot of obstacles. Sandy, even with you in front and paddling, this is not going to work."

"Yes, it will. We can make it work," Tom said slowly. "We can put Marty into one canoe and secure her. Then attach the two canoes like a catamaran. Sandy, Ralph and I will sit in the other canoe. It will be awkward, but Sandy will have room to move and it will certainly be more comfortable for Ralph. I think we can do it. You and Chris walk out to the road and get help, and we meet up at the take out."

But Sam just shook his head again. "No that won't work either, we tried something like that once. Maybe in a more normal environment, but in this river full of obstacles you won't be able to maneuver around. Sandy can handle a canoe okay, but we need to balance it right for her."

From the look in his face I could tell that his mind was made up. Suddenly I felt very angry.

"What do you mean walk out?" I shouted.

The others "shushed" and pointed to Ralph.

"What do you mean, walk out?" I lowered my voice. " We have no dry clothes, our shoes are just basic, cheapo canvas shoes and we are tired. I have never hiked, let alone in the dark, in unfamiliar terrain. And what about the Army? You were the one that told us about the territoriality of those bastards. Now, what makes you think that we can just walk out of here?"

I was furious. Sam just pointed at the overturned canoes by the campfire.

"See that? I have spread out our clothing. I don't know if it is dry yet, but if not then it will be shortly. Including the shoes. Yes, I agree that what we have here is less than perfect, but we can't just sit here either. We don't have three canoes anymore. Have you looked at Ralph and Sandy's? It's all shot up. We'll have to leave it behind."

"Yeah, and whose fault was that?"

I shot an angry glance at Sandy.

"Come on Chris," Tom put a hand on my shoulder. "Being angry right now doesn't help our situation."

I shrugged his hand off and walked away. Being angry may not help our situation, but it sure as hell made me feel better.

The light of the fire had bathed everything in a golden glow and the warmth felt good. We had only packed lightweight stuff. Maybe we do have some dry clothing to wear, I thought. It would be nice. I felt something touching my arm and realized that a mosquito had started to feast on me. I stopped; this was the second time this evening that I had noticed mosquitoes. Not nearly as many as I would have expected, but still it represented a slow return to normal. I touched the clothing hanging from the overturned canoes. A couple of T-shirts were dry, and the spandex shorts Marty preferred were dry as well. The shoes were still a little damp on the inside. I took a deep breath and returned to the group, taking the dry things with me.

"Okay Sam," I sighed. "Okay, I give in. Let's talk about walking out of here."

We gathered by the fire and Sam showed us on the map where he thought we were. "See this little squibble? We are in this area. My guess is, it's about three, maybe four miles to the highway. And 'highway' is really pushing it. It's just plain blacktop, but on a Monday morning it should see some traffic."

He took a sip from his coffee and pointed with a small stick.

"Here is the boundary for the base. We are off it and on the other side of the river, so we shouldn't run into any problems from them. I figure it's going to take us until daybreak to hike those three or four miles." He gave me a little smile. "I know you're in pretty good shape, but we will be walking in the dark. That's different."

I nodded, but I wasn't sincere. I did not want to go. I wanted to stay with Tom. I was scared. You see, I may appear tough and strong, but I don't see myself as very brave at all. And right now I just wanted to be with my husband and hide in his embrace. It helped just to feel his hand on my shoulder. He gave a little squeeze.

"You can do this, babe." He whispered in my ear. "I need you to do this. Get us home, honey."

I felt my eyes fill with tears.

"We'll start out walking as fast as we can," Sam went on to say. " We'll slow down when we start uphill. I'll lead and all you have to do is follow me. We'll stay very close together, and we won't be using a flashlight. With the full moon, our eyes will adjust nicely and we should be able to see well enough to get by. If I move too fast, let me know. Don't let me find out after I've lost you that you can't keep up." I nodded, still not convinced of the sanity of this idea.

"Ok, then let's get this show on the road." We ate some candy, drank some coffee and helped Tom and Sandy with the supplies. Everything we had left was redistributed. We transferred Marty's body into the canoe Sandy would be taking. For Ralph, we built a soft area in the middle of the second canoe. He wouldn't be of much help to Tom, and I knew that Tom could handle it. I was not so sure about Sandy. Finally, Sam and I changed into dry clothes and took a flashlight, a pocketknife and our wallets. My heart was pounding so, I could hear every beat in my ears and I felt as if someone were strangling me. When I hugged Tom for the final, time tears poured down my face. I tore my self away from him and grabbed Sam's hand.

"Come on. Let's go and get this over with."

We started out into the woods, initially blind and feeling helpless. It took about 10 minutes for our eyes to adjust to the darkness and when I realized it happened, I was really surprised at how much we could see. As our vision improved, our pace increased. Occasionally, Sam would point out stars to me, but mostly we walked in silence. The first stretch was fairly clear and only at a slight incline. I had no trouble seeing trees, but the bushes got me, and so did the holes in the ground and the tree stumps. I never noticed that Sam ran into anything. When I commented on this he just chuckled.

"Practice, my dear, practice. I've done this before. Just concentrate on what we are doing and tune out why we are doing it. Ouch!"

Now it was my turn to giggle. "Concentrate, Sam".

The night air was getting cooler, but not at all uncomfortable. I was sweating from the uphill hike, and the light breeze felt good. There was a nice, woodsy scent in the air and, for the first time in two days, I heard animal sounds off in the distance. The woods became denser and it was harder to see stars. We walked through a patch of low brush and my legs got scratched up. I wanted to stop and clean up. Even more, I wanted to be at home in my soft comfy bed and in my husband's arms.

When I looked around, all I could see was Sam's form and the trees and bushes. I felt lost and lonely. Come on now, I said to myself. Don't be such a wuzz. Pull yourself together. Focus on going home. Concentrate on Allen and Tom. Just focus!

Finally we took a break. Somehow Sam had found a grassy spot and we sat down next to each other. I wanted to say something, reassure Sam and be reassured, but I suddenly felt completely exhausted.

"Chris," Sam said softly. "Take your shoes off and massage your feet. It will help some."

I did and it really felt good. Sam checked his watch.

"We've been at it now for more than three hours," he said. "It's a little after one, but we still have a ways to go."

We must both have smelled it at the same time.

"Sam, I smell wood burning."

"Me too," he whispered and put his index finger across his lips. I nodded my head in agreement. His lips were on my ear as he whispered: "Let's just be careful. We don't know who else is out here. Let's figure out where the smoke is coming from. Follow me and be very quiet."

Very slowly and carefully, we followed our noses. Fortunately, that also meant continuing toward the highway. Just before we reached a flat spot, we started to hear voices. I couldn't make out what was being said, but the voices were male, loud, and rowdy. We moved closer, then Sam signaled to stop and we lay down on some grass.

Directly ahead of us, maybe a hundred feet away, was a nice, big campfire. I counted five people, and judging by the voices they were all male. From what I could see they were wearing uniforms.

"Army?" I softly asked Sam.

"Could be. Listen, but try not to look at the fire or you'll lose your night vision."

I heard the "pssst" of a beer or soda can being opened, and watched as cigarettes were lit. Before too long, judging by the scent, I realized that it wasn't tobacco.

"This has been one weird day." I heard a male voice say. I thought, "Amen brother."

"Today was Sunday. Man, I had a date lined up for yesterday, but instead I ended up out here. With you assholes!"

"Lucky date!" followed by raucous laughter.

"Aw man, you wouldn't believe who with."

"Tell, come on"

"That little supply clerk over at Battalion."

"The blonde with the big tits?"

"Yeah, that's the one, Brenda."

"I hear she gives great head, man."

"Yeah, she swallows."

"I can vouch for that piece."

"Oh baby, yeah!"

"What do you mean?"

"I went out with her one time. We went to a real nice place, you know. Had dinner, a couple of glasses of wine. Then we drove around a little and ended up in this little park. I get to foolin' around a little, and then she wants to go to a motel. Well, gee whiz, nobody needs to say that to me twice. Mr. and Mrs. Jones checked in. Man, it was great – one hot piece of ass."

"I don't believe you."

"You want the details?"

"Yeah man, spare me nothing."

"Well, we're in this motel, see. Before I get the door closed she has her clothes off. Man, them knockers just jumped right out at me saying: 'suck me suck me'."

A voice laughed.

"Well did you?"

"Let's just say I was very accommodating."

More laughter and the sweet-smelling smoke drifted over to us.

"I had her on that bed lickety split and oh, man, did she ever taste sweet. Always have been a tit man. And her pussy, man, she was so wet; she practically came on my hand right there and then. I gave her some of that big black dick of mine to suck on just to slow her down a little, but only a little. I couldn't believe it, man. She was hot, ready, willing and most certainly able. Once we got going, anything went, man. Anything. I kid you not! She sucked my dick like there was no tomorrow; oh sweet Jesus was it ever good. And then I rolled her over and fucked her from behind."

"Did you fuck her in the ass?"

"I'm sure she would've let me, she was that hot, but, I don't go for that shit. No, that pussy was so sweet and so wet and when she stuck her ass up in the air and showed me that thing, it looked so good, I could have sworn it winked at me. She was goin' along with anything I wanted, man, anything. It was a great piece of ass."

"I can't believe I missed my date with her. I could fall in love with someone like that."

"Well next time you're just gonna have to come along with us and join the fun. Make it a threesome. I'm sure she won't mind. You just let me get her motivated."

"All right, yeah."

"I saw something wild last night right out here."

"Oh yeah? What?"

"Did you have a wet dream?"

"You been out here too long when the trees start to look good to you."

"No, you perverts. We were down by the river. Sarge didn't let us build a fire and I was with some square guys, so I didn't dare smoke. But one time I took off by myself for a little while and just sat close to the water."

"Come on man, admit it, you was beatin' your meat."

103

"There were some people on the river. I watched them skinny-dipping and then I watched them fuck."

"Cool, how many?"

I could feel myself blush, but Sam just took my hand and squeezed it.

"Just two, man, a man and a woman. Nice looking chick, big tits. Nice. I watched them fuck, man. I wish I could've gotten in on that."

"Did he fuck'er in the ass?"

"No, dickhead, not everyone is perverted like you. These looked like pretty normal people. They had no idea I was there. It was cool! This dude, you know, he played with her tits! And, awh man, I know she was coming all over him. I heard her moaning and begging him for more."

Sam squeezed my hand again. I still felt myself blushing.

"You two did get a little loud." Sam whispered in my ear with a chuckle.

"Hey, why didn't you go over and partake?"

"I was with these weird people, man. Some suits from DC or some place, I guess. Couldn't just swim over and say hi, lemme fuck the bitch too."

Sam squeezed my hand so hard I thought my fingers would break. It hurt, but it also helped. "I'm sorry," I told Sam. "We didn't know anyone was there."

"It's ok. Really, it doesn't matter. Be quiet now. I'm trying to figure out a way to get past those idiots."

"Who was with you?" One of the male voices asked.

"I really don't know. They wasn't introduced to me. It was all hushhush and supersecret. I was just the driver. They didn't even set up camp. They had put up some electronic equipment earlier in the day. Computers and that kinda stuff. And then they waited. I guess it was around lunchtime when something turned on. Then, after a couple of hours, some of the stuff got loaded up again and a couple of these dudes went back to base. One of them spent the night and came back with me just before dawn. I'm telling you, it was weird."

"Didn't they talk at all?"

"They was probably aliens!" followed by raucous laughter.

"Aw man, I'm serious. No, these guys wore suits, man. They was talking to each other all right. You know. 'Bout this satellite and that it had already sent some kinda rays. I guess I musta looked lost, cause one of them had coffee with me and told me that they were doing some field tests on some kinda rays that would come from some satellite. Those rays would be sent to farming areas and then the farmers could harvest sooner. He said that in their lab, they had gotten an extra crop per growing season."

"Yeah, some kinda Startrek stuff?"

"Find out how it works, we'll increase my pot harvest." More laughter.

"You're a bunch of assholes! I don't know how it works, I'm no fucking scientist. But I tell you, they was serious. This dude I was talking to, he said that he'd been involved with this project for a bunch of years. He said that they'd been working in a lab all this time. Then they got money from the Feds and suddenly everbody wants in on it. They practically had this field test crammed down their throats."

"What do you mean?"

"He didn't think that they were ready. Said he was worried about it, how it would effect humans. But his company had made all these arrangements and wouldn't back off, and then the Army was nice enough to let them use this dump. Now that they had their field-test everything looks real promising."

There was silence on the other side. Finally a new voice could be heard.

"You mean to tell me that somebody did some secret testing here, with us right in the middle of it and just up and tells you? Come on."

"I'm serious. He told me that the actual test had been earlier in the day and they were monitoring. Nobody was in the area. They made sure of that. The Army leased some of the farmland over here on this side of the river for this test. They paid some old farmer a fortune for the use of his land. They picked that section because you can't really get into it on this side; there's no road."

"And then they got us running perimeter guards to keep people away. As if there are any people! No, no, none of us was on this side of the river at the time of that test. We were all on the other side. Besides, this was just a split second thing. Real superfast! Now hey're just watching for changes, make sure it worked. Don't get so fucking hostile with me. I'm just telling you what I heard last night."

"Did you tell Sarge about that?"

"Naw, I didn't want to get the dude in trouble."

"I don't understand this. These people have this weird shit they shoot from a satellite and it's supposed to make stuff grow faster?"

"Hey Tony, they shoulda told you earlier, you coulda put your dick in, make it grow."

More rowdy laughter followed. Sam motioned for me to follow him and we slowly moved to the left, away from the fire. Finally Sam stopped and whispered

"I don't know if they have somebody working guard duty, so I think we need to make a little detour."

I nodded in agreement.

"Look over there to the left. Can you see those two little cedars? Directly to the left the ground slopes up. I think we need to head that way and see if we can keep going toward the highway."

Going uphill was slow. The vegetation was dense and there were lots of dried, broken off tree limbs. We had to be careful and quiet, which was very difficult and time consuming. I wondered how Indians managed to sneak through the woods without making any noise; we certainly didn't. Finally we did reach the top. Looking down and slightly to the left, I could see the campfire we had just avoided. Sam was focused on the horizon even further to our left. He tugged on my shirt.

"Look at that, looks to me like somebody is coming."

I turned and looked to where he was pointing. A light was moving fast and in our general direction.

"Sam, that has got to be a car. Wanna go check it out?"

"Maybe," Sam's response was slow. "I'm not so sure that would help us. Look at the headlights. I think that's a military vehicle and that means whoever is coming this way is going to connect with those idiots down there. Let's wait."

We watched as the single bright light became two headlights of a vehicle. We watched as the headlights came to a stop a couple of hundred yards away from us. A horn sounded and we watched a light moving from the fire toward the vehicle. When it reached the vehicle a lot of shouting followed but I could not make out what was said. The horn sounded a couple of times and we watched as the fire went out and then several small lights moved through the darkness toward the vehicle.

"Party's over" said Sam.

"Yeah, but now we're stuck again." I was feeling very tired.

"Stuck? Not really, watch. As soon as the vehicle leaves, we'll go to where it was and see if there's a path we can follow out of here. Walking will be much faster if we can follow a set of tire tracks. Okay, there we go. See they are turning around and now they are heading back. Let's go – it'll be easier now."

I reluctantly followed him as we moved at an angle toward the path of the slow moving vehicle. Sam must have had some super powers, you know, able to see in the dark as he did. We found a narrow dirt path, well worn with heavy treaded tire marks. Up ahead we could see the vehicle top a rise, and then it was gone.

"Do you need to rest a little?" Sam asked.

"I need to pee," I said with conviction. "I didn't feel like dropping my drawers in front of that bunch. They knew too much of my anatomy already."

Sam chuckled and pointed to a couple of cedars, clearly visible in the pale moonlight. Considering all we had been through, it was good to hear him laugh.

"You can go behind those."

"I'd rather stay a little closer to you if you don't mind."

Sam didn't mind; Sam is good people. He just turned his back and waited for me. I felt much better as we moved on. It wasn't too much easier following those tire tracks. Instead of running into trees and falling over stumps and getting scratched by bushes, we now stumbled over rocks and roots and both of us almost fell into a hole a time or two. But we made progress and the thought of reaching the blacktop, reconnecting with Tom and finally getting home to Allen, kept me going. Sam and I didn't talk, we just walked as fast as we could and focused on the ground ahead to find a safe place for the next step.

My feet were hot and the flimsy little canvas shoes did not provide much support. I twisted my ankles several times when I stepped onto what I thought was solid ground, only to find myself sliding off a root or big field rock. My calves were sore, as if on fire. I noticed that I was beginning to lean forward more than was good for my back, and tried to stretch while I walked.

The farther away from the river we walked, the more I noticed the noises around us. There were choirs of frogs or bugs or something. Whatever it was, it was noisy. I even heard a cow. And there were whippoorwills. Our feet were beating a rhythm on the earth, and I felt myself becoming hypnotized by it.

Then Sam suddenly froze and grabbed my arm. Startled I said "What?" only to feel his hand firmly clamped over my mouth. "Shhhhhh" he hissed, then moved his hand off my mouth and pointed up ahead. I stared, but I couldn't see anything. Then suddenly I saw it, two small red lights. I looked at Sam.

"I think it's our friends from earlier, maybe they needed to take a break?"

"Now what?"

"Now we get the hell off the road, and let's hope they make enough noise to cover any noise we may be making."

Sam led the way, slowly, carefully, off the path and under some cedars growing to our right. There we sat down and waited.

The red lights blinked a time or two, once even seeming to come closer. I could hear voices.

"You clowns owe me a big favor, I hope you realize that. The lieutenant sent me out to locate you turkeys. You need to replace Third Squad for now. I'll get you guys relieved as soon as I can, but if you had any plans for tomorrow, forget it. Something big is going down. I don't know what, just that Third was pulled off guard duty and they are all in the dispensary. Just be careful out there."

"You mean to tell us they all got sick on duty?"

"Maybe they did, I don't know. Mess hall food ain't all that bad and they couldn't all be hung over at the same time. Oh, if you need to piss, do it now. It's a ways off and I ain't stoppin' until we get there."

"Come on Sarge, what's going on?"

"I honestly don't know. The Louie got a call from Colonel Stevens and went off to check on all the squads pulling perimeter guard. He radioed back for me to meet them at the south gate and when I got there he had me haul one half of the squad to the dispensary and he hauled the other half. They didn't seem all that sick to me. A couple were pretty sunburned and probably a little overheated, too. My guess is, they partied a little too much the night before and couldn't handle the heat. Must be pretty embarrassing for the Louie to get called on the carpet in the middle of the night, and by the Big Boy himself."

My mind was racing: That's how Marty got started. I thought of Tom and Allen. Sitting there in the middle of nowhere, the world suddenly seemed to close in on me and I could feel my heart beating faster. I was afraid, and I felt tears welling up within me. Yes, I was very scared at this moment and wanted nothing more than just to be out of there.

"Sam," I whispered in near-panic. "Sam, I'm so scared, I've got to get out of here. I can't handle this anymore. I wanna go home."

"I know," he whispered back and put his arms around me. "I know you're scared, and so am I. But let's just sit here a while and wait. You heard them; these clowns will be gone pretty soon. They have no idea that we're here. So we're okay where we are. Eventually, they'll leave. Our guys on the river are still sleeping, and I think we've made it pretty close to the road. So, just sit back and try to relax. Close your eyes and snooze a little if you want to, while I keep watch."

I leaned back against the broad base of an ancient cedar tree, laid my head on Sam's shoulder and closed my eyes.

Chapter 20
Monday morning

I must have slept a little. When I suddenly heard the rustling of dry leaves close by and slowly opened my eyes, I found myself curled up on the ground with my head on Sam's thigh. Sam was snoring softly.

Some protector! It was not quite daylight yet, more of a golden dawn with a promise of what to come. Dew was settling around us. I looked around for the source of the sounds that had awakened me and watched a little gray squirrel move about, at times scratching the ground for some unseen delicacy. Birds were chattering everywhere and I could not detect even a hint of the oddities we had seen down by the water. Next to me Sam was stretching and moaning.

"I can't believe I fell asleep."

"Me neither."

Sam looked around.

"Which way were those taillights we saw last night?"

I pointed to my right, just up a little rise and just a couple of hundred yards away at the most.

"That was close."

"Yup."

We brushed the dirt off and shared the last of the candy. I would have preferred to brush my teeth, but...

Then we slowly and carefully walked up the incline. You could clearly see where a vehicle had gone up the hill and where it had parked. The tire marks were deep and there were chunks of grass missing. Obviously they had problems going uphill. On the top the ground was level again and we found candy wrappers, cigarette butts and assorted trash strewn about carelessly where the vehicle had parked.

"What a bunch of slobs."

"Definitely no Boy Scouts. At least they are gone now."

Directly ahead of us was a drop off and when we reached it, we were looking at the black top road.

"Yes!" I said with conviction, "Yes, Yes, Yes!"

Chapter 21

Dawn found Ken Messer and Dave Smith busy at their computer consoles; Jeff Craft was curled up on a little 2-seater couch at the far side of the lab.

Smith stretched and turned to Messer.

"Hey, I think I've got it."

"What's that?"

"We'll get some satellite pix next time JA44P passes, which will be in exactly 5.5 minutes. We'll know if your calculations are correct and we can let Jonathon know."

"JA44P? Is that the designation for one of our satellites?"

"Well, no not exactly one of ours. Let's just say I have a contact and my contact has a contact and we've had to call in a couple of favors, but we are getting those pictures. I've done all the configuring and lining things up here. We're ready. "

"I still don't understand."

"Ken, my boy, we'll get real time transmissions of everything this bird high up in the sky sees and it's a lot. I learned that this little piece of modern technology is routinely used to monitor large unpopulated areas for illegal crops. So it should be possible for us to locate any unusual appearing vegetation."

More or less patiently they waited, finally Smith began to work the keyboard and they saw images appearing on the monitor in front of him.

"There. What's that? That brown stuff in the middle of all the green. What have we got here?"

It took another hour of tedious work and they gathered around a huge table, covered with papers. Dave Smith slowly attached the papers to each other with little pieces of tape.

"OK," he said. "Gather around and let me show you what we have. Over here, I have circled in red where our intended target area is. As you can see it's lots of green, our cornfield is growing nicely. Here are some enlargements of the area. Pretty nice straight rows. But this corn is still a long way from being ready to be harvested." He looked at them and they all nodded in agreement. Then he continued,

"But over here, about 8 miles to the west, is an area that is totally different. See," he pulled a large print out of the pile. "This area is full of trees and brush and stuff. The trees are covered with brown foliage, the brush is huge and I really don't know what some of the other stuff down there is. But this here looks like autumn foliage. This gentlemen, is the actual target area."

"Where would that be on our map? Where is the base?"

"Is that a river?"

"The base is right here." Again he pointed using a long ruler. " This is that little river we flew over. See, right here, the river is in the middle of the target zone."

The moment he spoke those last words, he realized what he had just said. All three men stared at each other.

"Oh, my God!" said Ken Messer finally. "There were people in the target zone. The blonde in the pink bikini."

His companions were quiet. He stared at them.

"Well, say something! What now?"

Dave Smith had been silent. He looked at his companions.

"Now we find these people. We need to find them and we need to find them fast. Let's face it; we have no idea what the IMPB does to human beings. We only tested plant life. If anything has happened to these people, SERPAC will be gone, finished, finito, kaputt. The lawsuits will never end, we'll all be finished, lucky if we can sling hamburgers at the nearest greasy burger joint to earn a living."

"Now wait a minute, just wait. How can you jump to such a conclusion? We just saw one person. Suddenly you're making a quantum leap from one person to multiples. I just don't see a reason to get so excited."

Jeff Craft looked around the table for support, but didn't find any. His companions just looked at him in disbelief.

"Do you seriously believe that one woman, in a hot pink bikini, will be sunbathing in the middle of nowhere completely alone? In this day and age? No, there were others close by."

Ken Messer ran his hand through his hair. "I was afraid of this, guys, I was afraid of this."

"Give it a rest, Ken."

"We can't go to Jonathon with one babe in a hot pink bikini. You all know that. We might as well prepare for what's to come. Come on, let's plot this one out and let's do it by the numbers." Craft sat down and motioned for them to follow suit.

"Ok, the way I see it, we have an AMAG mishap here. Not necessarily a system failure, but strictly failure of the targeting module. I'm not even sure that it's a programming issue. I really think it may be a hardware problem. But whatever it turns out to be, we have had the scheduled IMPB burst, but targeted at the wrong zone. And we have people right in the middle. We don't know what an IMPB burst does to humans and so we don't even know what to look for. Any suggestions?"

"We need to go to the area, see if we can find them, one of us at least needs to go. After we see them we'll have a better idea."

"We may have to bring them here, you know isolate them, observe them."

"Oh, come on. We can't just go snatch people off the river! They call that kidnapping you know! "

"I like the idea of getting them and observing them. We have just inadvertently stumbled onto some human guinea pigs. I could see that as a little surprise bonus."

"You are sick."

The shrill buzz of the phone interrupted them. Jeff Craft responded and after a meek

"Yes Sir" switched the speakerphone on.

"This is Jonathon Brooks. I had chosen the three of you to handle this project for SERPAC, because I felt you were the most capable, most responsible, most trustworthy! And then I get a call from my old friend Col. Stevens to let me know that he has eight very ill young men in the base hospital. Since nobody can figure out what is wrong with them he wants me to assure him that our AMAG did not malfunction and accidentally hit his men. What can you tell me?"

There was a moment of silence. Then Jeff Craft cleared his throat.

"We've had a problem. It appears, that for reasons unknown, AMAG targeted an area different than planned. The IMPB burst went off on time, but into the wrong target zone."

"Holy shit! Why didn't you tell me?"

"Sir, we just finished the analyses. I was just getting ready to call you when you rang through."

"How far off is the target zone?"

"Sir, the target zone shifted by about eight miles. It now includes the southern tip of Camp Crowder, the river dividing the base from the civilian farms and of course some of the farm lands."

"Well, shit! Then Stevens' boys were right in the target zone. I want one of you to make contact with Stevens, go see those boys, try to tape everything. Seems we have some human subjects we hadn't planned on. Might as well make the best out of this situation."

"That's not all, Sir. There also were civilians on the river."

"What?"

"There were civilians on the river. When we did the baseline fly over right after the IMPB burst, we also flew over the actual target zone." He blushed. "The pilot gave us the scenic tour. We saw at least one person on the river."

"Was the tape still running?"

Craft looked at his companions. Ken Messer nodded, "Yes, I believe so."

"Well, find out. Beliefs belong in church; we deal with facts. Make sure. Get the tape and transmit it to me pronto. I want to see what you saw. Civilians, Jesus, what else went wrong?"

"That's all we know of, Sir."

"Craft, find those damned civilians. Locate them, question them, and detain them if you have to. I don't care. Spend money, do whatever it takes to get control of this situation. Do not allow any of this to leak to the media. If we handle this right we can still salvage AMAG."

"Sir, this is Ken Messer from Seattle. We have no experience with humans exposed to the IMPB. We never even factored human exposure into our calculations. Wouldn't it be better to alert the public to this mishap so we can..." He was rudely interrupted.

"Mr. Messer, I believe you are on my payroll and SERPAC doesn't do public service announcements. I suggest you remember that when your conscience acts up next time. Now clean up this mess you've made and report to me that all is under control when you call me back."

It clicked and the line went dead. The three men stared at each other.

"Ok, you heard the man," said Jeff Craft. "I'll get ahold of this Col. Stevens and see if they can give me a pilot to cruise this godforsaken river until I find someone. Ken, get ahold of our corporate pilot, whatever his name was. I'll find out from Stevens where those men are, and then you go there. Observe everything, tape what you can without being too obvious, and find out what's going on. Okay?"

Ken nodded. Craft turned to Smith.

"Dave, rerun everything while we are out. From the first moment. We need to know what happened and why it happened. Plus you'll be our communications center. Ken and I will check in with you. Send the rest of the techs home until further notice. Tell them we're having lots of computer problems and to enjoy a couple of free days. Okay?"

Chapter 22

Our spirits soared as we reached the black top highway, and we walked with renewed vigor at a faster pace. But not for long, soon my feet were burning; those cheap, light canvas shoes provided no support. I could feel blisters forming, but somehow I kept going.

"I hope you have at least a basic idea of where you are going?" I said, just for the sake of saying something.

"Well, I do. I'm trying to keep us going down river, because that's where Tom is headed. Somewhere along the way I'm hoping to find a farm or maybe we'll run into someone, anything."

My feet were on fire now, every step like salt rubbing in an open wound and I knew that some of my blisters had burst. I wouldn't allow myself to stop, I couldn't. I thought of Tom and I thought of Marty and I thought of Allen. I missed him and Tom so much. Automatically I just set one foot in front of the other without thinking, left, right, left, right, Tom, Allen, Tom, Allen...

The sun burned merciless down on the tar and the heat and humidity combined with the noise of the cicadas hypnotized me. Somewhere along the way I had lost my hat and although we walked on the shady side of the road, I was sweating profusely and swatting at flies. I focused on Tom and Allen. Although I missed Allen, at this moment I missed Tom more. I could feel my heart racing whenever I thought of him. What would I do if something happened to him? I could not imagine my life without him. Funny, I never once thought that something could happen to me and how he would live without me. I thought of our early days, before we were married, before we had Allen. And suddenly I felt very old, sad and scared.

Tom has always been such a gentle, caring person. I used to think of him as my knight in shining armor, he was always there to rescue me from the fierce dragons. It didn't matter what dragons I was up against, problems at work, problems with my parents, a speeding ticket, Tom was there for me.

Mostly he listened and let me talk, and he'd hug me, hold me and rub my back and everything would come right back into focus for me.

What had seemed a crisis, suddenly no longer was of importance. I wished for time to stop, for us to be able to go back to before this horrible trip and for us to choose not to go. At least for time to stop long enough for Tom to catch up and be with me. I knew I could handle anything and everything if Tom was with me. But he wasn't and I was still walking along a hot blacktop country road out in the middle of nowhere, wishing for someone to come along, anyone, so we could get to our destination faster and put this nightmare behind us.

Being with Sam was better than being alone, but it wasn't the same as being with Tom. Right foot, left foot, right foot left foot, I kept walking, one foot in front of the other. I no longer cared about the sweat pouring off me, plastering my hair to my head. You can do this, I told myself. Remember what Tom always says, you're strong, you're tough, you can do anything you make up your mind to do.

Sam, a few steps ahead of me looked dazed and just as sweaty. Right foot, left foot, right foot left foot. I noticed that my steps were in synch with Sam's. Without noticing it, I had even matched the length of my strides to his. I chuckled and tried deliberately to change the rhythm and the length of my steps, but it didn't work and so I gave up.

Where would Tom be now? Did he get enough sleep last night? Did he miss me last night? Is he missing me now? What would I do if he too were killed on this trip? Would Allen and I be able to make it? Right there and then, on that hot country road I decided not to think that thought, ever again. We would be together, Tom, Allen, and I. I would see to that. I squared my shoulders, took a deep breath and felt a burst of energy.

What would Sam do now? How would he explain what happened to Marty to their kids? How would he go on? He had always seemed so devoted to Marty. Once he got home, everywhere he looked there would be reminders of her. I really felt sorry for him, poor man. We used to tease him mercilessly about his devotion to Marty. Right foot, left foot, right foot, left foot...

I remembered how Tom and I had talked about Sam and Marty, how we had wondered what they talked about or if they even talked to each other. What did Sam see in Marty? How could such a bright, outgoing fella be married a narcissistic airhead?

My feet were beyond sore, they felt numb and I told myself, that once we all were back in our homes, I would not take another step and eventually I would never again wear another pair of cheap, flimsy canvas shoes. Period.

Suddenly Sam jumped into the road, frantically waving his arms. I almost ran into him, my mind took some time to recognize what he was doing, while my feet kept on beating a rhythm into the pavement. But there was Sam, in the middle of the road, waving his arms and jumping up and down. I finally heard the vehicle approaching, glad Sam had pretty good hearing. It was an old, banged up, scratched up, dull brownish - orange pick up truck, the driver a man of undeterminably age, most of his wrinkled face hidden by the visor of his cap. He pulled over next to Sam and yelled out of the passenger window.

"Mornin! Y'all need help?"

"Yes!" We both shouted in unison. "Can we get a lift?"

He just waved us into the cab, pushed the passenger door open and we hopped in. Sam sat in the middle and once I slammed the door shut and hung my arm out of the open window I actually had plenty of room. The old man extended his right hand to Sam.

"The name's Elmer Stubblefield, just call me Ben. You folks not from around here, are you?"

Sam and I shook hands with Elmer called Ben.

"No, not really, my Grandma used to live over near Hooper's Ferry, 'til she passed away a couple of years ago."

"Is that right? What's your Grandma's name?"

"Alma Louise Evans, she had a little farm, couple of miles from the old ferry, by the old Buckner place."

"Is that right?"

The old man pushed his cap back revealing a pair of sparkling blue eyes and a head full of thick snow-white hair.

"You must be the little rascal that used to go squirrel hunting on my place all the time. Shot out a couple of windows in the process."

Sam turned and looked at him closer, a look of recognition on his face. "Hey, how about that. Isn't that something?"

The old man shifted and the truck slowly started to move.

"And who's that pretty young lady there with you? The wife?"

I had to laugh. "No," I said. " No, I'm just a friend."

That was greeted with a raised eyebrow and a noncommittal, "Oh

I see."

Sam had tensed up. I could only imagine the emotions churning in him.

"No, Mr. Stubblefield," he said quietly. "A bunch of us went floating on the river and there's been an accident, my wife died in that accident yesterday. Chris's husband and the rest of the group are still on the river, we walked out to get help."

There was a moment of silence, I could only see portions of the old man's face, but he suddenly looked tired.

"Accident? What happened, if you don't mind me asking?"

"I don't mind." Sam's voice calm, too calm. "I really can't explain it. We had this trip pretty well planned. Marty got sick the first night out. I kinda think it was a combination of too much sun, too much heat and some new medication she been taking. We got into some rough water. Didn't realize how much the river had dropped while we were planning this outing. Couple of our canoes collided; Marty fell in and was too sick to keep herself above water. We got to her in time and at first she seemed to be ok, but then she just died on me. Real strange. Real strange."

We continued on in silence, I certainly didn't know what to say.

"Yep," the old man finally said as we continued to roll slowly down the road. "I can remember when my Emily died. It was real hard to keep going after her passing. And you don't have any idea what happened?"

I wished he would step on the gas, speed up or something, anything. I did not want to go through a lengthy conversation about something I could not comprehend let alone explain. I just wanted to get this trip over with, I wanted to be back at home, with Tom, with Allen and feel safe and clean again.

Sam did not seem to be nearly as troubled as I was by the conversation.

"I don't rightly know what actually happened, Mr. Stubblefield. We started out on that trip and everything was fine, but by the first evening she was feeling pretty lousy. She had been on some medications and we've been thinking that she may have had some kind of a reaction to that medication, but I'm not so sure. She just kept getting sicker and sicker and then she just died. Right out there."

"And she was fine before you all left?"

"Yes sir, sure was, everything was ok, until that first afternoon actually. She just suddenly got real sick and she kept on getting sicker, no matter what we tried. Of course we did not have a lot to work with. We never expected anything like that to happen."

"And you have no idea what could have caused her death?"

"No, sir. I sure don't. Marty was healthy, she was a real health nut. Sure, I have my quirks, but she was real serious about it. Always taking vitamins, and eating low fat food and going to exercise classes, all that stuff. Then she just got sick on me. First she just had a headache. She thought that she might have had too much sun. You know how that is. When your haven't been outside much and suddenly you sit in a boat on a river in the bright sun all day, you can easily get too much of it. But she took a couple of Aspirin we had with us and that didn't help at all. Then she started to run a real high fever, I think she may have even had seizures from the fever. We gave her some more Aspirin, but it didn't help much. In the end I think she just died in her sleep."

There was a moment of silence. I shifted around in the seat and looked out of the back window into the truck bed. There was a little, black calf in the back of Mr. Stubblefield's truck. It was just lying there on some straw. I couldn't help but stare at it. When I first looked out the back window, I had thought the little thing was sleeping, but then I looked a little closer and saw that its chest wasn't moving, it wasn't breathing. Its black fur was dull and dirty and its nose all dried up looking.

"You all have kids?" I heard Mr. Stubblefield ask of Sam.

Sam just nodded. "Yes, sir two, boy and a girl."

"Ain't gonna be easy raisin' them alone."

Sam just nodded.

"Mr. Stubblefield," I interrupted, in a way hoping to rescue Sam from this obviously painful talk. "What happened to this little calf?"

"Well now, that's real strange."

He lit a cigarette and inhaled deeply. I was beginning to wonder if his truck ever made it over 30mph, but as slow as he spoke, it would be just natural for him to drive slowly as well.

"I went out yesterday, you know, just to check on my animals. Have a couple of little calves." He paused and inhaled.

"I had brought most of my cattle down to the river for the summer. When I got here yesterday, I thought it just was kinda queer, I didn't see any of them. So I went looking. I found that little one right away. It was still alive then, but pretty sick already. I stayed here for the night. I got me a little shelter out here. Then I found my other cows too. They were sick too and now pretty much dead. I'm taking this one in to the vet's maybe the vet can figure out what killed them."

He finished his cigarette and pitched the butt gracefully out of the window.

"But that's not the only weird thing. The cows that were on a pasture closest to Joe Bennet's land, they died first. Ol'Joe had leased his pastureland in that area to the

Federal Government this year. I don't know why he did that, being how he feels about paying his taxes. Maybe they gave him a pretty penny; Joe likes money. But them cows, they died first. When I first found them they was all bloated, but then they just dried up, kinda like old bread. You know what I'm talking about? I saw that. I was there on that pasture when they died, one after another. If I hadn't known better, I would have thought that them there cows were a bunch of old ones. But they were young and healthy," he paused to light another cigarette.

"Yep, I figure I have just lost about 33 head of cattle. $25000. - to $30 000. - all lost in one night."

I looked at Sam; surely he was beginning to see the connection between what had happened with the cattle and Marty and all the wildlife down by the river. Or was it just my imagination in overdrive? But Sam was quiet, lost in thought, staring out of the window.

"Mr. Stubblefield," I said. "Mr. Stubblefield, when we walked up from the river last night, we stumbled onto some soldiers from the base. We listened to them and they didn't know we were there. They were talking about some secret testing the government did on this side of the river. They said that the Army had leased some land from a farmer on this side and then conducted some testing."

"Is that so?"

I couldn't figure out if he had even understood what I was saying.

"That farmer would have been ol'Joe Bennet. What kind of testing?"

"Well, those guys were not real specific, they were drunk or something. They said, it involved some satellite and some sort of radiation aimed at a specific plot of farmland, supposed to make the crops grow faster, you know mature quicker. Something like that. Right Sam?"

But Sam didn't respond. He just sat there. So I poked him in the ribs, startled he looked over his shoulder at me.

"Sam, would it be possible that this secret testing killed both the cattle and Marty? Come on, you were there too last night when those men were talking?"

"I was just thinking about that myself. It's pretty outrageous for the government to conduct testing of this sort in a populated area such as this. But then take a look at some of the other equally outrageous stuff our government has done in recent years. Look at the Gulf War Vets that have strange health problems that even an idiot can link directly to the Gulf War, except the government.

I have been thinking about what those solders said last night, yes, I see the connection. You bet. But I also know that we will never be able to prove anything. And if we did, would it bring Marty back? Would it bring your herd back? No. I am so angry; I'm ready to take on the government, hell I'm ready to take on anyone at this point. If I had known that they wanted to do testing here, we would have never floated the damn river. I dragged you guys out here because I knew that it was quiet and remote and I thought safe. Now Marty is dead and I have no idea how the others are."

The old man had pulled over into a narrow, almost overgrown gravel path. "You hold on a minute here!" he said. "I got a few more cows out there I want to look at real quick."

He climbed out of the cab and lifted up the gate in front of us, pushed it open and walked through. I was curious and despite my blistered feet I followed him. He stopped in the middle of a grassy meadow that gently sloped away from us and lit another cigarette.

"See down there?" he pointed down the slope. " If you keep going in that direction, you run right into that river of yours. I got some more pastureland all around here and I like to keep my cattle here for the summer, let them roam. Then come fall, we round them up and bring them back closer to the house, so I have a little easier time feeding them in the winter. We are a little ways away from where you guys ran into them soldiers. Let's see how my cows are doing out here."

We stood a while looking around and then I saw movement in the brush and the trees bordering the meadow. Slowly several huge black cows moved toward us. Now that I knew what I was looking for I could see more of them in the grass under some trees, their huge jaws in constant motion. Mr. Stubblefield silently watched them approach and walked closer. I was amazed at the size of the creatures. But then I've never been around farm animals, so anything would have amazed me. He rubbed a couple of noses and seemed to know several by name. Finally he turned back

"Well, all seems to be ok out here. But I sorta expected that. We're a bit down river after all. Let's get you into town and get some help to your friends."

We were back on the road in no time and I was glad to see that the old man could coax more than 30 mph out of his truck. I leaned against Sam' s shoulder, the little dead calf in the back of the truck looked back at me; I closed my eyes and wondered how Tom was doing.

Chapter 23

Tom sat for a long time staring in the direction Chris and Sam had taken when they left.

Suddenly, he did not feel so sure that their decision to split up had been a good one. What if something happened? He wouldn't be able to protect her. Would he ever see her and Allen again? He never thought of himself, or what could happen to him. He knew Chris could handle raising Allen by herself. Don't even think this way, he told himself.

He walked over to check on Ralph and Sandy; glad Sam had helped him load Marty's body into one of the canoes.

The three of them stayed close to each other and close to the fire, although none could explain why. The night seemed endless and increasingly noisy, and Tom recalled his earlier conversation with Chris. What if she was right? What if, for some unexplainable reason, the world around them had changed? He tossed and turned in an attempt to get comfortable, but sleep never came.

Damn the what-ifs, he thought. With the slightest ray of light appearing in the sky, he gave up and went to tend to the fire. He quickly had water boiling, and the three of them ate what little was left and drank the last of the coffee. Then they doused the fire and gathered their belongings. They decided it would be best if Sandy took the canoe with Marty's body and additional gear as ballast, while Tom would ferry Ralph downriver. His greater skill at handling the canoe would provide a much smoother ride for Ralph. Comfort, after all, would not be an issue for Marty. Just as sunlight appeared on the water, they pushed off.

"Pace yourself," Tom kept telling Sandy. "Stay close and pace yourself. It's going to be a long, hot day."

He was right. When the sunshine hit, the temperature climbed rapidly. Before too long, they were both sweating profusely. There wasn't much of a current any more, so much of their forward motion came from paddling. They missed their partners. More often than they liked, they entered water so shallow Tom had to get out and wade,

124

towing the canoe behind him.

Shortly after ten o'clock, they stopped for a moment in a section of the river that was particularly wide and shallow. Tom had been dragging the canoe behind him for what seemed like miles and, finally, even Sandy had to get out and pull. They stopped and just sat on a rock in the middle of the river. Then they heard a mechanical thudd-thudd-thudd-thudd.

"A boat?" Sandy turned to Tom. He shook is head. "No, I don't think so, it sounds more like a helicopter."

"What do we do?"

"Absolutely nothing. Ralph, just keep that shirt over your lap and lay back. Close your eyes and pretend to sleep. Sandy, you just be your usual, obnoxious self. We'll play it by ear. We're just friends out for a day of frolic in the sun."

"You think it could be the army looking for us?"

"Could be. It's too soon to expect any help from Chris and Sam."

They could hear the helicopter approaching before they could see it and, as expected, it was dark and obviously of military origin. It hovered a little distance from them, and then a figure jumped out into the shallow water and waded toward them.

The figure was dressed in plain, dark green coveralls, and wore an oversized helmet with mirrored visor. Based on the way the figure moved, Tom decided it had to be a man. He still would have preferred to see a face.

"Good Morning."

That sounded friendly, Tom decided.

"Mornin'," he said. "What's up, you all have engine trouble?"

The two men laughed,

"No. Actually, we are doing a kind of survey of the folks using this river for recreation. Just want to ask you a couple of questions, if you don't mind."

"If we don't mind?" This was Sandy at her best now, and Tom only hoped that he could still call her off in time.

"If we don't mind? Well, if that isn't something! We get out here on the river to get away from all the hassles of everyday life, especially from you fucking survey takers. You rank right up there with used car salesmen and lawyers. Do you have nothing better to do with your

pitiful lives than to bother people who are trying to relax? Why didn't
you interrupt us at dinner last night? That's what guys like you do best.
Well, sugar britches, we ain't interested in your damn survey and we
do not care to answer your questions, and what we do or why we like
to use this river for recreation, it ain't none of your business. So get
back into that ugly green thing there and buzz off."

She did have to take a break to breathe, but there was no mistaking
it: Sandy was hot and Tom enjoyed the role of the silent observer.

But the man was unruffled, and just turned to Tom and Ralph.

"Sir, how long have you been on the river now?"

Tom was undecided. Should he get equally nasty, or play along?
He decided to go along with the questions, at least for the time being.

"You talking to me now? Oh, I guess since about daybreak."

"Have you noticed any other people?"

"No."

"That's what we came here for, asshole!" Sandy just couldn't back
off now.

"Did you notice anything unusual at all?"

"No."

"Yeah, you showed up."

"How many are in your party?"

"Just us. Count," Tom invited.

"If you know how to count." Sandy was in rare form.

"Where did you start?"

"A little ways upriver"

"Where do you plan to end?"

"A little ways downriver."

Sandy giggled.

There was a pause while the man took notes on his clipboard. Tom
was starting to get irritated.

"Just a few more questions, sir, if you don't mind."

"I do mind," Tom said calmly, but with conviction. "You stand
there with the sun behind you and those damned mirrored visors over
your eyes and interrogate me like some low life scumbag. You don't
extend me the courtesy of an introduction and now you want me to
answer more questions? Screw you."

He picked up the rope and started walking on. Sandy, never one to be outdone, flashed a smile and extended her middle finger as she grabbed her rope. Together, they moved on toward deeper water. Fortunately, the shallow part ended and up ahead they could see the river narrowing and beginning to look deeper.

"Hurry up" Tom hissed between his teeth. "Come on Sandy, move it."

They did not turn around. They just moved on, leaving the man standing in six inches of water, his clipboard dangling from his left arm.

They were just entering deeper water and picking up the rhythm of stroke after stroke, when Tom turned back and saw the helicopter leave.

* * *

Back in the helicopter, the man was already talking on the radio when the pilot lifted off. When he ended his conversation, the pilot said: "Sir, we need to get back to base. I am having some abnormal temperature readings and need to get that checked out."

"Come on, Lieutenant! Let's go downriver a little further. We are just getting started. Didn't you just check this bird out this morning?"

"Yes I did, and no we can't. This is not the type of problem I can just ignore. I'm sorry sir, but we're headed back."

Chapter 24

"Dave, Ken here. Can you find a way to patch me through to Jeff?"

"Jeff? Hello?"

"Go ahead, Ken, we're on a secure system."

"I sure hope the scrambler is functioning properly. Jeff, we have a problem at my end. I just taped three dead men. These were supposed to be young guys, but what I saw were three dried out and mummified corpses. The medics on duty said the men came in sick, looked like heat stroke. Then they just shriveled up and died. But that's not all. The bodies continued to dry up right before their eyes. At the moment they are waiting for an Army pathologist to perform autopsies. Families have not yet been notified." There was silence. "Jeff? You still there?"

"I'm here, I'm just thinking. I just got back to the base myself. I didn't get much done. The chopper developed engine problems. But I did connect with some people on the river. They were okay, healthy. Just pretty nasty-tempered, and no babe in a pink bikini among them."

"If we really had civilians on the river, they are dead by now. Based on what I saw, their bodies are decaying at an accelerated speed. How do we explain this to their families?"

"We don't. You heard what Jonathon said. SERPAC has very, very deep pockets. We need to find the bodies, and we need to take control of them. In the end, it'll be just a couple of people who had an accident. Happens all the time. After the dust settles, we resume AMAG and we still win. I'll talk to Jonathon. He is friendly with this Colonel. Maybe he can take over the military end of this clean-up, and you and I can concentrate on the civilians."

"Listen, Craft. Are you telling me that if we find these people, and if they are not yet dead, we'll detain them and just watch them die?"

"That's precisely what I'm telling you."

"Well, count me out. I will not be a participant. These people need to be found, I agree. But if and when we find them, we need to help them. No Jeff, I'm out. This has gone too far. I'm done. I'll head back to the airport. Tell Jonathon he'll get my resignation from

128

Seattle."

"Ken, don't do this. You can't just jump ship in midstream. I can understand your reservations, but what do you think we can do to help these people? You saw the soldiers, you tell me."

"Nope. I told you, I'm done. I don't want to have anything to do with the deaths of those people. This has gotten way out of hand. I'm outta here." He hung up the phone.

Jeff Craft stared at the dead phone in his hand, and then he dialed another number. It was promptly answered by a familiar male voice.

"Jeffrey, I hope you have good news."

"Not really, Sir. Messer has been to the base dispensary. The three soldiers are dead and Messer got cold feet and jumped ship. He said you'll get his resignation from Seattle."

"Is that so."

"Yes, Sir. I've not been able to locate those civilians on the river. Based on what Messer described of the soldiers' deaths, I do not believe that the civilians are alive anymore. Messer said the soldiers' bodies continued to decay at an accelerated speed after death occurred. I think if we just wait this out and let nature take its course..." He paused for a moment.

"You didn't see any sign of the civilians? No boats or such?"

"I did run into a small group, but these were most definitely healthy people. When I tried to talk to them, they were pretty hostile. I don't think these were the people we're looking for."

"Well, don't be too sure. I've had an opportunity to view the tape of your joy ride right after the IMPB burst. You all buzzed a nice looking young woman. She was sunbathing in a small boat of some sort. Put that tape into your machine and view it one more time. When you get to the young woman, look closely. You have to enlarge it a bit, but focus on the shoreline. You'll see her boat tethered to something, and you will see two more canoes full of gear. Jeffrey, you are looking for three canoes and however many people can be packed into them. Call me back when you have news. And don't worry about Messer, it'll be okay."

Jeff Craft had already slipped the videocassette into the player.

More than five hundred miles away, Jonathon Brooks signaled his oriental servant to bring him another drink. He dialed a number. A

129

male voice answered.

"There is a situation that needs cleaning up. Messer has become a liability. His services are no longer needed. He is headed back to the airport, take care of him. Let me know when you're done."

Chapter 25

The rocking motion of the truck changed, and my head hit the back window. It woke me up.

"Where are we?" I asked, sitting up and rubbing the back of my head.

"We're going to stop off at the Vet's," Sam said. "I thought it would be interesting to hear what he has to say, and we still have plenty of time. Besides, the Vet's bound to have a phone and we need to get help."

"I just want to get to the car. I don't want Tom to get there and we're not there." I knew I was whining, but I didn't care. I was hungry, and suddenly very thirsty, and my head ached and my feet ached worse. I wiggled my toes. Oh man, were my feet sore!

"Hang on," said Elmer-call-me-Ben. "We're almost there."

He turned off the blacktop onto an unmarked gravel path, and then turned to the right and into the driveway of what looked like a neat, clean, little farm. The house was a small white frame bungalow with pink flowers and a big welcome sign on the front door. Ben just pulled up to the big, red barn, honked his horn and got out.

Sam and I followed. A slender figure, maybe 5'6 tall, emerged from the dark of the barn. The visor of the baseball cap covered much of the face, and I was surprised to see a long brown ponytail sticking out of the back of the cap. A bit unusual, I thought, to see an old farmer-veterinarian with long hair.

"Howdy, Ben. What brings you out here?"

"Mornin, Ginny. You real busy this mornin'? I got a problem with my cows and I was hopin' you could look at this calf and maybe tell me what you think."

How could I have done that? I asked myself. How could I just automatically assume the doctor would be a man?

"What kind of a problem, Ben? And who are these folks with you?"

"Oops, I'm sorry. These are some folks I know, Sam Evans and Chris Landly. This is Ginny Page, she's not only the best vet anyone could want, she's also a very dear friend."

We said hello and shook hands, but it was obvious that Ginny didn't warm up to strangers easily. Sam and Ginny unloaded the little calf from the back of the truck onto a cart and wheeled it into the barn where the neat, clean examining room had been set up in a niche. I was impressed, but not knowing much about animals, dead or alive, I just stood in the background.

"Well," said Ginny looking at the calf. "Why don't you all help yourselves to some lemonade back there in the fridge. You look hot and thirsty. Then you might wanna go ahead and tell me what happened."

I had forgotten how thirsty I was until she mentioned something to drink. Sam and I emptied the pitcher in record time, then found the lemonade mix and made another pitcher. Taking off his cap and wiping sweat off his forehead, Ben took a long gulp of the cool, wet delicacy.

"I was out checking my cattle yesterday evening, you know, down by the river. Well I have to go past Ol' Joe Bennett's pastures to get to mine and I could see right away that there was something wrong with his cows. Actually most of them were dead. I couldn't find mine right away, but when I did find them, they all were pretty sick. Since it was getting dark outside, I decided to spend the night down there."

He paused and wiped his forehead again.

"I'm kinda glad I did. Wouldn't believe it otherwise. Ginny, I watched my cows die. I had thirty-three head of cattle down there on that pasture by the river. All of them's dead now, and I want to know how come."

Ginny continued to check the calf. "What did you see, Ben?"

"That's just what was so queer. These cows were too quiet. They didn't move around or nothing. The calves I had, they didn't run and play. They just all laid down and stayed down and then they died. I went looking to see if there were any injuries to any of them, but I couldn't tell. There wasn't any bleeding or anything like that. If I didn't know any better, I'd say that I just had a bunch of old cows that finally died of old age. But that herd, heck, none of them was over three years old, not counting the calves."

Ginny didn't answer right away; she was touching and poking on the calf.

"Sam, go ahead, tell her what happened to you all," said Ben. Sam told Ginny of our float trip, how Marty had gotten sick, how Marty died and how he and I had walked through the woods to get help. Since I don't really know that much about animals, let alone cows, I was kinda left out of the conversation. The others talked and talked for what seemed to be an eternity while Ginny examined the little calf.

I was beginning to feel strange. I was just standing there, right next to them, but their voices were drifting to me through an invisible fog. And there was this nagging buzzing sound. I turned and looked at Sam, and it seemed that I was looking down a long tunnel. I felt sort of numb all over and started to look for a place to sit down. I couldn't see one, and the buzzing was almost overwhelming.

Suddenly everything went black around me. I could hear Sam's voice call my name, and I could hear a female voice say, "Just ease her on down to the floor. Probably got too hot. Stay here, I'll get some cold water." The next thing I remember is feeling a cold cloth on my forehead. Slowly, the buzzing in my head faded.

When I opened my eyes I looked straight into the greenest eyes I have ever seen and a very warm, friendly face. "Feeling better?" asked Ginny the Vet.

I struggled, trying to get up. My legs and arms felt like rubber and seemed to get tangled up, and I wasn't able to coordinate any movement.

"What happened?" was all I finally brought out, and the raspiness of my voice surprised me.

"I think you were trying to pass out" said Ginny the Vet, "but these guys here kept you from hitting anything vital, and you came around again once we had you horizontal

"I'm sorry," I didn't know what else to say. I looked at Sam and at Ben and they were smiling.

"Just stay down for a little while. You're not missing anything."

"But I feel like an idiot."

"Okay, so you feel like an idiot. Just stay down anyway."

They just laughed and went on discussing the calf. I pulled the cool wet cloth over my eyes, adjusted the pillow under my head, and decided to take the advice and just rest for a moment. I felt I had no choice. Sure I would have rather been with Tom, who suddenly seemed so very far away. The relative coolness of the barn, the steady humming of the conversation, and my exhaustion, all suddenly hit me and I felt myself drifting off to sleep.

An unmistakable urging woke me up after what seemed to have been an eternity.

"Sam, we have to get to the river."

I felt panic, and I know my voice must have been full of it. But Sam just said, "Relax, Chris. We've only been here a moment and we have several hours yet."

"And I really need to use a bathroom."

I couldn't think of anything more intelligent to say. Everyone was smiling at me and I felt pretty embarrassed. With a little help from the vet, I managed to sit up.

"Thanks Doctor," I said finally, with a more normal voice, and she just winked at me.

"To the folks around here I'm just Ginny. Please call me Ginny."

Ginny helped me into the house and to the bathroom. I instantly fell in love with the little house. It had shiny wooden floors and a small-patterned, flowered wallpaper. There were lots of antiques and plants. It smelled of spices, cinnamon and cloves.

The bathroom was very white, very bright and very clinical looking. It had a huge, tiled walk-in shower and a separate tub, white with a neat dark blue trim. From the looks of it, that must have been a whirlpool tub. The room's only window had been extended outward in a greenhouse-like bubble. This space was filled with plants. I recognized spider plants and a red flowering hibiscus, but I didn't recognize any of the others. The window area could be closed off on the inside with white wooden shutters, should privacy ever be an issue out here. I decided that someone had spent a bit of money on the restoration of this house, and had done a great job.

I splashed some water on my face and washed my hands with soap and warm water. Ahhhhhhh. I felt so much better. I took some sips of the sweetest-tasting cool water I could recall.

The little house was truly as beautiful as it had first appeared. One wall of the living room was built of rocks, with a fireplace in its base. There were exposed wooden beams in the ceiling, and comfortable-looking, overstuffed couch and chairs. Lots of windows let in lots of sunshine and, although I could not detect the humming of an air conditioner, it still felt comfortably cool. I felt completely intimidated and out of place. I had to move slowly, since every movement made me dizzy. I managed, though, and rejoined the others in the barn.

Chapter 26

Tom was satisfied with the progress they were making. They had finally reached a section of the river that was deep enough and fast enough to give them a little respite from their labor. They continued to paddle along. Tom deliberately stayed slightly behind Sandy. He didn't want to let her out of his sight. After all, every bit of disaster on this trip seemed to originate with Sandy. Ralph didn't care. He was stretched out in front of Sandy, in pain every time he moved, and tensing up at the slightest hint of motion. But Sandy was doing okay. She worked the paddle just as hard as Tom did and, to his surprise, maintained their pace. Finally, she pulled onto the bank.

"Okay, that's it. I have got to go to the little girls' room. You guys may have ten-gallon bladders, but I don't." With that, she disappeared into the woods.

Tom and Ralph looked at each other. Ralph shrugged.

"I wouldn't mind that myself, but I can't make it into the woods."

The two men stared at each other. Finally Tom handed him the old coffee can they had used to boil water. Ralph held it out in front of him, looking startled.

"Don't look at me, man," said Tom. "I'm not gonna hold it for you. I know you're hurt, but this you're gonna have to do for yourself." Then he went into the woods to take care of his own business.

Before he returned, he heard Sandy and Ralph arguing with each other.

"Just remember, I did not want to go on this fucking trip. Just remember that. It's the last time I ever do anything with you. Never again, never, never, never."

Sandy was loud and mean-sounding.

"I'm the one who got shot, not you. I'm the one in pain, not you. Why does everything have to go your way all the time? Besides, you wanted to come too. Yeah, you did, admit it! You wanted to see Sam's butt in a swimsuit. Just admit it. This one time in my life I'm counting on you to do something for us and what do you do, you bitch about it. Well, I've had it with you."

"You? You've had it? I'm always the one who does everything for the family. I haul the kids around. I remember the birthdays in your stupid family. Who do you think sends your Mom flowers for Mother's Day? Me, did I get flowers? No. Okay, you got shot. Was that my fault? Did I shoot you? Did I tell those fucking idiots to shoot you? No, I did not. I may have thought it and it may have seemed like a pretty neat thought, but no, I didn't. So don't go accusing me of something. That's the way you are, accusing me of something I had absolutely nothing to do with. Then when I get all upset you change the subject and try to get me to feel sorry for you. Well, bud, it ain't working. I'm done with that silly mind game. Fuck you."

"My fault I got shot? If you, stupid bitch, hadn't flipped those dickheads off, they wouldn't have gotten pissed and shot at us and I wouldn't have gotten shot. So, yeah it's your fault. Just once in your life I'd like to see you think about someone other than yourself, think about what repercussions your actions could have, engage your brain before you act. That would be a nice change. But you wouldn't, you couldn't! You are just 'damn the torpedoes, full speed ahead' all the time. No thinking involved. How you managed to stay alive as long as you have amazes me!"

"Oh, I forgot you are the brain in the family. I'm sorry. Should I ask you which hand to wipe with next time I have to go?"

"Awh, shut up you two," Tom said as he stepped out of the woods. "Isn't there ever a time when you don't fight?"

There was no response, so he motioned for Sandy to get back in the canoe and get going. Ralph had turned slightly to his side. He had closed his eyes and looked half-asleep. Tom took one quick look at the map and his watch.

"How much longer do you think?" Sandy's voice was almost soft. Almost.

"Well, it's hard guessing." Tom shrugged and passed the last water jug. "I think about two or three hours, tops. Now don't hold me to that. I've never been this way before and I'm only guessing!"

"You're probably pretty close," said Ralph, not opening his eyes. "We left at daybreak, around five. Now it's noon, and we had estimated about six to eight hours on the river. We've hit some real bad spots, when you had to get out and pull, and that really slowed us

137

down. So I guess about two or three more hours is a pretty close estimate."

"Ahh, he speaks to us mere mortals."

"Knock it off, both of you." Tom was losing his patience with both of them. He shoved off, following Sandy. In no time at all, had they once again found their rhythm.

Chapter 27

The little calf was on a large, metal table. It had been cut wide open. Ginny had a big rubber apron on, and long heavy rubber gloves. Nobody said a word when I approached, so I assumed that whatever they had been doing was done.

"Sam, I brought you some water."

He took a big gulp. "Ohh thanks, I was so dry."

"We about ready to leave now?" I asked.

The three of them just looked at me kinda funny.

"Did I say something wrong?"

"No, no," Sam said. "The Doc here was just explaining things to us."

"I don't really have an explanation," Ginny shrugged. "You are telling me you watched this calf die less than twelve hours ago. With what I can see so far, I'm telling you this calf died several days ago. Actually, when I look at this carcass, I'd think it's some old cow. See here," she pointed at something Sam could see but I didn't care to. "This animal has started to decay at an accelerated rate. You say it died within the past twelve hours, and I say it's been dead a lot longer than that."

Ben Stubblefield took off his cap and ran a hand over his white hair. "Now Ginny, I was right there with that calf. When I got there, it was still up and moving around, looking for his momma. Within the hour, it was laying down in the grass, and then it was dead – graveyard dead."

"I don't doubt you, Ben, but what I'm looking at here just doesn't fit."

"Well, what about the rest of my herd? I've got about thirty-three dead cows up there. What killed them? I can see us having one little one die and we can't determine how come, but thirty-three of mine and god knows how many of Joe's? Ginny, something isn't right here."

"Didn't you tell her about the soldiers?" I asked Sam.

"What about soldiers?" Ginny looked at me.

Sam just nodded to me, looking very tried and worn out.

139

"We were on the float trip, you know. It was just supposed to be a fun little outing. But then everything went wrong. Marty died, Ralph got shot, and Sam and I had to walk out and leave Tom, Ralph and Sandy behind. They're bringing Marty's body, and we need to go to meet them at the takeout point."

I knew from the look in her eyes that my story made no sense at all. I inhaled deeply.

"When we walked out last night, we stumbled onto some soldiers from Camp Crowder. They were talking about some top-secret government testing right in the area we had floated through."

I waited to see if there was a reaction, then I continued. "The test is something about a satellite that sends beams of some sort to earth. They're supposed to speed up the maturation of crops and allow the farmers to bring in more crops in a regular growing season."

Sam was nodding all along, but Ginny just stared at me and made me feel like one of those alien abductors.

"When Marty first got sick, there were suddenly no more animals. Small stuff, like squirrels, birds, bugs, turtles, that sort of thing. But that's not the only spooky thing. There weren't really any dead animals laying around either, at least not for long. One day I saw animal corpses when we stopped for lunch, then later the corpses were all gone."

I took a deep breath. I would have to bring up the subject of Marty, and I didn't want to hurt Sam doing it.

I turned to him and he just nodded at me as if to say 'go ahead'.

"And about Marty. She started to get sick Saturday, the first day of our trip. By afternoon, she was pretty sick, and she was hurting, all over. She had been out in the sun a lot, really more so than the rest of us. Anyway, I thought at first that it's bad sunburn or something. But it was different. She got much sicker. Oh it was just horrible! She was just shriveling up, right before our eyes. At first her skin was all puffy, and then it got wrinkled. She just got real old looking."

Sam had turned and walked away from us. I continued. I thought the vet should know.

"She became delirious and then she became comatose. At one point, she almost drowned when our canoes capsized. And then she died, just died."

140

IN LIMBO

I paused and drank another glass. Nobody said a word. Sam returned and looked at us.

"There is more," he said. "Rigor mortis set in very fast and only lasted a few minutes, then her body started to dry up. I don't know how to explain what I saw. So weird. Her body just dried up. I'm not even going to guess what shape it's in now after a full day in the heat." He paused. "I hope to bring enough of a body back for the authorities to autopsy, maybe find out what really killed her."

After a long and uncomfortable pause Ginny looked at us.

"Let me see if I got you right," she said. "You guys were on the river, on a float trip. One of you gets sick, she dies. You see weird looking trees and bushes and all the little animals and insects are dead. You think that her death and all those changes in nature, had to be caused by some secret government testing done at Camp Crowder?" We nodded.

"You may think it sounds like an outrageous story, but I happen to believe you. A couple of years ago we had something similar going on when I was in Vet School. I had already bought this little farm and was cleaning it up in my spare time. One day I was in town, picking up my mail, and I overheard some people talking about having tainted wells. Ben, you ought to remember that! Well, when I got home, I read in the paper that there had been some kind of training exercise on that base. Involved some petroleum-based products, I believe.

"Well, whatever it was, the stuff somehow got into the wells of two farms and ruined them. Sure the government paid to have new wells drilled, but a lot of folks around here still are leery, and boil all their drinking water. And strangely, the government is paying for these two families' medical care, all three generations living on the farms! You figure it out. So, you see your story is not all that strange to me."

I wanted to hug her. I wanted to cry. I wanted to be with Tom, and I couldn't say anything. Everything got stuck in my throat. So I took Sam's hand and squeezed it instead, letting the tears run down my face.

141

Chapter 28

They were progressing nicely. Although it was hard for her, Sandy maintained her pace. The river was moving swiftly, and there was always plenty of depth. Initially, Tom had ignored the surroundings and had focused fully on staying behind Sandy and urging her on. Finally, even he couldn't deny it any longer. It was getting very hard to keep those arms moving. He focused on his rhythm instead, counting along, breathing with it, and trying to think of Chris and Allen.

But there was Ralph in front of him, moaning, and he couldn't help but think of the wound he saw earlier. It was nasty, and there wasn't any doubt in his mind that Ralph's leg was infected. He hadn't said anything about it to Sandy, and they hadn't stopped anywhere long enough for Sandy to notice the swelling and the nasty looking, foul smelling drainage.

Tom continued to paddle, his motions mechanical. He heard the noise, but his brain didn't register it at first. Then he recognized it: rotor noise; helicopter.

Oh, no, he thought, gotta get out of the open. Frantically he looked around searching for fast and effective cover. The only thing close was the tree-lined bank. Fortunately, the trees were huge, old ones with giant branches that extended well over the water. Not perfect, but it was better than out here in the open.

"Sandy! Saannndeee!" he yelled. She slowly turned and he frantically pointed to the sky and waved toward the tree-lined bank. To his relief, Sandy nodded and immediately started paddling toward the bank. In a moment, both canoes were under the overhanging trees, and Sandy and Tom were holding on to branches to steady themselves.

"Why are we hiding from helicopters?" Sandy asked.

"I'm not sure," said Tom, peeking out, watching the two small, dark green helicopters approach from around the bend in the river just behind them.

"I just know that I have a very bad feeling about this, and I'd like it a lot better if they do not know where we are."

The two helicopters were skimming the water, slowly moving downriver. Holding their breath Tom and Sandy watched in silence until they went by.

Sandy looked at her watch.

"We should be getting pretty close to where our cars are. Do you think they will spot the cars? Do you really believe they were looking for us? What on earth for?"

Tom slowly and carefully let go of the tree branch he had been holding, allowing himself to drift toward her.

"Which one do you want me to answer first?" he asked. Before she could answer, he continued. "Yes, I think we are close to the takeout, no I don't think they'll see the cars, yes I think they were looking for us. No, I don't know why. Sandy, you were with us the whole time, what do you think?"

"I'll tell you what I think. I think we are in the middle of a giant alien experience. The government knows all about it, but is trying to keep it from the public. But we somehow stumbled into this mess, and now they are trying to catch us and kill, us or vaporize us, or something like that. So far, we have avoided them, but they won't let us off the river. We know too much, bud! You just mark my words! They will find the cars and they will find us, even if they don't catch us on the river. No matter what we do, we are toast. Alien toast. There you have it, just remember you asked."

Tom just sat and stared at her. He didn't know what to say. "You really believe that?" he finally asked.

Sandy stared at him for a moment. "Tom," she said patiently. "Yes, I believe that. I believe it, because that way I can explain everything that happened with Marty and the trees and all that stuff. Neither my head nor my heart can believe that the federal government just conducts a test of this magnitude and does not alert the public. So, that leaves aliens as the only acceptable option."

"Come on, Sandy! You can't possibly mean that. Aliens! I can just see it on the next daytime TV talk show. Or on the news: Innocent campers harassed by crazed aliens, details at ten! Let's just get out of here, okay? The heat is frying your brain. There are no aliens dropping by to harass us, and I'm not even sure that all the weird things we think we saw really did happen. So just come on and move it. The faster we're out of this area, the faster Ralph will get medical help, and the better I will sleep. I don't know about you, but I am tired and sore and I really want to get this over with."

But Sandy wasn't easily stifled. "Do you think you are the only one tired?" She glared at him. "Shit, I passed tired a couple of miles back. I'm not tired, I'm dead." She stopped and looked at the plastic wrapped body of Marty in front of her.

"No offense, Marty," she mumbled. "But I hate this whole fucking mess we are in. We couldn't just go to some amusement park, could we? Six Flags, maybe, or even Silver Dollar City. No, we have to rough it, and now look at what's happened. I hate this river, I hate this trip and if I ever see another green uniform it will be too soon." She stopped to take a breath.

Tom dipped his paddle and doused her with water.

"Shut up, Sandy!" he said, but this time not really meaning it.

"I'm not happy either, and bitching won't get us anywhere soon. Put your energy to the paddle and we will be home the sooner."

The movement of splashing Sandy woke up Ralph. His eyes had a feverish glaze and his face was flushed looking. He moaned, shifting his body weight in an attempt to get more comfortable. Oh shit, thought Tom, that's how Marty got started. Now Ralph? He didn't have the guts to say anything. If he talked to Ralph and asked him how he felt, he would get a horror story which Sandy would hear. She would panic and then he would have to take care of all of them. He sighed loudly and began to paddle even harder. Sandy was getting ahead of him. Can't let her out of my sight, he thought.

Every stroke of the paddle brought them closer to the end of the journey, but every stroke of the paddle also felt like someone stuck a hot knife in his shoulder. Yet he continued on, there was no choice. Block out the pain, he told himself, focus on the goal, focus on what matters, and focus on Chris and Allen. And he continued to lower the paddle and pull it through the crystal-clear water, again and again.

Up ahead, he could see Sandy occasionally sitting up straighter and stretching her back, wiping sweat off her forehead, rubbing her neck. He caught himself constantly evaluating his surroundings for potential hiding places. They were surrounded by the most beautiful scenery he had ever seen. He conceded that much, and he did enjoy the steep pale bluffs with their dark green dots where cedars were growing. Sprouting on sheer rock walls framed by the bright blue sky and the multiple shades of green of the surrounding forests. I would like to come back here some day, he told himself. Maybe, if everything works out well. Maybe it's all just a bad dream, maybe Marty isn't really dead, and maybe Chris is just up ahead. But he looked at Ralph's pale, sweat-covered face, and knew this was reality. If life were ever to become normal again, he would have to get them off the river first. Suddenly a change in Sandy's movements caught his attention. She had stopped paddling, had cocked her head to one side and seemed to be listening. Suddenly, she frantically paddled toward the bank, to the cover of the trees.

Must be the choppers coming back, he thought, and put every ounce of energy he could muster into each stroke.

He had barely grabbed hold of an overhanging branch when one small green helicopter came into view. This time it was flying even slower than before, just above the water. He could make out two figures, and he watched as they scanned the bank with what looked like binoculars.

Oh God, he thought, I hope Sandy found a good hiding place. Please, please, Sandy, keep your cool. If he hadn't been holding on to the branch, he would have crossed his fingers. He stared at the side of the chopper, willing it to lift up and speed away. But it didn't. Instead he watched the figures scanning yard after yard of shoreline. Don't move, Sandy, he thought. Don't move. After what seemed like an eternity, the chopper slowly moved on upriver.

Chapter 29

"Sir, we need to head back." The pilot said to Jeff Craft. "They couldn't have drifted this far. I'd like to go back to where you had the contact and start from there once more."

"All right." said Jeff Craft. Then he pulled out his cell phone and dialed a number. After a couple of rings, a young male voice answered.

"Hey Ron," he said. "Did Messer get back to the compound yet?"

"No, he sure didn't. Is he on his way here?"

"Well, he called me from the base, and he was pretty unhappy. He said he would be on his way back to Kansas City, to the airport. I just wanted to see what he was up to. It's been a couple of hours. Actually I was hoping he had calmed down."

"I'm sorry he's not here. Haven't seen him. He probably caught a ride from the base, or maybe he's in some little tavern having a beer."

"He better not. I could use his help. Have him call me when he shows up."

"Sure will. Perhaps I could be of help?"

Chapter 30

As the chopper moved on, Tom began to slowly move his canoe down river. Keeping under the cover of the overhanging trees made it harder, but his pounding heart admitted what his mind refused to accept. He was afraid to take the easy route downriver, out in the open.

Carefully, he made his way to where Sandy was holding on to a branch. He worked hand over hand, trying to avoid any undue rocking motions that could wake up Ralph or cause him pain. Finally he reached Sandy. She was clinging to a thick, exposed root of an old sycamore. Her eyes were pinched shut, and the knuckles of her hands were white from clinging to the tree. He saw her lips move, and wondered if she was praying. Sandy, praying?

"Sandy," he said softly. "Sandy, they're gone. It's okay now."

Sandy slowly opened her eyes. They were red, and the lids were puffy. He could tell by her sniffles that she had been crying.

"Oh come now, it's not quite that bad." He reached out and gently rubbed her arm. "We are almost there. Everything will be all right, and by tonight you'll be home and Ralph will be taken care of. So go ahead and let go of that root so we can get moving again."

Sandy sighed long and deep. "I know," she said, "I know. The logical, rational side of me says so too, but the irrational side just wants to go kick butt and take numbers."

Tom saw that despite her smiles, she was shaking all over. Tom carefully maneuvered their canoes side by side, and then he hugged Sandy and held her for a moment.

"You've held up beautifully," he said. "I have to give it to you, kid. You're one tough cookie!"

She smiled at him. "Thanks Tom," she said. "I needed that."

"What about me, huh?" Ralph was carefully turning over onto his left side.

"Shut up Ralph," they both said simultaneously.

"We should be at the take out pretty quick now. Actually, I think it's just up ahead." Tom was all business again.

"Let's just stay together now, we are too close to the end. Give

147

some thought to a contingency plan in case Sam and Chris aren't there."

"God, I hope they're there, and I hope they have lots of cold beer! What side is the take out supposed to be on anyway?"

Tom pointed across the river to the opposite bank. They sat in silence for a moment.

"We will have to get out there and cross the river."

"Yes, we sure do."

"Let's be quick and get it over with."

"Sam said we would be passing a huge cliff. You know, steep white rock. No trees between it and the river, just rocks and water. Sam said there's a cave up in that cliff, he had hoped to climb up and explore it with us." Tom pushed them away from the sycamore.

"Well," said Sandy. "Let's just go and say we did. I am not stopping for any caves, never again."

"I didn't say we should. I'm just giving you some landmarks. You need to help me look for the spot where we can beach the canoes and get Ralph out, okay?"

"Sorry."

He didn't like crossing the river. The other bank had no cover for them. Should the chopper return, they would have nowhere to hide. And where the hell was that second chopper anyway?

"Come on, kiddo. Put a little muscle into it. Let's get across and out of the open."

"You're worried about that second chopper, aren't you?"

Sandy could be intuitive if she wanted to be.

"Yeah, two went downstream, only one came back. It bothers me."

"If they come back and we have no place to hide, why don't we just play the old tourist game and wave? You know, Hiiiii! waving and taking pictures? After all, we are just a couple of people out on a little float trip."

Tom looked a little skeptical.

"I don't know. I'd just as soon not meet those assholes again."

He carefully studied the far bank. Lots of trees, but too far from the river to not give them cover if they needed it. He felt his stomach cramping; his chest was getting tight. Then he saw a big wall of rock up ahead.

"Yes," he said, almost too loud. "Yes, baby you are beautiful!"
"Is that Sam's cliff?"
"Yup, I do believe so."
It was just as Sam had described. An overwhelming wall of vertical white rock rose straight up and out of the water. Several large boulders lay in the water at its base as if tossed there by a giant.

Tom thought he could make out crevices in the vertical wall, but at the same time did not want to slow down to look. He couldn't help but feel excited. At the other end of this rock wall were the cars. Chris and Sam would be waiting for them, and then they would be home.

They paddled on in silence. The river was wide at this point, wide and shallow and slow. They were almost in the middle of the river. Really easier than I thought, Tom said to himself. We'll be okay!

At that moment, just as they reached the middle, the second little green helicopter came around the big bluff. Tom saw it almost before he heard it, and from the look on Sandy's face he could tell that she had seen it at the same time.

"We are tourists!" he yelled to her. As if on cue she raised her arms to shield her face from the sun, squinting at the chopper. He quickly checked on Ralph. A towel conveniently covered his injured leg, and his floppy fishing hat was pulled over his face to block out the sun. All propped up, he looked like a guy who's had too many beers and is taking an afternoon nap.

"Ralph," he hissed. "Ralph, don't move. We have trouble. Pretend to be asleep. You've had too many beers and are taking a nap. You understand?"

"Okay, I hear you," Ralph said quietly. "I'll be okay."

The chopper slowly moved closer and Tom grabbed hold of Sandy's canoe with one hand.

"Don't change anything," he said. "Look friendly."

"I know, just tourists out on the water for a little R and R.," she said. She smiled at the chopper and waved her hand.

"Do you think they'll put that damn thing down in the water?"

"I doubt it," said Tom. "It's not that shallow. My guess is about two or three feet. I don't think they can land in that much moving water, but I think they can hover and let someone get out."

"Must be what they are trying to do. We're drifting toward them but we're not getting closer. As we drift downstream, they are moving downstream. I do not like this at all."

"Me neither." Tom could feel his heart pounding.

They watched as a figure climbed out of the helicopter and jumped into the water. The figure stood up and was about thigh deep in water when the helicopter lifted up and moved away its rotors beating the water.

They slowly drifted toward the figure and as they came closer they were able to see it was a man. He had short brown hair and a bushy mustache, and his green jumpsuit was void of insignia or emblems of any kind.

Nice looking fella, thought Sandy, somewhat familiar looking. The haircut, although short, was too stylish to be military, the sunglasses too expensive looking.

"Hi there." He called out to them when the helicopter was at a comfortable distance and they could hear each other.

"Hello," said Tom. "That's one helluva way to bum a ride. Helicopter is definitely faster than a canoe. What's up?"

The man had found an even shallower spot. He waved for them to come over. They didn't have to paddle; the current carried them. He grabbed the bow of Sandy's canoe, but not for long. Tom climbed into the water and took control over both canoes.

"Hi there," the man said. "My name is Jeff Craft. I'm from Camp Crowder. I need to ask you something. It's really urgent or we would not trouble you folks."

Tom nodded for him to go ahead and looked at Sandy, his eyes begging her to keep her cool. Let's just wait and see, he seemed to say to her.

"The military is conducting a top secret training exercise a bit upriver from here, and we had pretty much sealed off all roads leading to the river. We were surprised to see you folks out here. Would you mind telling me where you accessed the river and how long you've been out here?"

"Oh that's no real big secret, Jeff." Tom scratched his head. "We paddled upriver for awhile and now we're just drifting back down. Had a couple of cold ones, and are just out here enjoying God's country. We're on the way home now. What's the problem?"

150

Oh my God, thought Jeff Craft, these are the same people I ran into earlier. And he said, "We just want to make sure there is no problem. One of our patrols reported a group of civilians on the river and thought they had drifted into the middle of a live fire exercise. We just want to make sure nobody got hurt. Would you mind giving me your names, sir?"

Tom looked past the man in the water and saw the end of the big bluff. Play along with him, he told himself. We are too close to the end now.

"Sure," Tom smiled at the man. "I'm Roger Jones, these are my friends Susie and Joe Carmichael."

"Nice to meet you, Roger. And Susie, Joe." The man nodded in their direction.

"Nice to meet you too, Jeff." Sandy could be civil if she wanted to be. Ralph just pushed his hat momentarily out of his face, glared at Jeff, and then covered his eyes again pretending to be asleep.

"Where are you folks from?"

"St. Louis. We're teachers. High School, you know."

"Teachers?" Jeff smiled, but his eyes remained cold. "My teachers never went canoeing. You all do this a lot?"

Sandy laughed. "No, we don't," she said. "But during the summer months, running away seems to be the only way to regain our sanity. This way we can let our hair down. You know have a couple of cold beers and not worry about running into any of our students. Those inner city kids wouldn't leave their air conditioned sanctuaries at this time of year." She laughed.

"What do you teach?"

"Oh, I teach biology. Susie teaches PE and Joe over there does math."

"Impressive."

Again Jeff smiled and again Sandy felt that the warmth of his smile did not match the iciness in his eyes.

"Have you folks seen anyone else out here? A larger group, more like six or more people?"

Jeff Craft carefully scanned the two canoes, trying hard not to be too obvious. Three people, two men and one woman. The two men were together in a canoe; the woman seemed to carry all the supplies, yet she is married to one. That one seems to have had quite a bit to drink, by the way he is lying in the canoe.

"No." Tom shook his head and looked toward Sandy, who also shook her head. "But then we haven't been out here all that long and we're already on the way back."

"I see. Would you mind giving me a phone number where I could reach you if I have any more questions? You know, you may have seen something and don't realize that it is of importance to me."

Before Tom could say anything, Sandy spoke up: "Why, certainly Jeff, let me give you my home number. At least I have an answering machine. Do you have anything to write with?"

Jeff produced a small notebook and a pencil, and Sandy proceeded to give him what sounded like a legitimate St. Louis phone number.

"Thank you, Mrs. Carmichael. Sorry to have troubled you all and I hope you enjoy the rest of your trip." He handed Tom a business card. "Please feel free to call me if you notice anything unusual."

As if on cue, the helicopter approached them. Jeff turned and carefully waded through the water. He snatched at a rope ladder dangling from the aircraft. The tourists were once again alone.

"What did you make of that, Roger Jones?" Sandy had a tremble in her voice. "And by the way I hate the names, Susie and Joe? How did you dream them up?"

Tom shrugged, "I just didn't want him to have our real names, that's all. For some reason I just don't like that guy. So, if you don't mind, let's get out of here."

Tom had already started to paddle again and they fiercely dug their paddles into the water.

"Sandy, look straight ahead, where the bluff ends right there." He pointed, "Right there is our spot."

Then the rock wall receded and gave way to a small sandy area.

"That's it. Oh baby, you are beautiful."

Sandy picked up speed and Tom had to work hard to catch up with her.

Chapter 31

They beached the canoes. Tom carefully climbed out and pulled both further out of the water.

He looked around, Sam and Chris should be here by now. I hope this is the right place, he thought.

"Sandy, stay here with Ralph a moment. I want to make sure this is really it. Our welcoming committee hasn't rolled out the red carpet."

"Hey, you want your shoes? They're over here."

But Tom just waved her off. "Nah," he yelled back. "I'll just be a minute."

Wearing his thin, plastic canoeing sandals, he walked toward the trees. They certainly looked familiar. Okay, and now to the right and that should be his Blazer. Yes, there it was, nicely stashed under the trees. Supposed to be hidden from the burning rays of the sun, it was also effectively hidden from the helicopters. And right next to it, Ralph's old truck.

OW! A sudden sharp pain startled Tom in his left foot. He stopped and looked down just in time to see a snake vanish into the tall grass. Damn, he said to himself, all these years out in the woods, a damned snake bites me now. Why here and now on this godforsaken trip? Shit!

He sat down to take a closer look at his foot. I know better, he thought. I know better than to walk into tall grass with just flimsy sandals on. I could have made some noise. I know there are snakes around here. Damn! A closer look at his foot revealed a single bite mark on the outer edge of his left foot, at the base of the little toe. It was just about where the strap of the sandal had been. The area was already swelling and getting numb. Tom took a closer look at the shoe, and there in the rubber of the strap was a tiny hole. It was not deep enough to completely perforate the strap. That's good news, he told himself. I got bit by a snake, but only with one fang.

He reached into the Blazer's glove box, where Chris kept a well-stocked First Aid kit. He carefully cleansed the area around the fang mark, and then covered the wound with a large Band-Aid. Okay, he said to himself, now what? If I tell Sandy, she'll freak out. If I tell Ralph, he freaks out. So I'm damned if I do and damned if I don't. Shit! Why me, why now? And what kind of snake was it anyway? He couldn't remember. He felt dizzy when he stood up, and now he felt his heart racing.

He climbed into the car. The comforting scent of the familiar surroundings was almost overwhelming. He gripped the steering wheel, to give himself a chance to catch his breath. Then he turned the key and the engine came to life. At least you had the decency to bite me in my left foot, he said to the now-absent snake. He carefully drove across the field to get as close as possible to the canoes. The shorter the distance to Ralph, the better.

"What now?" he asked Sandy, without expecting an answer. "Sam and Chris should be here by now. Let's load Ralph up and get back into town."

Sandy looked at her watch.

"Yeah, I think so too. Let's load Ralph and figure out what to do about Marty. We can always come back for the canoes."

Tom nodded. Marty! Damn, he had forgotten all about Marty.

"How bad is she?" he asked.

"I can't smell her." Sandy wrinkled her nose "If that means anything."

"Oh well," Tom said. "Let's get Marty loaded into the back first, then we'll put Ralph into the back seat where he can lie down. With the air conditioner on, it'll be cool in no time. I think there's an old tarp I keep in the back in case I have car trouble in bad weather and don't want to get messed up. We can wrap Marty in that."

He retrieved an old blue plastic tarp from the back of the Blazer and spread it out in front of the canoe. Slowly he rose up, feeling tired and old. He was acutely aware of an ache in his back he had never felt before. He also was missing Chris, suddenly and intensely. He felt his heart racing, heard every pounding beat inside his head. Gotta make it home, he told himself. Just gotta make it home.

Sandy grabbed hold of his forearm, tightly, like a vise.

"I don't want to drive back by myself." She had an edge in her voice and looked panic stricken.

"You won't be alone. Now let go of me. I need that arm, dammit!"

154

"Sorry. I'm just suddenly so scared. I don't know why."

"Try to lighten up a little, okay?" Tom tried to sound more confident than he actually felt. His heart beat so hard and fast, he thought he'd choke.

"Come on Sandy, let's get Marty moved. Sam and Chris should be here pretty quick, and we'd best be ready."

"Couldn't we just leave Ralph's old clunker here and pick it up later?"

"It's pretty secluded." Tom nodded. "If that's what you want to do."

"I do, I do!"

"Let's get Marty moved now, before Sam and Chris get here."

They stood staring at the small body wrapped in plastic.

"Somehow, I remember her bigger than that." Tom scratched his head.

"Well, I'm just glad she's not a two-ton woman."

Sandy still had that edge in her voice, Tom thought. Probably pretty tired, but then so am I. He patted the plastic wrapper.

"This seems to be the feet. Here, you take this end I'll take the upper half."

"Story of my life, I always get stuck with the ass end."

"Sandy, if you want the top, just say so. I just thought it'd be easier on you."

"No, no, no. Don't worry about it. Let's just get this show on the road."

But it wasn't as they had envisioned. When Tom lifted Marty's torso from the canoe to the tarp, it felt as if he were picking up a bunch of dried up-sticks, only lighter. He didn't dare grab just the bag; the plastic just wasn't strong enough to support any weight, and the last thing he needed was for the bag to rip.

He straightened up again. He felt dizzy and lightheaded, and his left foot felt like it was on fire. For a moment, they stood staring at each other.

"That felt weird." Sandy looked at Tom. "What happened to her? That felt like a bag of feathers, just skin and bones. I know that Marty weighed at least hundred and forty pounds. What we just lifted wasn't no hundred and forty pounds."

"I don't know, and right now I don't care." Suddenly Tom felt very

155

very tired.

"How did you come up with those names anyway?" Sandy asked as they were gathering their belongings together.

"Just made 'em up. How about that phone number in St. Louis? Do you know anyone in St. Louis?"

Sandy laughed; for the first time all day, she really, heartily laughed.

"It's the number for the zoo. I had to call it for the Boy Scouts to set up an outing, and I memorized the number. I thought that was a nice touch."

Tom had to smile. Yes, he thought, a nice touch. Ralph hadn't said a word since they arrived. He just watched as Sandy and Tom gathered everything up. He looked pale with deep, dark rings under his eyes.

"How are you planning on getting me into the car?"

Tom stretched. "Hey man, relax. We've got the motor running and the air conditioner cooling things down in there for you. We'll drag the canoe, with you in it, right up to the car and then we'll help you up. You just put your weight on your good leg. That's how we're gonna do it."

"It'll hurt."

"Yes, it probably will."

Tom knew he sounded harsh, but he didn't care. They had the army chasing them, Ralph shot, Marty dead, and Chris God knows where. To top it all, he was snake-bitten. What a mess! They positioned the canoe at a ninety-degree angle to the Blazer's back door, and together they lifted Ralph out of the canoe and stood him up. While Tom steadied him, Sandy climbed into the back seat. When they were done, Ralph had to admit that he was pretty comfortable.

"Let's leave the canoes behind." Tom looked around, feeling dizzy and lightheaded. "And let's get out of here."

"But what about Chris and Sam?"

"Let's leave them a note."

Tom dug into the glove box and produced a scrap of paper and a pen. On it, he wrote, 'Been here and headed back.' He stuck the note under the windshield wiper of Ralph's old truck. Together they carried the canoes into the underbrush, closer to the river. Leaving them upright, they pushed both canoes into the dense growth. Then they left.

Chapter 32

I was grateful when Ginny volunteered to take us back down to the river to meet Tom and Sandy and Ralph. It's not that I didn't want to ride with Ben. I liked Ben Stubblefield. But right now I was very impatient. I wanted to be reunited with my husband, and I wanted this nightmare to end. I just couldn't stand it any longer. I felt tired and dirty and I know I smelled bad. No, I wasn't patient enough to ride with Ben. Ben just didn't drive fast enough for this occasion.

Ginny had one of those big four-wheel-drive trucks. In her practice, I guess she needed that. It had four doors, and lots of stuff in the back seat area. I'm sure Tom could give a more intelligent description, but as tired as I was, I can tell you this much: The three of us fit nicely into the front seat. The air conditioning felt heavenly, and when she stepped on the accelerator the truck lurched forward with its big engine roaring. Yes, we were going somewhere, finally! I let Sam give directions to Ginny. I just bathed in the cool air, soaking it into every pore, listening to Sam.

"Wow!" Ginny exclaimed. "That was a pretty good size trip you had planned. Underestimated the distance a bit, didn't you?"

"It wouldn't have changed much, even if we had gotten off the river yesterday. Marty was already dead."

"Quite true."

"Watch out, up ahead. See that huge hollow tree? That's where we need to turn to get into the river-bottom. It's still a little ways, but here's where we'll need to turn."

Ginny never even slowed down as she made the turn. I doubted that she knew any speeds besides "go" or "go faster." Despite the rough road, the ride was remarkably smooth. Must be the size of the truck I thought.

Then my heart skipped a beat. Out of the trees up ahead came a familiar-looking vehicle.

"That's Tom!" I screamed so loud, even Ginny jumped. I just about crawled out of the passenger window, waving my arms and screaming. Ginny turned her big truck without seeming to slow down, and after a perfect ninety-degree turn blocked the road with my side facing Tom. Before Tom had even come to a full stop, I was out of the truck and at his door. I yanked the door open, almost causing him to fall out. I didn't care – I was happy! Finally I was back together with my Tom, and nothing else could possibly bother me any more. Nothing else could happen. I hugged him, kissed him, touched him and tasted him, savoring his scent, even his stubbly chin rubbing on my face.

"I love you." I repeated over and over. "I was so worried about you."

"Later, babe," Tom said, as he firmly held me to his chest. "Right now we need to get away from here. We need to get Ralph some medical attention and we need to get Marty taken care of. And if I am not mistaken, we will have this whole area swarming with people searching for us, and pretty damn soon."

I know my husband. When he uses words like 'damn.' something is greatly upsetting him.

"What happened?" asked Sam.

"We were stopped twice by guys in helicopters. No mistaking, they were searching the river. We saw them actually three times, but they didn't see us. I mean it, let's go!"

I climbed into the Blazer, cherishing its familiar feel. I also wanted to check on Ralph. He had propped himself up on one side, obviously curious. He still looked bad, but not as bad as I had expected. When I tried to undo the bandage, he reached out and stopped me. "Just trust me when I say it's bad," he said. "Don't waste our time here."

"Let me check this out."

"Why? There is nothing you can do about it out here. Leave it alone for now and end this goddam kaffeeklatsch and get me to a fucking hospital. Maybe I won't loose my leg after all. Marty is dead, there's nothing anyone can do for her, but I'm still alive."

I didn't know what to say. Here I was feeling giddy and happy, and Ralph sounded bitter and harsh. What he said was like a cold shower on my feeling of elation after being reunited with Tom. But he was right. We were so preoccupied we didn't even think about him, and he should have been top priority. I jumped back out of the blazer. With my first deep breath outside the car, I knew he had been correct. The fresh air was in stark contrast to the foul putrid odor inside the Blazer.

"Listen, people," I said. "We still need to get Ralph to a hospital. We can't save Marty, but we really need to do something for Ralph. That leg's in bad shape."

They all looked at each other, and I could tell each one felt badly about forgetting Ralph. Then I saw Tom's foot.

"Oh my God, Tom what happened to your foot?" His left foot was swollen and a large band-aid had come loose and was just dangling.

"A snake bit me."

"A snake? What kind of snake? When?" We all spoke at the same time.

"I don't know." He was pale and sweaty and wiping his forehead. "I don't know what kind of snake. I only saw it for a moment. It was kind of brownish, sort of. No rattles. Maybe a copperhead. I really don't feel well at all."

"That's bad enough," said Ginny. "Tom, Chris, Sam you are all wonderful people, but right now I'm going to take charge. So listen up."

I helped Tom sit down and he put his head between his knees.

"We need to get medical attention for two people, and do it fast. Sandy, that's you, right? Sandy, you take the blazer and head for on the freeway. I'll lead you that far. I know a shortcut. Drive north to Holsum about thirty or so miles away. They have a pretty decent hospital, and you can take your husband there. Tell them it was a camping accident. You two were fooling around with his rifle and it went off. It took you until now to get back to civilization, okay?"

Sandy nodded. "But, what if someone recognizes the bullet?"

"Stick to your story and be very very polite. Polite people never shoot each other on purpose, but pay attention to what you are doing. They will call the cops. Even the rural ER doctors know they have to report all gunshot wounds. We want to be sure and give them enough detail, but not too much and definitely nothing about Marty and the military. Got that?"

Sandy nodded.

"What about you, Ralph?" Ralph nodded, his eyes closed, I'm sure he was in pain, but I was only worried about Tom at this point – Tom and only Tom.

"Sam, you and I are going to move Marty's body from the Blazer to the back of my truck. Then we'll put Tom in the backseat. We'll drive some back roads. I know an old country doc over in Muncie. I happen to know that he is very experienced with snakebites, and always prepared to handle a snakebite emergency. Sandy, we'll connect with you tomorrow. Just stay put at the hospital."

We all nodded. "Any questions?"

"We need to get to our other vehicles upriver, also."

"Whose cars are up there?"

"Well, this Blazer here is Chris and Tom's," Sandy said. "Sam's van is upriver, and ours is back there. We can't just leave them there forever. They'll attract attention."

"We'll pass by there and Sam can pick up his van. Sandy, your husband has priority over your truck. Get him to the hospital, and be glad you have friends who trust you with their car. Let's go."

Sam had already walked over to the Blazer and had opened the back door. He flung Marty's plastic-wrapped body over his shoulder and hurriedly walked back.

"She feels light as a feather. I can feel her body, but her arms and legs feel like sticks." He gently put her down in the back of Ginny's Suburban. Then we helped Tom up and into the back seat. Ginny was still talking with Sandy and Ralph. I saw her gesturing and I could just imagine the argument going on. We were used to Sandy and Ralph. Ginny wasn't, and I watched to see how long she could hold on to her temper. She didn't strike me as a timid person at all.

I was in the backseat with Tom. I had found a medical bag which contained a skin cleanser. Ginny may be the vet, but some things are the same even if your patient is not a human being. I took off Tom's sandal and started to wash off his foot. He had lain back and closed his eyes, flinching every time I came near the bite. I could clearly see the single bite mark. The skin in the area was puffy and slightly red. Other than that, it didn't look nearly as bad as I had thought snakebite ought to look.

"How you doing babe?" I asked and Tom just shrugged.

"I feel cold and sweaty. I feel so odd. My heart is racing and I can't seem to catch my breath. And if I open my eyes I get so dizzy, I could just throw up."

"Oh Tom, I love you and I want to help you and do all the right things. But I have never seen a snakebite before. I don't know what to do." I checked his pulse at a hundred and thirty, but had no way to check his blood pressure. He felt warm, but I suspected the thermometer in the bag was not meant to be put into the mouth of a human. I just held him.

Sam and Ginny climbed into the cab. Ginny did not look happy. I sort of sat in the middle facing backward to Tom.

"I hope Sandy isn't as ditzy as she comes across. I'll lead her to the interstate and we'll pick up Sam's car along the way. From there on, she's on her own. Sam, you can just follow us when we cut across to Doc Humphrey's. Chris, keep an eye on Sandy, will you?"

I nodded.

"There's a little cooler back there with it has a couple of sodas in it. I don't know how cold they are. See if Tom would like one, it might help him feel better."

She stepped on the gas and we took off in a shower of gravel.

"Snakes don't often bite humans," Ginny said. "They use their venom to paralyze or kill their prey or to defend themselves. Snakes don't hold a grudge against people, but when someone gets too close or seems to threaten the snake, he gets bitten. Usually a snake releases just enough venom to do the job. That's where a human gets into trouble. We're too big, and so the snake gets confused about how much venom to use. It may release no venom at all when it bites in self-defense or it may release all of the venom in its glands. Usually if a snake bites you in self-defense, like when you almost sit on it, it releases less venom than when it hunts. It just wants to get rid of you. You are too big to be dinner."

"I guess that means the snake and I had a communication problem, eh?"

Ginny chuckled, "You've got it! Usually you see local swelling and tingling or numbness, then nausea. It just depends. Some venom destroys the red blood cells and other venom affects the nervous system. Any dangerous snakes around here would carry the haemotoxin, which causes the blood poisoning.

"That's why I want to take you to Doc Humphrey. He knows about snakes. He should, he's been bitten too damn many times himself." She looked at Tom in the rearview mirror. "Right now, my friend, you are in no trouble. Your foot is immobilized and, although it is swollen and probably hurts like hell, I've seen far worse! Relax and calm down. That will slow down your pulse and the spread of the toxin. It will take us about thirty or forty minutes to get there. Doc likes to use antivenin, within 4 hours of the bite. We have plenty of time."

"I am feeling a little better," said Tom. "It's reassuring to hear you talk. How come you know so much about snakebites?"

"She's the local veterinarian, Tom," said Sam. "Ginny, do you know that little gravel road that used to be called Possum Squat Road?"

"Yeah, I believe I do. Runs right by the old Brenner place, doesn't it?" Sam nodded.

"I know the one you're talking about. Had to deliver a couple of calves out that way. Why?"

"A long time ago, my Grandma used to take that road and cut across to the highway on it. It may just save us some time if it's still in decent shape."

"It's in good shape all right. We shouldn't have any trouble at all. I was over there just recently. Someone in Chicago bought up a couple of the old farms down that way. They built some sort of corporate retreat. I can't recall the company's name, but they're from the Chicago area. Since they'll be flying all their big shots into Springfield and then haul them all the way here in a limo, they fixed that road up nicely. They even petitioned the county commissioners to make it a private road and stop all the through traffic. But the commissioners are local people and a lot of local farmers need that road to access some of their fields. Then there's deer season! So the private road deal didn't pass."

The ride was fast and bumpy. Sandy stayed right on our tail. I was totally disoriented by now. Things are different when you're looking backwards. I was worried about Tom, and I trusted Sam and Ginny to lead Sandy to the interstate and get us on down the road. I felt completely inadequate. As a nurse, I should know what to do. We're always camping, so why was I not prepared this? I wanted to cry, but I bit my tongue. Tom didn't need tears. He had closed his eyes and seemed to relax. I felt his pulse again and it was still fast and pounding.

Ginny made one more fast turn and then came to a stop. She

jumped out. I turned around to see what was going on. She walked over to our Blazer and talked with Sandy, gesturing and pointing to her left. Then she was back.

"Okay folks" she said to us, "Sandy is headed to the hospital with Ralph, and I hope she'll do okay. We're off to pick up Sam's car and to see Doc Humphreys."

She accelerated sharply and we were on the way. The road was bumpy and I don't think I would have driven it quite as fast as Ginny did, but I'm sure she was used to that stuff and her truck was prepared for it. We left one gravel road and followed the blacktop for a short while, and then we turned off again and back onto another gravel road.

"Sweetheart, I don't want you to get car sick," Tom said to me. "Go ahead and face the front, I'm really okay and I do not want you to get sick."

He was right, of course, as he always is. I do get carsick easily. I'd never ridden backwards, and so I wouldn't know if I get sick that way, but if anyone's gonna get carsick, I'm the one! So I sat with him on the backseat, looking out of the front window. We had turned off the blacktop and were driving down a hill. There were lots of big, old oak trees on either side of us. The road was still gravel, but remarkably smooth and wide.

"You're right," said Sam "They did fix this old road up a bit. But where is this corporate hideaway?"

"Oh you can't see much of it from this road. There's just a little road that leads up the hill. They pretty much kept the farms where they were. Smart, since utilities were already in place. The buildings still look old and rustic, but don't let that fool you. They pretty much gutted everything and rebuilt from the inside. I kid you not! One of the old farmhouses is now just a couple of big wide-open rooms downstairs and a couple of rooms upstairs. Must be bedrooms, and every one has its own bath. The barns have become meeting rooms, and the smaller barns are used as bedrooms as well. The other buildings are living quarters as well, but only the old Brenner place has the meeting rooms. It was the only place with a couple of big barns."

"How do you know so much detail?"

Ginny laughed. "I'm just incredibly curious. Call me nosy. I wanted to know why a big corporation would come to this extremely rural area and set up shop. Why didn't they stick to the cities? They could have gone to Rolla, Springfield, Jefferson City. Why here? So I made a point of driving by a time or two, and I got to talking with some of the people who worked there. And then one day I just drove over and walked around. Pretty interesting what they have done. I wanted to get into the basement, but it was locked up. I really just wanted to see if I could borrow some ideas from them for my house. But they were operating with a different budget!"

We passed the little road leading up the hill.

"Well, now isn't that interesting," said Ginny. "Look at those tire tracks, they have been busy little beavers."

The curve leading from the main road up the hill to the houses showed well-worn ruts where many cars must have come and gone. Just a few minutes later we bounced onto a blacktop road, and after a moment turned back onto another gravel road. Shortly we came to a stop where our nightmare had started. There was the van, just as we had left it.

"Hop out, Sam, and keep up with me with your car." said Ginny.

Sam did just that. We waited until he had his van started and then we took off. With Tom relaxing, I had crawled up front with Ginny. Without ever moving her eyes from the road, she punched a series of numbers on the keypad to her car phone. I heard the ringing. Cool, I thought, a speakerphone. As if she had read my mind Ginny said, "When I'm making house calls this truck is my home and my office. It's safer to use the speakerphone, you know, keep my hands on the wheel."

A male voice said, "Hello."

"Hey Humph, you old goat." Ginny giggled and winked at me.

"Ginny, love of my life, what's up? Did you finally decide that I'm the man for you?"

"You know you are my one and only! Do you still keep that antivenin around the house?"

"I sure do, what happened? You get bit?"

"No, not me, a patient. I'm on my way over to you right now. Just wanted to check first, you know."

"Come on over baby, I always enjoy your patients. Bye now."

Chapter 33

The two men looked at each other.

"Well, I warned you," said the one with short blond hair, graying at the temples. "I told you people in this area would be out and about on weekends. But no, you didn't believe me. So now you're monitoring the airways, as if anybody in this outback would own a cell phone. These people are so poor, they probably still use smoke signals."

The other man was younger, with thick dark hair, cut stylishly short. His coat was draped over the back of a chair, and he had rolled up his shirtsleeves. He held his finger up to his lips and silenced his companion. Together they listened to Ginny's conversation.

"So what do you make of that?" He asked the first man. "Sounds to me as if someone is going for medical help for a snakebite victim. The chopper reported people on the river, said there were at least two parties. Well, I think one of those people got bit. All we need to do now is send our people out to monitor the ERs in the area, we'll have our snakebite victim, and we'll have the people on the river. Bingo."

But the other man shook his head.

"No," he said. "Ginny is the local veterinarian. I've run into her a time or two. She drives past here quite a bit, uses this as a shortcut. She's taking a patient to be treated for snakebite. The vet, bud, the vet! Her patient is an animal."

* * *

Doc Humphrey lived right at the edge of Muncie. To call Muncie a town would be exaggerating. The sign announcing the Muncie city limits gave a population of eight hundred and eighty-seven, and I'm sure that included a few stray dogs and cats. Muncie was a quaint little place. We drove straight through the middle of it. The town square reminded me of an old western movie set with its boardwalks and fancy wooden storefronts. I could envision cowboys on horses. There was the Muncie General Store and the Muncie Post Office. There was a diner, a bar and a barbershop. Finally, at the very end of Main Street,

165

was a small white frame house with a sign: Michael Humphrey M.D. I looked at my watch, and it had been more than an hour since I learned of Tom's snakebite.

Ginny parked directly in front of the house.

"Wait here" she said "I'll go get him, he can give us a hand with Tom." Sam pulled into the driveway at the side of the house and joined us.

Chapter 34

"Ron, Jonathon Brooks here. What news do you have for me?"

"Well, Sir, it seems that Mr. Messer was quite upset when he left the base. He must have stopped at a little tavern along the way and had a few drinks. Unfortunately he made a few wrong turns, and since he's not familiar with our roads, he overestimated his ability to drive. He rolled the vehicle. Some passerby saw it all and called it in to the Highway Patrol, but didn't stick around. The Highway Patrol notified us, since it was a company vehicle, and I'm waiting right now for a call from the Emergency Room in Holsum."

"I'm sorry to hear this, sure hope Mr. Messer is okay. But drinking and driving? Are you sure of that? It just doesn't sound like him at all."

"Oh yes, quite sure. The Highway Patrol said this witness saw him leave the tavern and he was quite unsteady on his feet then. Because of the curvy roads, he couldn't pass and was able to see the whole thing. He couldn't help, because the vehicle went down a ravine."

"Well, you and I have preached to our city slickers time and time again to be careful when they get into these little four wheel drive things. On those curvy roads, they flip in a second.

But that's not what I'm calling you for. Ron, I've been thinking. A lot has gone wrong down there, and I will feel a lot better when all those lose ends are tidied up. Our hot shots are not thinking." He chuckled. "I'd like to do some checking of my own, and that's where you fit in." He paused.

"Sure, I'd be delighted to help you, Sir. Just tell me what you want."

"We know that a civilian was shot by a military patrol, see. Now I'd like for you to find out if any dead body has shown up somewhere. Surely you have a contact at the Sheriff's office, someone reliable."

"I just happen to have a weekly poker game with the sheriff – not for money, mind you. Let me make some calls. I'll get right back to you."

It took Ron just a little more than 5 minutes to reach the sheriff, and in less than 10 minutes he was back on the phone.

"Ron here. Seems the Holsom ER is treating a man for an accidental gunshot wound. There is a deputy on his way over. I'll have the name, address the everything else in a little bit."

"Good man! I knew I could count on you! We know where the real brains in the company are, don't we? See what you can find out. Be discreet and keep me posted. Oh, before I forget it, do let the others know about Messer. Perhaps it will get them motivated to think better. Bye now."

Ron sat quietly for a moment, and then dialed another number.

"Mr. Smith? Ron here. I thought I'd let you know that I have news about Mr. Messer."

"Oh yeah? Did he calm down yet? When will he be back? I hope he knows he's leaving us in a real pinch."

"Well, I hate to say this, but he was in a pretty serious accident on his way from the base to the compound. The Highway Patrol called here, since he was in one of our vehicles. I'm actually on my way over to Holsum, to the ER to see how he is doing."

"Oh wow! What a bummer! I'm sure he's okay. Keep us posted, Ron. Did you let Mr. Brooks know?"

"I'll call him next, just wanted to let you know first."

"That's nice of you. We need to let his family know too."

"I'm sure Mr. Brooks will take care of that."

"Well, thanks for the bad news, Ron. Keep us posted, okay?"

Dave Smith stared at the receiver in his hand. Finally he looked up at Jeff Craft,

"Ken Messer had a wreck on his way from the base to the compound. They have him in the ER in some place called Holsum. Ron will be on his way over there shortly."

"Shit! I counted on him. I was so sure that once he calmed down he'd be back. Damn, now we are really up against the wall. Let's see if we can get some coffee and let's talk. Is he going to notify Jonathon?"

Chapter 35

Doc Humphrey was not what I expected. I had expected an old man with white hair, but what I got was a man about our own age with flaming red hair and bright green eyes. His hair was long, curly and pulled back in a ponytail. He wore faded blue jeans, a tie-dyed T-shirt, and Birkenstock sandals.

"Hi!" He said in a warm and friendly voice. "Now, who lost the fight with the unfriendly snake?"

"My husband. He's in the back seat." I opened the door for him and hoped he didn't notice Tom's skeptical look.

He climbed in, looked at Tom's foot, and started asking questions. By the time I made it to the driver's side to climb in and watch, he had Tom up, and together they walked into the house. I noticed that Tom walked pretty straight and didn't seem to have any trouble putting weight on the injured foot.

Ginny grabbed my elbow and waved for Sam to come and join us.

"Tom will be okay," Ginny said. "I know Doc looks like a long lost hippie, but he's about as square as you can get, and pretty knowledgeable. Most of all, he went into medicine because he loves it, not for the money. I've known him for quite some time, and he's never been wrong. So relax."

I nodded, but it's not easy to relax when you know that your husband's been bitten by a snake, could possibly die, and the doctor you have to trust looks like a reject from the sixties.

We joined them in an examination room. The furnishings were stark, white enamel and stainless steel. No frills; strictly basic; white, clinical and very clean.

Doc had Tom on an exam table and was just adjusting the big light when we walked in.

"I hear you are a nurse?" He smiled at me and I nodded. "I had a nurse working with me once. I couldn't pay her what she was worth and what she needed and she started to commute to Holsum. She still helps me out once or twice a week. I try to schedule most female appointments for those times, you know, to have a chaperone present.

Otherwise, I just keep the husband around. Let's take a look at that bite. How did you manage to get that snake to bite you?"

"Oh that was pretty stupid." Tom flinched as I took off his sandal. "I was walking through some pretty tall grass and stuff and I wasn't watching, and I guess I stepped on it or got too close. I didn't see the damn thing until it had already bitten me and was leaving."

"Hm," Doc studied the foot close up. "I see only one fang mark."

"The other one is in the strap of my sandal."

"How did you do that? Tackle a snake with bad aim?" We laughed.

"I don't know, it just happened. Do you have the antivenin here?"

"Yes I do, but first tell me about that snake. What did it look like?"

"It wasn't all that big, sort of brownish with a bit of a pattern in it. I didn't see any rattles and I didn't see the head. I guess, maybe one or two feet long, but that's a guess."

"How do you feel?" And he checked Tom's blood pressure and listened to his heart and lungs.

"At first it hurt like hell. Felt like my foot was on fire. Then, once I had chance to lie down on the way over here, my foot didn't hurt so much anymore. But my heart was racing, and I couldn't catch my breath. It's better now, but I'm still a little out of breath. What do you think?"

"Weeeeelllll" He managed to draw that word into an incredible length. "Well, I think you will be just fine. I don't know what kind of snake you tangoed with, but I don't think you need any antivenin. See, you had your sandals on and when she bit you, by chance one strap of your sandal moved in the fang's way. That also kept the other fang from penetrating too deeply. Must have frustrated her a bit."

He moved the light around and pointed to Tom foot.

"As you see, that area is a little bit swollen, but I believe that's just from the injury and not from the venom. Snakes can cause a lot of damage because of infection, not just venom. I think if you got any venom it was very little, not enough to justify the antivenin."

"Are you sure?" I had my doubts and I wanted to make sure my husband would be ok.

"Yes, I'm pretty sure. Let me explain why. Someone very wise and with a lot of free time once determined that there are about forty-five thousand snakebites in the US annually. Of these, only about eight

170

thousand involve a venomous snake, and of these, only about ten result in death. Unfortunately most of those are children. What a lot of people do not realize is, that just because a snake has bitten you doesn't mean that the snake has injected you with venom. In this area, we need to concern ourselves mostly with Copperhead bites. We also have rattlesnakes and cottonmouths, but most of the bites I see are copperheads. And about a fourth of those bites do not result in envenomation, they are dry. Getting bit by a snake is a pretty terrifying experience. I know; I've been there. You were bitten about an hour and forty-five minutes ago, correct?" We all nodded." Usually you see a marked local reaction within thirty to forty-five minutes following the bite. You know, pain, swelling, redness and sometimes blistering around the fang marks. You can see that we don't have that here. We have a little puffiness and a little pinkish color. I think that's just from the tissue trauma. You felt faint and felt your heart racing and felt short of breath. Is that better now?"

"Yes, it is." Tom's voice even sounded better.

"Never underestimate what the stress of that situation can do to your body! Like I said, there is no doubt that a snake bit you. Unfortunately we don't have the snake to positively identify it, but we know a little bit about it. My guess is that a copperhead bit you. That, in itself, eliminates the need for antivenin. It's unnecessary in most copperhead bites. But we need to get you a tetanus shot, and we need to get you started on a broad-spectrum antibiotic. Then we'll all share a pitcher of iced tea and you can tell me about this float trip."

"Are you sure about this antivenin?" I don't know anything about snakebites, but I wanted to be sure that Tom was okay.

"Oh, absolutely! Every month I have someone in this office with a snakebite of some type. Have lost only one. My statistics show that I see more snakebites than most other providers, but I think that's because people around here take these bites more seriously now. We had one of these religious sects passing through a couple of years back. I'm sure you've heard about them, handling snakes during their services. A good-sized rattler bit one of the handlers. He chose not to get medical help, and kept with the faith healers. When they brought him to me, he was having seizures. It had been several hours since the bite. He died here in the office a short while later. Word got out. I was pretty upset. I was new here and I didn't need that. So I went and educated myself about the subject, and I've been seeing snakebites ever since. When was your last Tetanus?"

He talked and listened and talked, and while he talked he cleaned Tom's foot thoroughly, gave Tom the tetanus injection and started him on antibiotics with some professional samples he had. I liked the man.

Then we regrouped to his porch. He had a big porch swing and Tom immediately lay in it. Tom has a hammock at home, and loves it after a hard day at work. He swings, and relaxes almost instantly. Doc brought out a big pitcher of iced tea and some glasses. He seemed to enjoy the company, and declined to answer our inquiries about his fee. Sam and I told him about the float trip, and Ginny filled in a few things too. He listened quietly. Then:

"Ginny, you and I have talked about this before. When I first came to this area, I was fresh out of med school and I was pretty wet behind the ears. I saw myself as a modern day Albert Schweitzer. I was determined to save the world! Why go to the jungles of third world countries when there is such a need in our own rural areas?

"Well, some corporate headhunters were after me. Including the military. But that was out of the question for a variety of reasons. I'll tell you some other day. I'm from the east coast, but I came out here while I was in college. I visited some friends, went fishing, and I liked it here. Later on, I returned and stayed. Then, over the course of several years, I noticed that more and more testing was being done at Camp Crowder. It was usually very hush-hush. But in a rural area like this, you hear about everything. It seemed that if the feds wanted to test something for its environmental impact, they tried it at Camp Crowder. I read in this morning's paper that the Army, together with a private corporation, conducted some testing at Camp Crowder over the weekend. Yes, here it is." He read aloud:

"The US Army Public Information Center has announced that agricultural experiments conducted at Camp Crowder over the weekend were successful. A spokesperson for SERPAC, the company conducting the experiment, said that the results indicate the artificially induced rapid maturation of crops may increase harvest yields significantly by allowing farmers additional harvests in the regular growing season. No negative impact on the environment has been determined, and further testing is scheduled."

I didn't know what to say. Neither of us did. Tom was softly snoring, which didn't surprise me. Doc had given him some Benadryl, which always puts Tom to sleep.

But Sam was sitting upright, and Ginny had put down her glass of tea. "Now let me see if I got that straight," she said. "They conducted some testing and it involves rapid maturation of crops, and it was successful and had no negative impact on the environment?" We all nodded.

"Let me show you a negative impact." Sam got up and walked out to Ginny's truck. He picked up Marty's plastic-wrapped body and easily carried it up to the porch.

"Is that Marty?"

"What's left of her." Sam sounded angry. "Look, even though she is dead, her body is continuing to change. I can tell you right now, in the short time I've been away, there's less of her now, than there was a couple of hours ago."

"Tell me one more time exactly what happened to Marty."

Sam carried Marty into the exam room and we again started to tell the story, filling in for Tom, who softly snored on the porch swing. While we talked, Doc cut open the plastic wrapping. There was no more odor, there wasn't anything resembling Marty anymore. It looked like the extremities had come off and the dried up tissues really resembled shredded beef jerky more than anything else I've ever seen. Everything was crumbling under his hands when he touched it.

"Ashes to ashes, dust to dust." I heard Sam say. Doc went into another room and came back with a very heavy-duty plastic bag and we transferred everything including the plastic into that bag.

Silently, we returned to the porch. It was dark outside, and we were serenaded by a choir of bugs and frogs and God knows what.

"It's getting late and none of you has had any decent sleep. Why don't you stay here tonight? I have plenty of room, and plenty of clothes to share."

We were a ragged-looking bunch. A shower, clean clothes and sleep sounded heavenly. I looked at Sam and he seemed to think the same, I didn't bother with Tom. He was asleep and wouldn't care either way. I was worried about Allen. I called and talked to him for a while. He didn't mind staying at Grandpa's another day, and Grandpa didn't mind it either. They had been fishing together and had lots to tell. I didn't tell them about Marty or about Tom. I just said that Tom had hurt his foot and we were staying at a friend's house for the night.

They didn't ask for details.

Chapter 36

Sandy didn't have any problems finding the Holsum Community Hospital. There were plenty of blue directional signs. She pulled up in the Emergency Room sally port and honked. Several people responded and helped get Ralph out of the Blazer.

While they were wheeling him in, she started to move the vehicle to the designated Emergency Room parking area to clear the driveway. But just as she turned toward the patient parking, area the Blazer's engine died. Swearing, she looked at all the gauges and found herself with an empty gas tank. When the engine died, so did power steering and brakes. Unable to control the heavy vehicle, Sandy let it roll downhill, easing it into the employee parking lot at the bottom of the incline.

Her disposition did not improve as she climbed back uphill to the emergency room entrance. There, she had to fill out paperwork and, although she had expected a mountain of it, she felt overwhelmed and appalled. All she wanted to do was to be with her husband. When she was finally allowed to see Ralph, she was shocked. In the brightness of the ER, he looked pale and frail, truly very ill. The staff had undressed him and cleaned him up a bit and an IV was attached to his right forearm. She desperately searched for something to say to him, to cheer him up, but couldn't come up with anything. So she just pulled up a chair and sat down silently. The ER doctor was an older man with thick, snow-white hair and kind eyes. He introduced himself and took a seat.

"Well, folks," he said. "Looks like we have a pretty nasty wound here. I'm sure you already realize that it is infected. We've taken some wound cultures and we'll get you started on some antibiotics. I've also prescribed some pain medication for you, so please don't be a hero. Let the nurses know when you need it. I have also asked a surgeon to look at your leg and I will be turning your care over to him when he arrives.

"We've notified the Sheriff's office, as we are required to do so by law, and have shared your personal data with them. They took note of it, but it is doubtful that anyone will come by to see you; it's just such an obvious accidental shooting. So now we'll concentrate on getting you back on your feet."

"Doctor, how long will he have to stay in the hospital?" Sandy asked.

"Oh, at this point that's hard to say. I'd like to see how he responds to the antibiotic first, and I'd like to get culture results before we make that decision."

He saw them both frowning.

"Is there a reason why you are in such a hurry? Keep in mind that this is a wound that has been without medical attention for almost forty-eight hours. We're talking about two days of less-than-sanitary conditions. Merely suturing it is not an available option anymore. Who knows what kinds of bugs the river water has introduced into this wound. No, I think you will be better off planning to spend a few days with us, and then we will know more. Once we're sure that you are on the road to healing, we'll send you home, okay?"

Sandy nodded, but Ralph just closed his eyes.

"Oh come on, Hon," said Sandy. "It's not that bad. I'll get hold of my sister and have her come down to meet me. Then she and I can drive back and get the car, and I'll go home and get some clean clothes for you. I'll call work for you, and I'll let Dr. Miller know so he can help me arrange the transfer for you. In a day or two, we'll have you home. Okay?"

"No, it's not okay." Ralph sounded bitter.

The doctor looked at them both. "I'll leave you to work the details out with the nurses. There's also a social worker who can help you. For right now, I'll have one of the techs clean this wound once more and bandage it. Take care, now, and I'll check on you a little later."

A few minutes after he left, a burly young man with an extreme crew cut entered their cubicle. "Hi," he said. "My name is Tim. I'm one of the paramedics, but I also help out in the ER. I need to work on this wound a little." He turned to Sandy. "You can stay if you want to, or maybe get a cup of coffee over in the cafeteria. It's free, and it's pretty good."

Sandy looked at Ralph, his eyes were closed, his lips pressed tightly together.

"Do you want me to stay?" She asked.

"No," he said, almost with a whisper. "No, call your sister and make the arrangements to pick up the car. The sooner we have transportation, the faster we are home."

Sandy shrugged but managed to smile at Tim. "Take good care of him. He's pretty special."

Tim measured sterile saline solution into a steel washbasin and added an equal amount of peroxide to it. Then he arranged sterile gloves and gauze sponges. After donning the gloves, he began gently to wash Ralph's thigh.

"So, you got yourself shot? How did that happen?" Ralph didn't even open his eyes. He sighed, and said, "You wouldn't believe it."

"Try me! I've heard all sorts of stories."

"We went floating with some friends, and we ended up in an area that had been closed off for some top-secret experiment. Somehow, we were exposed to something and one of the women died, I don't know where they are now. When we were on the way downstream, headed home, some gung-ho GIs stopped us and they shot me. There you have it, the short version. I'm saving the gory details for the media and my attorney."

"That's quite a story, Mr. Holtzer," said Tim. "But it says here that you were accidentally shot when you and your wife were having a little too much fun in the tent."

"That's just a cover story. Shit, do you really believe I'll tell everyone about this? They'd have me in the funny farm in a New York minute. I don't even know why I'm telling you. I just feel like I can trust you, I guess."

He grimaced as Tim began wrapping his thigh with stretchy gauze. "Take it easy, will you. This hurts like hell."

"So what kind of experiment did you stumble onto?"

"Actually pretty interesting, but the fact is, it killed one of my friends and got me shot. It's something agricultural – supposed to make the crops mature faster. But when I get done with the sons-of-bitches, I'll own the company and the patent. You just don't conduct this type of experiment in a public area where it can endanger people.

"No, there'll be hell to pay. As soon as I can get to a phone I'll call the media and my attorney. Hell, maybe I'll go to one of those TV talk shows. That would be fun."

Ralph paused and took a couple of deep breaths.

"What would you do, man? Put yourself in my situation. You're out with the wife and friends, just a little float trip. A little leisurely trip down Coon River, overnight camp, campfire, the works! There were some things the wife and I had to work through and this would have been perfect! But next thing you know, your friend's wife is dead and you are shot, all because you are on a public waterway. In the wrong place at the wrong time. No way am I gonna just roll over and take it."

Tim remained silent, and finished dressing Ralph's wound. After taping the gauze to hold it in place, he said, "It's been a pleasure meeting you, Mr. Holtzer. You get some rest now and get some pain medication. Just relax and you'll feel better soon. They'll take you up to the second floor in a few minutes and put you into a more comfortable bed. In a day or two things will look much better."

Tim walked away shaking his head, thinking, what a nut! And if he's not nuts, then he's gotta be hallucinating. He shook his head again and went into the dirty utility room to dispose of his trash and wash his hands. Suddenly, a thought entered his mind. Bobby just had the weekend off because of his Reserve thing and he said he would be out at Camp Crowder. Perhaps he's home? Maybe he knows something of this crazy story?

Using the phone in the utility room, he quickly dialed a number.

"Hey, Bobby! Tim here. Got a question for you. You were out at Camp Crowder this weekend weren't you?"

"Yeah, sure was, why?"

"I'm at work right now. We've got a man here who says he was out camping with some friends and got shot in the leg by some army personnel. It's really a bizarre story. That wound is pretty infected, and I was just wondering if you might have heard of a shooting out there. Otherwise I'm gonna ignore it as hallucinating."

"What? He says he was shot while camping at Camp Crowder? What a dumbass! Camp Crowder was closed to all civilian traffic this weekend. He was probably trespassing and got caught."

"He said he and his friends got caught up in some secret testing. One of them died, and that's when he got shot."

178

"Secret testing? Man, what a crock! I was out there this weekend. We had a busy weekend and that's that. There was no secret testing going on. He's hallucinating; I hope they admit him to psych. He sounds sick."

"Yeah, they're waiting for wound cultures, you know. That leg looks pretty bad. Anyway, sorry to have bothered you on your day off. Bye."

Tim left the utility room. Bobby would have known if anything had happened out there. He rounded the corner, just as two nurses' aides wheeled Ralph into the elevator. Good riddance he thought. Now you're somebody else's problem.

Fifteen miles away, Bobby stared at the receiver. Weird, he thought. He clearly recalled hearing some radio traffic during the weekend about civilians getting shot. After a moment's deliberation, he dialed. A friendly male voice answered on the second ring.

"Ron here."

"Hey Ron, what's up."

"Bobby! Did you have a good weekend? Play soldier again?"

"It was ok, it's my patriotic thing to do, you know. We all have our vices."

"What can I do for you my friend?"

"Gotta question for you."

"Sure go ahead." Ron sounded curious.

"You know I've been part timing it for SERPAC for quite awhile now. Helped you locate the farms for your fancy retreat and all that. You know I have a corporate security clearance."

"What are you getting at?"

"Did SERPAC do any top-secret testing out at Camp Crowder this past weekend?"

"Bobby, Bobby, Bobby! You know I can't answer that on this line. Come over, and we can talk in person."

"I can't today. I promised Cheryl I'll run her up to the mall. But let me tell you a story I just heard from a good buddy. There in the ER in Holsum is this man, his wife brought him in. He is shot in the leg. The wound is infected he says it happened out at Camp Crowder. He, the wife, and some friends, they were out on a float trip and somehow ended up in the middle of some sort of top secret testing being done.

179

One of them dies, he gets accosted by the army and ends up shot in the leg."

"Is that right?"

"Well, that's all I know."

"Sounds pretty crazy to me, he probably had too much sun."

"Well, just thought I'd check this out with you. I know how paranoid you guys can be."

"Go take Cheryl to the mall."

Ron pulled off the road to think. Finally he dialed, and the voice of Jonathon Brooks answered.

"We have a problem. In the ER in Holsum is a man who says he was shot at Camp Crowder. He is singing a loud and annoying song! I am on my way over there now. But I think you might want to get a couple of people to look at the civilian bank of Coon River, downstream from the base, see what we can find. I have a couple of guys in mind, like John Schroeder, Tim Miller, Rudy Melton. They are pretty loyal and their silence can be bought.

"Do you want me to take care of that song bird if necessary?"

There was silence for a moment. Then:

"Ron this whole mess is getting out of hand. We need to regain control. Far too many people are involved. We do not need any publicity. AMAG has had problems, and we're not ready yet to go public. If this clown is for real, then we must deal with it. Neutralize the situation. Just be damn sure that you cover your tracks well. You have everything you need?"

"Yes I do. This has been a very long day. It's going to be more complicated and could possibly involve more than just one target. Think about increasing my bonus."

"I understand fully, and I agree. I will personally take care of that, and will double it. Will that be okay?"

"That's fine. I'll call you later."

* * *

In the hospital's main lobby, Sandy listened to her sister's answering machine in frustration. Why couldn't she be home tonight? Finally she left a cryptic message that she had been involved in an accident and

180

desperately needed help and could be found at the Holsum Community Hospital. Then she told the switchboard operator where she could be found, and went off to find Ralph. She found him in the small Intensive Care Unit. This ICU had only six beds; each in its own little cubicle. Ralph was hooked up to a cardiac monitor, and seemed to be asleep. The nurses told her firmly, that visits were limited to immediate family only and only for ten minutes on the hour. At this point Sandy didn't care any more. She was exhausted, and the only feeling remaining was her profound sense of accomplishment for having brought her husband to a hospital. All will be well now, she thought. In a day or two, we'll be back at home and everything will be back to normal. She curled up on a reclining chair, using one of two blankets left behind by someone as a pillow and the other to cover up with. Her final thought as she drifted off to sleep was how nice the cool air-conditioned air felt.

* * *

A very well dressed young man approached the registration desk just inside the entrance to the Holsum ER.

"Excuse me," he said. "I'm with SERPAC, and I was notified that one of our executives has had an accident. Kenneth Messer. Where would I find him?"

The young clerk smiled, an open friendly smile that revealed discreetly attached braces, and touched a few keys on the computer keyboard. Her smile vanished.

"Oh, Sir," she said. "You will have to speak with the ER supervisor. I'll get her." Without waiting for his response, she disappeared through a side door. Ron leaned back in his seat and took a deep breath. Just stay calm, he told himself, you are the upwardly mobile young executive and you look the part. The people here do not know you and after this will never see you again. The young clerk returned with an older, gray-haired woman in street clothes and a white lab coat.

"Hello" she said. "I'm Mrs. Webster the night supervisor in the emergency room. I understand you are looking for Mr. Messer. May I ask what your relationship to him is?"

"Mrs. Webster? Hi. My name is Reginald Salisbury. I am one of the vice-presidents of SERPAC. Mr. Messer is one of our executives, directly under me. He is from Seattle, here on a temporary assignment. He is scheduled to fly out of Kansas City in the morning, back to his home in Seattle. I'm here to see to it that all of his needs are met. I would really like to see him now, it's getting late and I still need to find a motel for the night."

Mrs. Webster studied his face for several minutes; finally she took a deep breath.

"Mr. Salisbury, I am very sorry, but Mr. Messer passed away about two hours ago. His injuries were quite substantial, and he really didn't have much of a chance. I'm very sorry."

Ron took a moment to look away.

"Oh no, oh no. Has anyone notified his family? What about his things?"

Mrs. Webster firmly took his arm and guided him to a chair.

"Let's sit down for a moment. Nobody has notified his family. He never regained consciousness, and we found nothing more on him than a corporate ID. That's why SERPAC was called. We will need some more information for our billing records. Do you wish to notify the family or do you want us to?"

"No, no SERPAC will take care of that. We will cover the bill, all of the expenses. Oh gosh, I don't know what to say! This is certainly a new situation for me. How would we get the body back to Seattle? Where is the body now? Can I see him? This is just so awful!"

"I'll take you down to the morgue, then we can notify a funeral home so you can work out the details with them. But first we'll stop in admissions and see what they need."

Before he could think of an objection, she had whisked him down a long corridor and around several corners into an office area. She briefly introduced him to the clerk and stood back while he tried to answer the questions as best as he could. In the end, they gave up and agreed that he would have the corporate personnel department contact the hospital with the missing information.

Then it was off to the morgue, in the basement of the hospital, far away from the bright lights, traffic and noise. Mrs. Webster produced a key and let them in. The room was much smaller than he had expected. The floor and three walls were covered with white tile, and the floor slanted slightly toward the center of the room, toward a grated drain. Pushed against a wall was a long gleaming stainless steel table on wheels. Mrs. Webster looked at a logbook, and then opened one of six metal doors in the one untiled wall. Inside it was dark and cold. She pulled out a metal stretcher, just far enough to allow viewing of the face. Then she pulled back the white sheet covering the head. Ron bent forward. "Yes," he said, making sure he had a slight tremble in his voice. He cleared his throat. "Yes, that's Kenneth Messer. No doubt about it."

It would be a bit of work for the Seattle funeral home to restore Messer for an open-casket funeral, he thought. The left side of his face was raw looking and studded with pebbles, and had several small, gaping lacerations. He did look peaceful, expected of someone with a broken neck. He turned away from the corpse and wiped across his eyes. Mrs. Webster patted his shoulder and told him to wait out in the hall while she locked everything up again. Together, they walked back to the front door, where he thanked her profusely for her kindness. As he walked out into the night, she returned to her little office, her mind already on staffing the next shift. She already had forgotten what Ron looked like as she flipped through her Rolodex.

Ron started his car and immediately punched a series of numbers into his car phone. "Can you talk?" he asked when a male voice answered. "Of course." Ron delivered his report.

"Good job, my friend, as always. I appreciate your services and I will see to the remaining issues from my end."

Chapter 37

The phone continued to ring and ring, a loud shrill ring, and it finally woke Sandy up. It took her a moment to become oriented, and then she jumped up and answered the phone. It was her sister. Sandy began to cry as she told her story, the whole story, exactly the way it happened.

She noticed the janitor entering the waiting room and busying himself with wiping off tables and countertops. She saw him, but her tired brain did not register his actions. It didn't matter. She was too tired to care. He was still in the room when she gave her sister directions to the hospital and explained to her where their truck would be parked. Then she returned to her chair and promptly went back to sleep.

Ron deftly returned the janitor's cart to the utility closet where he had found it and rushed out of the hospital, not bothering to change from the scrub suit he had also borrowed. In his car, he threw the wadded-up suit into the back seat, pulled out a detailed map of the area and plotted his course based on Sandy's directions to her sister. He needed to get to her vehicle before this other person could get there. They could use the vehicle to identify the woman and afterward they would still have time to decide what to do.

With tires squealing, he fishtailed out of the parking lot. It wasn't easy to find the back roads in the dark, and he wondered more than once if he had perhaps turned the wrong way. His car wasn't meant for this kind of driving, and he was glad to see a parked vehicle appear in the beam of his headlights. Leaving his car running and his lights on, he quickly walked through the grass to the old truck. It didn't take long. The old truck's doors had not been locked, and inside he found Sandy's employment ID card and a pay stub for Ralph, both with Social Security numbers.

"Bingo" he said out loud, as he copied all the information down in his little notebook. He returned the items to where he had found them and left quickly.

* * *

184

Sandy's sister arrived just before dawn. They hugged quietly for a long time. Sandy was disheveled and sweaty, in stark contrast to her well-groomed sister. As they held each other, Sandy whispered, "I'm so scared."

They visited Ralph, but only briefly, as he was finally asleep. After picking up a couple of coffees to go from the hospital cafeteria, they were on their way. They did not see the young man in hospital scrubs passing them on his way into the building.

Ron retrieved the janitor's cart once more and wheeled it into the ICU. He made sure the nurses all noticed him.

"Mornin' ladies," he said cheerfully to no one in particular. "Just stoppin' by to get you'alls trash. How y'all doin' this fine mornin?"

The nurses ignored him. The bulletin board at the nurse's desk showed him where he could find Ralph Holtzer. He quickly went from cubicle to cubicle, dutifully emptying bedside wastebaskets. He deliberately chose Ralph's cubicle last. All the nurses had seen him and, by now, were ignoring him completely. Piece of cake, he thought, piece of cake. As always, no one sees what's before his eyes.

He entered Ralph's cubicle and busied himself with the trash, all the while carefully slipping a pre-loaded syringe into his right hand. He inserted the small needle into a rubber stopper on Ralph's IV tubing and injected the clear liquid into the IV line. Ralph did not move, but just continued to snore softly.

He was just reaching into his shirt pocket for the glass tube, the syringe's container, when a nurse walked into the cubical. Damn jogging shoes, he thought. Didn't hear her coming. The nurse saw the syringe in his hand and paled. "Oh God, be careful," she said, much too loudly. "Was that in the trash? Here, let me dispose of it in the sharps box. You're not supposed to handle sharps. Did you stick yourself?"

"I, I, I ah, no. I was just gonna come get one of you," he stammered. But the nurse already had slipped the syringe into a wall-mounted gray container labeled "Sharps Disposal Unit."

She smiled at him, "See, all done, no problem for anyone."

"Thank you," he mumbled, and pulled his cart out of the cubicle. Head bowed, he continued to collect trash at the nurse's workstation, and then left the ICU again. Once in the hallway, he quickly pushed the cart back into the utility closet and left, again without changing clothes.

Chapter 38

It was well past eight in the morning when I finally woke up. My back felt stiff and I was totally disoriented for a few moments. But then it all came back to me. What a mess! I rolled over and snuggled up to Tom, who was also just starting to wake up. We just lay there for a little while.

"We really need to get going," he finally said. "We need to get into Holsum, stop by and see Ralph, and pick up our truck. Sandy probably needs a ride to get to theirs, and then we are going home. I can't wait to get there."

The delicious smell of fresh coffee drifted into the bedroom, and I heard a male and a female voice talking. I couldn't understand what was being said, but it was a comforting sound. I stretched and poked Tom in the belly, then went to the kitchen to get coffee.

Sam and Ginny were at the table, involved in a seemingly serious conversation. I wasn't awake enough for that yet. I threw them a "morning" and delivered Tom's black coffee. I went into the bathroom with mine. The sound of running warm water seemed to come from heaven. I shampooed my hair at least three times. My fingertips were wrinkled when I finally stepped out of the shower, just in time for Tom to use the little bathroom. Yes, life was returning to normal.

I dressed in the clothes we had borrowed from Doc Humphrey. The old, well-worn t-shirt felt unbelievably soft, as did the faded jeans shorts. Then I joined the others in the kitchen. Now I was awake and ready for the world. Apparently the discussion had centered on what to do about Marty. Sam needed closure. He needed to be able to bury Marty. But he couldn't just walk into a Sheriff's office and hand them a bag full of dust and say, " this is the body of my wife, and let me tell you how she died." We had to agree with that. But then, what could we do? Marty needed to die in order for Sam to have closure. We all must have thought it, but only Ginny spoke up.

"Go home, Sam, and let it be known that you are planning a little excursion with some friends. Then you rent a boat, maybe a houseboat, on the lake, and you, Tom, and Chris spend the weekend.

"Some time in the wee hours of Sunday you radio the Water Patrol that your wife is missing. Tell them that she had said something about wanting to go swimming in the moonlight and that you're worried. She may have had a little too much to drink. We know they won't find a body. But you'll have a record of the accident, and then after a while they will declare her dead. I don't mean to sound cold, but you'll have a little funeral service and eventually life will return to normal. You can bury the remains out at my place. There's an old cemetery way out on that property."

Sam's face was pale, his efforts to control his emotions an exercise in futility.

"I can't do this." He said, emphatically over and over. "I just can't plan this."

Ginny hugged him. "You're not planning anything. You're working on a solution that brings peace to everyone, especially Marty." He nodded, hiding behind a now wet paper towel.

While Tom, Sam and Doc worked out the details, Ginny agreed to run me over to Holsum to retrieve the Blazer from Sandy, and if necessary, ferry Sandy to get their car. When we got to the hospital the nurses told us that she had already left with her sister to retrieve her car. We were given an opportunity to visit Ralph briefly, and I'm glad we did. He was sleeping, but I managed to glance at a worksheet one of the nurses must have left behind on his bedside table. That didn't look too bad. The previous shift had recorded a fever but, all things considered, that wasn't too bad. They had him on pain medication, a decent antibiotic and were closely monitoring him. I tore a piece of paper out of my notebook and wrote on it:

CAME BY TO CHECK ON YOU, GOT THE TRUCK AND ARE HEADED BACK NOW. CALL! C &T.

I laid the note on the nightstand, by the phone. When I turned around to leave the ICU, I was startled to see a janitor just standing in the doorway to Ralph's cubicle staring at me. I looked at him closer. I did not know him, I was sure of that. So I just said, "excuse me" and went past him. I caught a whiff of an expensive men's cologne. I couldn't recall the name. When he pushed the unit's door open for us, I was quite surprised to see a fancy gold watch on his wrist. I turned around once more, but he was already gone and the door was slowly closing. Ginny had noticed all this, too.

"They must be paying their janitors very well in this place," she said, and we both laughed.

We looked for the Blazer in the visitor parking lot but didn't see it. It was just by chance that I looked downhill and spotted it sitting in the employee parking lot. I wondered why Sandy had parked there. I just couldn't give her credit for being sensible. My questions were answered when I turned the key and saw the gas gauge. Ginny, ever prepared, had a can of fuel in her vehicle and we were able to leave the hospital premises without attracting any more attention.

* * *

The janitor made rounds once more through the ICU, diligently emptying the trash in all areas. He lingered just long enough to glance at Ralph and to peek at the nurse's work sheet as she entered Ralph's cubicle to check on him. Last temperature was above 101 degrees, blood pressure hovering around 100.

He left the ICU, pushed his cart back into the utility closet, and rushed to one of the big picture windows looking out over the parking lot. He saw the two women who had been in Ralph Holtzer's cubicle putting fuel into a four-wheel-drive vehicle. He could not read the license plate or clearly identify the vehicle. Before he made it as far as the elevator, both women pulled out of the parking lot and disappeared. Ron swore loudly, racing down the stairs two at a time, but it was to no avail. Their vehicles were out of sight when he reached the hospital's entrance. He decided to hang around for a little while longer, sitting in his car, at times dozing off. Then he watched Sandy return in the old, slightly banged-up pickup truck. Still wearing a scrub suit she had borrowed, she entered the hospital without even glancing at him. That pleased him, and he smiled as he followed her into the hospital.

Sandy headed straight to the ICU. Her stomach growled, and after she checked on Ralph, she would get a bite to eat. He was sleeping when she got there. His face looked flushed and his skin felt hot and dry. She pushed the call button at the side of his bed and quietly asked the nurse how he was doing. The nurse was a young brunette, with medium length hair that she wore pulled back in a simple ponytail.

189

The maroon scrub uniform did not hide her obvious pregnancy; her nametag identified her as Mary RN. Mary stepped into the cubicle and glanced at Ralph. "Hmm," she said with a frown. "I've been keeping an eye on his monitor out at the desk. He was sleeping, and I didn't want to wake him up. But I think we need to. I'd like to check his temperature. He looks a little flushed to me."

His temperature had risen to 104.4 degrees. He didn't really wake up, but just mumbled when Mary called his name. Sandy got about the same reaction, although he did turn his head toward the sound of her voice. Sandy felt panic rising within her.

"What's happening here?"

"Well, his temp is pretty high, higher than it has been, and people do get delirious with a high fever. Mrs. Holtzer, I need to check a few more things, but you can stay right here by his side. He would probably like that a lot. Then I'll call the doctor and then we'll know more, okay?"

Sandy didn't answer. She just sat down. Don't say, "okay," she thought. It's not okay; nothing connected with this weekend has been okay. This is how Marty started, only sooner. She was confused and feverish, and from there went downhill. If Ralph dies, then I know I'll be next. Then it will be Tom and Chris, and eventually Sam. I wonder who will be last? Whoever that is, he or she will bury all of us first.

She didn't notice the nurse leaving the cubicle, but she suddenly became aware of her voice, obviously talking to someone on the phone. Then Mary returned.

"Ok, I just spoke with the on-call doctor. He wants us to do some blood cultures, and then he'll have the ER doctor come up and put in a central line. It's faster that way than waiting for him to drive over here. He'll be here himself in a little while."

"Blood cultures?" asked Sandy. "Central line? What for?"

"Oh, we'll do blood cultures to see if the infection in his wound has perhaps gone into his blood. That could be causing this high fever. And then he would need to get lots of medication. Some of that can be pretty irritating to the blood vessels, so we like to run it through a big vein. Unfortunately, all the good big veins are deep inside the body, and that's why it's called a central line. Now, excuse me a moment while I get my stuff together."

190

Sandy sat stunned. The she quietly began to cry. She stroked Ralph's hand.

"Don't you dare croak on me!" she whispered. "Whom will I fight with?"

The nurse returned and arranged several items on the bedside stand, and then she put on gloves.

After putting a tourniquet around Ralph's upper arm, she drew two vials of blood. These she handed to a young tech who had appeared behind her

"Tony, tell the lab this is stat. And I mean STAT."

Sandy fled from the ICU. In the little waiting room, she curled up in the recliner she had slept in and tightly wrapped the blanket around herself, rocking back and forth.

A tabloid tossed on a table caught her eye, the headline screaming something about aliens.

She sat staring at it. Under more normal circumstances, she would not have given the headline a second glance. These past couple of days had been anything but normal. At the bottom of the article about people who had encountered aliens was a phone number and the request to call if you had an unusual event you could not explain.

Sandy did not think twice. She walked over to the phone and dialed the toll free number. It did not take long to get someone to listen to her story, and she turned her back toward the waiting room door and told about the weekend, about Marty's death, and about Ralph's being shot. With her back to the door, she did not see Ron enter and stand listening. They wanted details, and Sandy was ready to deliver. How long would she be at the hospital? At least 24 more hours, she told them. They would send a couple of people over. Satisfied, Sandy returned to the ICU to check on Ralph.

* * *

The night had not brought them much rest. Dave Smith and Jeff Craft were impatiently waiting for daylight. At five a.m., the phone finally rang. The message was short and to the point: Be at the Camp Crowder airstrip by six o'clock sharp.

Both were bleary-eyed and unshaven when they arrived, David

191

carrying a large folded up map of the area. They found a young pilot waiting for them.

"Mornin'," he said, entirely too awake and cheerful. "Are we ready to roll?"

Smith and Craft nodded. Craft was a bit disappointed. He had expected the corporate helicopter. He wanted to keep an outside agency out of this. It would be so difficult to observe and take notes with some outsider right there. How would he explain what he anticipated? The young man calmly went through his takeoff checklist.

"Okay, let's talk about where we will be going. If you put these helmets on, you will have headphones and microphone readily available to you, and we can communicate with each other. I control the switch to communicate with the tower. As I understand it, you have some campers in a restricted area, and we will be flying over the area to see what we can find. We have a couple of ground crews out there also, but they are probably still sipping their coffee and trying to clear the cobwebs from their heads."

Dave Smith explained the map. The young pilot listened, but never stopped chewing his gum. Finally they took off. The view was spectacular. The clear blue morning sky contrasted nicely with the greens of the forest. They easily identified the targeted area. Its brown foliage stood out in stark and obvious contrast to the lush green of the surroundings. They saw a few vehicles traveling on roads in the area, but they did not see anyone in the targeted area. They followed the river, but still did not see anyone near or on the river. At lunchtime, they returned to the base. After thanking the young pilot for his efforts, they returned to the corporate retreat.

There was no longer any way to avoid the inevitable. They had to report to Jonathon Brooks. Obviously, he had been expecting their call, as he answered his phone on the first ring. He listened patiently, then said,

"Well, gentlemen, it seems to me you have done all that could be done. I'm not quite ready to declare the experiment a total failure. No, I 'd rather say we have come upon a few challenges and were unable to overcome all of them. Let's just move into Phase Two as we had originally planned. I'll dispatch the Phase Two teams. They have been standing by since Day One.

"They will continue to monitor and record everything in the targeted area for the rest of the growing season. Since we've had so many unusual events, I think we should monitor the area for a while longer. Would you consider three years to be an adequate length of time?"

Craft and Smith uttered agreement.

"Well, gentlemen, I must say I am very pleased. We've had a number of obstacles to overcome and we've had the unfortunate loss of Mr. Messer, but aside from that everything has gone well. Now comes the arduous task of sorting through the data. I'll have the corporate driver pick you all up in, oh about an hour. The corporate jet will be standing by at KC International and you'll be home in time for dinner.

"Oh, I almost forgot, you won't be expected in the office for the rest of this week, take some time with your families. SERPAC takes family life very seriously. Have a safe journey."

Both men looked at each other, somewhat relieved, somewhat puzzled. Jeff Craft was even a little disappointed. This was a far cry from the "Jeffrey, my boy." speech he had received earlier. Had he fallen out of graces already? David Smith just sat quietly.

"I want to get away from here as fast as I can. How is he planning to get us home with the corporate jet by dinner? You're headed to Houston, I'm headed to the east coast."

He stared at his companion. Jeff Craft just shrugged.

"At least we are headed home."

Chapter 39

The drive home was wonderful. I felt giddy, like a little kid. It seemed to take no time at all to get back. We stopped by Grandpa's to pick up Allen before we went home and I'm glad we did. He took one look at us in our tie-dyed attire and said, with mock sincerity:

"If this is what you look like after a little campout, don't go camping any more. You look weird in those clothes." I laughed, cried, and held him until he protested, and then I still gave him one more hug.

Nothing had changed at home. The coffeepot still had a drop or two left in it, and the beds were still as unmade as they had been on Saturday morning when we left. I deeply inhaled the familiar smells, cherishing every nuance. Allen just headed for the neighbor's house to make sure his friends had not abandoned him during his absence. Tom came up to me from behind and cupped my breasts with his hands.

"Glad we're home, babe?"

I nodded; my eyes were filling with tears.

"I'll go get our stuff and put it in the garage for now."

I nodded. "I'll check the phone for messages, and give Sam a call. I'm also thinking about calling Ginny and Doc to thank them once more."

"Good idea."

There was a message from Sandy, she obviously was bordering on hysteria. She said Ralph was in the ICU, that the leg was badly infected, and that he had a very high fever. She was saying something about Ralph possibly being transferred to the University Hospital, but she was rambling so much it was hard to tell exactly what she was talking about.

She said something about having talked to some sleazy tabloid about our weekend, and that she would be calling some TV talk show in New York if Ralph got any worse. And then abruptly she hung up. I was glad we have an answering service, not a machine with a time limit on the message. It took just two calls to get the number for the Holsum Community Hospital from Directory Assistance, and the

194

hospital's switchboard transferred me to the ICU. The nurse I spoke with was noncommittal. She just said Ralph's condition was considered guarded at this time, that his wife was with him and that she would put me on hold and fetch Sandy. Within moments I had a sobbing Sandy on the phone.

"Thank you for calling me. I am so lost here. This is like being on a different planet! Chris, I think he's dying! Oh God what am I gonna do?"

"Settle down, Sandy," I said. "Tell me what happened. You took him to the ER and then what?"

"We got here, and the Doctor said it was pretty nasty and infected from all the river water and whatnot. He had them clean it up real good, and then a surgeon came by to look at it, also. He said he didn't want to operate because of the extensive infection. He said it would be okay to leave it open for now, and that he'll deal with closing the wound after the infection is better.

"He had a little bit of a fever at first, but now it is over 104! They say they've done everything they can, but it's not coming down at all. They say it's the infection, that it's in his blood, and it's probably a bug that is resistant to the antibiotics they are using. Chris, what am I gonna do without him?"

"He's not gone yet, Sandy! Come on now, he needs you to be there for him. Tell him you love him! Tell him everything will be all right."

"He doesn't respond to me any more, Chris. They said it's something like a coma."

Oh shit, I thought, he is septic.

"Sandy, tell him anyway. Talk to him, no matter what. Okay? Promise me that."

"Yes, okay, I promise."

"Tell me Sandy, did they do blood cultures?" There was a moment of silence.

"What? Blood cultures? Yeah, they did that. They drew a bunch of blood, man! And they put in a central IV line. Is that good?"

"Yes, that's good. The blood culture tells them what kinds of bugs he has in his system. Did they tell you something yet?"

"Yes, the nurse said something, but I don't remember the name, E-something."

"E-Coli?"

"Could be, sounds like it. Is that bad?"

Oh what to say, what to say?

"Could be. And now they want to take him up to the University?"

"Yes, that's the last word I have."

"Are you okay to drive? Tom or I will come to Holsum and ferry you."

"No, no, no. I'm fine to drive. You're just the first sane person to talk to me in normal English."

I heard a loudspeaker announcement through the phone. "Code Blue ICU, Code Blue ICU, Code Blue ICU."

"Sandy, what's going on there?"

"I don't know, just a bunch of people running back and forth. Listen, I'm gonna go. I need to go to the restroom and then I'll get a bite to eat. I promise I'll call you later."

"Okay, then. See you. Hang in there!"

But she was already gone. My hand was shaking and I must have had "I'M SCARED SHITLESS" written on my forehead. Tom stared at me and asked what was going on.

With a sense of foreboding, I told him what Sandy had said.

"That doesn't sound all that bad. Am I missing something?"

"Could be. Just before she hung up, there was a code in ICU being announced on the intercom."

"A code?"

"Yes, a Code Blue. You know, you heard me talk about that. People crash and you resuscitate them. The code announcement brings the Code Team together. In a small hospital, they usually don't have enough staff in the ICU to run a code and still take care of the other patients. So, every shift has specific staff members designated as Code Team. They deal with the CPR, the resuscitation and all that."

"And the significance to Sandy and Ralph?"

"He's running a high fever they cannot control. They have a bad blood culture report, possibly with e-coli, and he is unresponsive. Yes, I'd say he's is at high risk for cardiac arrest."

"Did you tell Sandy that?"

"Are you kidding? I already had to scrape her off the ceiling, without that bit of news."

"So what do we do now?"

"I don't know, I suppose I could play dumb and call into the ICU for an update."

"Okay, let's do that."

I dialed the number and the operator connected me with the ICU, warning me that she'd come back on the line if the phone wasn't answered by the fourth ring: "They're kinda busy at the moment."

A male voice answered on the second ring. I said I was Ralph's sister from Kansas City, calling to see how he was doing. I was really listening to the background noises. to try to get an idea of what was going on.

The man on the phone said, "Holtzer? Oh, the man in Bed Four. I'm just helping out here right now. Hold on a moment I'll see if there is any news."

He didn't put me on hold, but just put the phone down on the counter. I listened to the familiar sounds of a cardiac arrest being worked. But I didn't like what I heard. Apparently someone was giving someone else a report fairly close to the phone, because I could pretty much understand everything being said.

"... male, I don't recall his exact age, early forties probably, gunshot wound to the, lemme see, thigh. He was on a fishin' trip with the wife, they were so far out in the woods, we didn't get him until more than twenty-four hours post-injury.

"Wound cultures grew an assortment of junk, just as you would expect. Yes, a pretty nasty wound. Started him on antibiotics, and he almost immediately starts to spike temps. He's been steady above one-oh-four for over twenty-four hours now. Blood cultures show e-coli. Yes, I think that's interesting. He's been pretty much unresponsive for hours now. Yes, I think so too. Well, about fifteen minutes ago he went into some arrhythmias. There was nothing organized at first, and then he became tachy, went into V-tach. A Code was called and he became asystolic. That's where we are now. We've had some electrical activity, but nothing cardiac. Yes, yes. We've been at it now, uh, at least 10 minutes. Yes, still asystolic. Yes, family is here. Ok, we'll wait for you then."

I heard a click and his voice became louder.

"OK, guys, I that's it, let's call it. Time of death..."

197

The male voice faded, replaced by a firm, slightly out of breath female voice.

"Hello, this is Mary, may I help you?"

I couldn't talk. I just hung up the phone. I don't know how long I stood there. Tom didn't say anything, but just took me in his arms and held me there, letting me cry.

It felt like an eternity had past when the tears finally stopped and I was able to talk. I blew my nose.

"Ralph coded, he's dead. I listened to someone give report."

"You sure?"

"Oh yes."

"What about Sandy?"

"Let's get hold of her sister."

We just stood in the kitchen, holding each other. I felt cold – so terribly cold. I curled deeper into Tom's embrace, shivering.

* * *

Sandy was running cold water over her hands and wrists. Awh, that felt so good. She stared at her image in the mirror, not really seeing anything. Her mind was adrift and far, far away as she let the water run. A nurse opened the door and said "Mrs. Holtzer?" It startled her, and she splashed water all over her front.

"Yes, that's me, what is it?"

"You need to come with me, quickly. There's been a problem with your husband."

They rushed back to the ICU. There, amid the white walls, beige curtains and assorted equipment, a young doctor took her aside.

"I am so sorry," he said. "I am so very very sorry."

She stared at him, her ears hearing what he said, her mind not believing. The doctor's voice came to her as if through a wall of cotton balls, in slow motion, fighting to overpower the buzzing in her head.

"Your husband developed unexpected heart problems," he said. "Certainly related to the massive infection present in his body."

She tilted her head to one side, what was he saying? The buzzing in her head was getting louder and louder.

"We tried some very powerful antibiotics, but the infection did not respond to them at all."

WHAT ARE YOU TELLING ME? her mind screamed.

"Your husband's heart just gave out. We tried to resuscitate him, but we were not successful. I am so sorry. Is there someone we can call for you?"

But Sandy just stared at him, not comprehending what was being said.

"Mrs. Holtzer?"

Finally she responded, "Yes? What are you saying?"

"Mrs. Holtzer, your husband passed away. Is there someone we can call? Someone to come and be with you?"

"Ralph, dead?"

He nodded patiently.

"No, no, no." Sandy cried out. "You must be mistaken! It's not possible. Marty is dead. Not Ralph! NO!"

A nurse gently hugged her.

"I want to see him." Sandy sobbed, pulling away.

"Of course," said the nurse. "Come dear, let's go see your husband."

They walked over to his bed. Sandy stared at him, not believing. There was a tube in his throat, IVs snaking across the sheet covering his chest. Slowly, she sank to her knees beside the bed. The nurse turned and pulled the curtain around them.

Sandy sat there on the floor beside Ralph, feeling so very lost, not knowing what to do or say. She felt an overwhelming sense of emptiness.

Then the tears began to flow.

"You were the only man I have ever loved," she whispered. "I know I have been such a bitch and treated you so badly. I just don't know how to love without fighting. You were always so patient, putting up with me. And now you are gone, and I won't even be able to tell you that I love you. What will I do without you?"

She reached out and took his hand out from under the sheet. Oh God, she thought, he feels so warm, he looks so peaceful. This cannot be happening. Surely he'll wake up and get mad at me for making such a fuss. She gently stroked his hand. He didn't wake up, and she buried her face in his hand, letting her tears flow.

The nurse quietly stepped around the curtain.

199

"Mrs. Holtzer, would you like to speak with a minister? One of the local clergy is here."

"No." Sandy almost shouted, feeling rage at the interuption.

"No, I don't want to speak with anybody. No minister will bring him back to me, and I don't want to hear that God knows what he is doing. Do you hear me? No, I don't want anyone. I want my husband back!"

She buried her face in Ralph's hand.

But the nurse did not leave.

"Mrs. Holtzer" she said gently " I know that this is a terrible time for you, but there are some things that need to be attended to. Would you give us permission for an autopsy?"

Sandy stared at her through tears and red-rimmed eyes.

"What? What things? Autopsy? Cut him open? Why?"

"It would tell the doctors what happened to your husband."

There was an awkward moment of silence. Then Sandy responded in a firm voice.

"Cut him open? NO! The damned doctors didn't want to cut on him when he was alive, and I won't permit anyone here to cut on him now that he's dead. Just help me get him home. I know what happened to him. We have said it all along. The damned army shot him, that's what happened to him and now he's dead and gone and now you want to cut him open so that you can tell me yes, he got shot and that's why he died. Well, fuck you all. No I will not give you permission."

A hospital social worker helped Sandy with the funeral home. Sandy was present, heard what was said, but did not comprehend anything.

Appearing calm and collected on the surface, but inside in a burning rage, she made the necessary arrangements with the funeral home. She politely refused their offer to ride home with Ralph.

"No, I need to be alone for a little while. You go ahead. I'll catch up with you."

She returned to the little waiting room, taking some comfort in the familiar surroundings, and retrieved a notebook from her purse along with a couple of coins. Her first call was to her sister. She was crying when she told her of Ralph's death.

She didn't notice the janitor, also present in the little waiting room, washing the same window, over and over.

The next call was more mysterious at first, but then she addressed the other party by name and that name was the name of a well-known TV talk-show host. The janitor gave up all pretense, and just stood by the window, listening to her.

Sandy's back was turned to him, but she would not have noticed him either anyway. Her mind was on the story she was telling. She told of their camping trip, how Marty died, how the world around them had changed. She told how they had learned of this big corporation, SERPAC, conducting testing without concern for the people in the area.

She talked for a long, long time. She did not notice when the janitor left without his cart. She was very, very angry now, and someone was finally paying attention to her. She did not reveal her friends' names "No," she said firmly when asked. "No, I can't do that. I need to talk to them first "

Finally, without so much as a glance at the ICU, she walked out of the hospital, climbed into the battered old truck and drove off. She didn't notice the man in the janitor's uniform, as he got into his car and followed her. She stopped for gas and a soda, and then headed for home.

Sandy was not familiar with the way home. Holsum had never really been part of her scene. When she set out, the highway was nice and straight. A few miles out of town, it became narrow and curvy. It had no shoulder, and certainly not designed for high speeds. Sandy didn't care about that at this moment. Her mind felt empty. She sipped her soda and turned the radio's volume up as high as she could stand. Between sips, she sang along with the radio. The noise helped her drown her thoughts.

She drove faster and faster. The man in the car following her had an increasingly harder time keeping up with her. But keeping up didn't really matter to him. He knew where she was going. Sandy rolled down the window, letting the wind play with her hair and dry the tears that had started to flow again. Slowly, she became aware of her surroundings and of her speed. She took her foot off the gas. When she stepped on the brake, the pedal went to the floorboard without resistance and without any braking action.

It felt as if she were stepping into Jell-O. No matter how much she pumped the pedal, nothing happened. Sandy reacted automatically, barely realizing what was happening. It didn't matter; she didn't care. When the brake didn't work, she just stopped pumping the pedal. Keeping her right foot off the gas pedal, she entered a tight curve at high speed and lost control of the truck. Her mind never registered the vehicle tumbling into the ravine She was numb and void of feelings.

The old pickup came to rest on its rusty top with Sandy dangling in her seatbelt. Then, out of nowhere, a man appeared. She saw him out of the corner of her eyes as he walked closer.

"Help me, please," she begged. "Please help me get out of here before the truck blows."

He did not respond. He stayed out of her full field of vision as he inspected the interior of the truck's cab. He saw how she was suspended by the seatbelt. She had a cut above her left eye. She must have hit the rear view mirror or something. Blood was trickling across her forehead and into her hair. Otherwise, she seemed okay. He finally spoke to her.

"I'll help you, just wait a moment."

"Thank you, thank you. Please hurry! I'm all tangled up in this damned seatbelt and I can't get it loose. Do you have a knife? I need to get home to my kids."

But the man already had walked to the back of the truck. He picked up a small red canister of gasoline, and systematically poured it over the exposed underside of the truck. Then he wadded up an old newspaper and placed it in the pooling gasoline. Then he stepped up to the driver's side of the truck and splashed Sandy and the inside of the cab with more of the fuel from the canister. He backed away and struck a match.

The roaring flames drowned Sandy's screams. The man ran back to his car and slowly backed up into the road, careful to stay in Sandy's tire tracks. A mile or two down the road, he pulled into an entrance to a field and dialed a number on his car phone. A male voice answered.

"Ron here."

"Tell me what I want to hear."

"Your problems are over."

"You are indeed a good man! Be sure to check with your bank later on."

Next, he dialed a local emergency number. He didn't have much to say. He just reported a car on fire, somewhere down Highway ZZ.

"No, I don't now exactly where. I'm headed into Holsum. I guess about ten minutes or so outside of Holsum, west bound."

He drove casually on. Not a bad day's work, he thought. Six figures in eight hours. He would need to return to the retreat to collect his baggage, but that would take all of five minutes. Then he would be off to a well-deserved vacation.

* * *

When the Holsum Volunteer Fire Department arrived, the overturned pickup was still smoldering. They had no trouble locating the fire. The black column of dense smoke led them. In the vehicle they found the charred remains of what could have been a person, and decided to get the Highway Patrol involved. The first trooper at the scene radioed for the County Coroner. The fire had been so intense that it had destroyed any identification on the vehicle. It seemed obvious that it could be a long time, in this rural county, before the charred remains of this truck would be identified.

Then one of the junior volunteers found a small brown handbag in the grass, just far enough away not to have been damaged by the fire. He opened it. There was a wallet, maybe ten or twenty dollars in assorted small bills, and some coins There was a check book with an ATM card, a driver's license and assorted pictures of kids and grown ups.

"Mr. Bodine," he yelled toward the group of adults gathered by the side of the road. "Mr. Bodine, look at this here." He held up the purse. They emptied the contents onto the hood of the Highway Patrol cruiser. The officer was on his belly in the grass, studying the interior of the charred vehicle from the passenger side. Curious, he joined the group

"It's amazing," he said to no one in particular. "This guy must have been unable to get the seatbelt off. It's buckled, but in the wrong place. He buckled into the connection of the passenger side. What do you have there?"

"Jimmy, here, found this in the grass, over there by the driver's side of the truck."

"Oh man, I think I know who this is." A young sheriff's deputy had just joined the group. He held the driver's license and checkbook in his slightly trembling hands.

Without saying anything further, he returned to his patrol car and started talking on the radio. He was pale and moving slowly when he returned to the group.

"Man, you are not gonna believe this. The other day we got a report from the hospital in Holsum that they had a man with a gunshot wound. The man had reported it himself as an accidental shooting. Him and the old lady were out in the woods, you know, foolin' around and the rifle goes off. Well, I just checked. He's dead. Just up and died. Complications, the hospital said. But guess what his name was?" He looked around. Nobody answered. Although they had seen the driver's license, nobody had paid attention to the name.

"His name was Ralph Holtzer, and he had a wife named Sandy Holtzer.

"This driver's license is made out to Sandra Holtzer."

Chapter 40

I read about Sandy's death in the newspaper the next evening. My supervisor had been nice enough to forgive me for not showing up at work two days in a row, and I owed her. So I found myself having to do a double shift. It was pretty busy at first, with lots of kids and adults playing ball and lots of kids and adults getting hurt. It was well after eight PM when I finally had a chance to take a break. Of course the cafeteria was closed by then. This always happens to me. I was stuck with having to eat one of those horrible vending-machine sandwiches, old and soggy.

Someone had left a newspaper on a table and I grabbed it. I almost choked when I got to page two. There was a picture of an overturned, burned-out pickup truck. The headline read, "TRAGEDY STRIKES AREA FAMILY TWICE. The story said that a local couple, Ralph and Sandra Holtzer had gone on a camping trip. Then the man accidentally shot himself and subsequently died of complications at a Holsum hospital. The wife was driving home, when she ran off the road for unknown reasons. The truck rolled and burned, and Mrs. Holtzer died in the fire.

The couple had two young children who will stay with relatives. A bank account has been set up for donations on their behalf.

My hands were shaking so hard, I could not hold the paper any longer. I sat there, with my hands folded in my lap to keep them from shaking. Marty dead, Ralph dead, Sandy dead. Only Sam, Tom, and me left. I dug a quarter out of my uniform pocket and dialed home. Tom had also seen the paper. He said there had been a story on the evening television news as well.

"Get hold of Sam," I said. "Let's meet him tomorrow, please."

I didn't have to beg. Tom had already contacted him, and Sam and his kids were on their way over. The grown ups would provide Pizza and videos for the kids. All would spend the night, and we would have plenty of time to talk. I went back to my supervisor, claiming a horrible migraine and cramps. I was able to talk my way out of that night shift.

I had wondered why nobody had called to tell us of Sandy's death. But then, I had never met any of Sandy's or Ralph's families. They wouldn't know us, or be aware that we had been together that weekend.

When I got home, Sam and the kids were already there and, so was the pizza. The delicious smell hit me when I came through the door. I was lucky, the guys had ordered three large pizzas and had plenty left. The kids were spread out in front of the TV watching some Disney movie. They had sleeping bags, and each had a special pillow. They all wore big smiles and had pizza sauce smeared on their happy faces.

I looked at Allen. I just love that kid. The emotions were simply overwhelming, and I retreated to the bathroom, just to be alone.

Chapter 41

The kids were asleep before we even gathered at the kitchen table. I had hoped they would be. My thoughts were racing in all sorts of directions. I deal with assorted crises everyday at work, and I think I handle them well. I have learned to stay calm and focused. Tonight, though, was completely different. It was too close to home. When it comes home, it's a completely different situation. Tom made one of his infamous pots of coffee, designed to resurrect the dead. And the three of us sat down at the round kitchen table.

"Well, guys." Sam looked at both of us. "It's just the three of us now. Sort of like we started out a long, long time ago."

"I just want to stop whatever is happening and get my life back." I blurted out. I felt tears filling my eyes. Tom held my hand.

"I've been doing a lot of thinking," He said slowly. Tom can talk real slow – slowly enough to drive you nuts if you let it.

"I've been thinking about everything that's happened and what we should be doing from here on. Rather, what we could do. I see lots of different possibilities here."

He took a deep breath. Sam knows him and just waited. I was nervous and tapped on the tabletop with my spoon.

"Chris, quit beating up on the table." Tom looked at me. " As I said, I have given this a lot of thought. I don't have an answer, just a theory."

"Come on, Tom." I made a face at him.

"Okay, okay. We know we stumbled onto some sort of experiment. What ever it really was, it's what killed Marty. We'll probably never know for sure what happened. Ralph and Sandy, that's totally different. Ralph got shot and then the wound got infected.

He looked at me.

"Chris, you told me while we were still on the river that you expected him to have problems. And Sandy also talked about an infection. So, let's just assume that Ralph's cause of death is the infection. Sandy, now, that's different." He took a sip of his coffee and I drummed faster.

"I talked with Sandy's sister this evening. Didn't really tell her who I was, just a friend calling and asking about the funeral arrangements. She said the pickup ran off the road and into a ravine just west of Holsum. The Highway Patrol had told them that she must have driven too fast, maybe fallen asleep, who knows. Either way, there were no markings on the pavement showing that she used the brakes. They did notice some fluid spots, just ahead of the curve, which could be brake fluid, but it's a well-traveled road. She also said that Sandy was buckled in wrong, and that they found her handbag, undamaged, outside the vehicle. That's how they knew who she was."

I was stunned! I didn't know these details. The paper didn't say anything about being buckled in wrong or about the bag.

Tom went on. "I think there was foul play involved. But I cannot figure out who is behind it." He paused and looked at us.

"What about the military?" I asked. "The SOBs shot Ralph, why not also do a number on Sandy?"

Sam shook his head.

"No, I don't think so. They saw us. They know we saw them, and they have too much to lose to come after us. No, they will maintain a very low profile. I think Ralph's getting shot was pure coincidence, the result of Sandy's behavior. It was wrong, but still I think that's the way it happened."

"You heard what Ginny and Doc Humphrey said about that corporation down there doing testing and all that. What if they are behind it?"

"I hadn't given that angle any thought."

"Try. It's just too much. They are testing something that is supposed to make crops mature faster, and what happened with Marty was a natural process, only in fast forward."

Tom started to sound angry.

"And besides, what does all this mean for us? Have you noticed any strange henchmen hanging around?"

He stood up and peeked into the living room to check on the kids.

"I haven't, but if there was foul play with Sandy, I doubt that she would have noticed."

We were quiet for a moment, waiting to hear what he had to say.

"I guess what I'm trying to say is that we won't know if there's someone after us until it's too late. We can't control this situation at all. We have nothing to work with. I just think we ought to quit panicking over something we can't control and get on with our lives. I doubt they even know who we are and, if we maintain a low profile, they never will."

There was silence. I wasn't all that convinced. Usually Tom is right, but...

"I need to take care of Marty," said Sam. "I need closure. This is all still like a bad dream to me, and it's hard to keep up a facade for the kids. They think she's visiting some friends and at some sort of beauty seminar. Some of her customers are calling the house and asking about her. I can't keep that up too much longer."

"What did you have in mind?"

"Like we talked about the other night. We'll go out on the lake and then report her missing. I'm not looking forward to it, but I really need the closure. It'll be rough on the kids." Sam closed his eyes.

"Did you have a particular weekend in mind?"

"No, just the sooner the better."

I looked at the wall calendar.

"I have to work this weekend, and I'm in enough hot water the way it is. So you guys might want to go without me."

"We'll need the kids along."

"I can't do this." Tom shook his head. "I can't just sit here and plot how we will let Marty disappear. It feels like killing her. I know we did nothing wrong, but it still bothers me."

Sam and I just looked at Tom. Sometimes he is really hard to figure out. Most of the time I agree with him, but not this time.

"Come on, honey," I said. "Look at everything that's gone wrong in the last couple of days. It's been horrible. The three of us are the only ones left of the six friends who started out. We are in this together and, if we are going to survive this, we need to stick together. That means planning things together. I can appreciate you feeling uneasy, but we need to talk about this. I need to talk about it."

"So, what's your theory?"

"Mine? I think we were in the middle of that big experiment. But think something went wrong and they need to get rid of anyone who could cause them problems. Somehow they identified Ralph and

Sandy, or they just waited until someone with a gunshot injury showed up in the ER. Then they somehow killed them both. I have no idea if they know of us or not. Anything's possible. But I do think, that since Sandy's sister didn't know any of us well enough to call us, we should be ok. There is no way to trace us to that damned river, is there?"

"Well, we did leave our canoes in the brush down there. I know ours is registered with its serial number. That can be traced."

Sam shook his head. "I really doubt that we'll have any problems. The area is just so remote, and we were not at a regular river access, just off an old gravel road the local farmers use to get to their fields. I doubt that it's even on any maps. We could go back down there in the morning and get the canoes."

The idea sent chills down my spine. I shook my head.

"Oh no, we don't!"

"I'd just as soon leave well enough alone, at least for now." I was glad to hear Tom agree with me.

"So what do you suggest?" Sam seemed frustrated.

"I think I'll call the police and report the canoe stolen. Other than that, I think we ought to just live as normally as possible. Maintain a low profile and don't draw attention to ourselves. Let time be our friend and take it one day at a time."

Tom looked at us. Sam nodded and so did I.

"Yes," said Sam. "I like that. Maintain a very low profile and let's see what comes up. But we still have to deal with Marty. We can't go to the authorities with the real story. There's not enough of a body anymore, and I'll end up in the funny farm.

"The kids and I need closure. I'd like to do the boat thing and do it pretty damned soon. Get it over with. Let's seriously talk about this weekend, guys."

"I'm out," I said. "At the most, I could trade and do a double on Saturday and then join you on guys on Sunday."

"Sounds good." Tom squeezed my leg under the table.

"What about the kids?"

"They'll be very busy! I have spent a little time thinking about this You see, there's a water park complete with one of those huge slides and a wave pool and all that. We'll take them there and run them ragged. I will tell mine that their mother will be joining us after work

They know that can be after dark, so it's no big deal. They have only asked me a couple of times so far where Marty is, and I told them she is at some seminar. They're cool with that. Your kid will be there and, with Chris joining us the next morning, it will all seem very normal. What do you think?"

I nodded in agreement, the plan sounded good.

Tom, my reborn smoker, lit a cigarette and said, "Are you going to make the boat arrangements or do you want me to?"

"I can do it, I have lots of down time at the moment, and it will help me get through this week. Thanks for the offer."

"So we'll reconnect by Thursday evening and confirm everything?"

"Sounds fine. Hey, would you mind if I call Ginny and ask if she and the Doc would like to join us?"

"Great idea," I said. I liked Ginny and had hoped we would maintain contact with her. "But, just in case, mind you, let's not go into details on the phone, okay?"

Chapter 42

The week flew by. It seemed that either Allen or Tom had a ball game every evening, and I had work. Sam, Tom and I decided not to go to the funeral for Ralph and Sandy. We wanted to, but after some hard thinking we had to admit that we were worried about being identified and decided it would be better to stay away and not be connected with them.

Neither Ralph's nor Sandy's families had ever met any of us, and staying away was easy. Ginny did go to the graveside service. She admitted being nosy. She promised to tell us all about it, but I was not looking forward to that conversation!

I had to do some serious sucking up to get back on my head nurse's good side. By managing to work an extra nightshift and rearranging my schedule for next week, I managed to get scheduled to work seven a.m. to seven p.m. Saturday. That put me back on my boss's good side and worked out well for all of us, as it would get me down to the lake by eight p.m.

As we had planned, Tom, Sam, and Ginny spent pretty much of the day with the kids at the water park. They stuffed them full of junk food and kept them running until the adults finally ran out of energy. I reconnected with them on the pontoon boat Sam had rented for the weekend. By the time I got there it was almost nine p.m. and the kids were cleaned up and ready for bed. All three greeted me with hugs. Sam's little girl told me that her mommy would be there pretty quick too, that she had to go to a special class to learn how to make people pretty. It tore me up to hear that, and I had to remind myself that there was nothing I could do to change what had happened to Marty.

We motored out toward the center of the big lake and got away from the parties at the shore. Close to midnight, we stopped the engine and sat on the deck, drinking wine coolers and looking at the stars. Had it only been one week since the river? I found that hard to believe. It seemed like a bad dream from a different life. I saw a shooting star, closed my eyes, and wished for Marty to come out of the cabin and whine. She didn't. We were on our second wine cooler when Ginny finally told us about the funeral.

"It was a simple service. Nothing fancy, just family and friends gathered at the graveside. The minister said very little. I got the impression that the two families did not get along very well. Makes me wonder how the kids will do growing up. Right now they are with Sandy's sister. I heard they will stay with her during the school year, because that keeps them from having to change schools."

"Did anybody ask you who you are?"

"Yes, as a matter of fact I was asked that. And Chris, you will not believe who asked."

"Who?"

"Remember when we went to the hospital in Holsum to get your Blazer? The janitor who came out of the ICU, the one with all the gold and expensive cologne?"

I couldn't remember.

"Come on," said Ginny, "surely you didn't forget so soon? Good-looking fella, early thirties. Wore hospital scrubs with some serious gold on him. I mean bracelet, necklace and that cologne! I still can't remember the name, but it's a three-digit price tag."

I seemed to vaguely remember something about a janitor, but nothing solid. Ginny gave up on me.

"Well, anyway, guys, you will not believe it, but he was at the funeral. Dressed up, in a nice dark suit. Silk, probably. Nice, tasteful and expensive! I have never encountered a janitor with that kinda taste and the wallet to support it! He's the one who asked me if I was family or friend? Acted as if he belonged to the family. Even offered me a seat with the family. But he was dressed too classy to fit in with either family. I told him I was just a co-worker of Sandy's and was paying my respects, and didn't need special seating. I didn't stay long after that."

"Where do you think he fits in? Army?"

"No, definitely not. I really don't know where he belongs. It took me a while to place him. He has this really ordinary face. You can look at him all day long and not remember what he looks like. If it hadn't been for that cologne, I would never have made the connection. I think its Halston."

"Halston? What is Halston?"

"The cologne, men's perfume whatever. I think its Halston. I don't know if it's really a three-digit price tag, but it's definitely not in your average janitor's budget."

I didn't care about Halston, or whatever perfume the janitor wore, but I cared that someone who had seen Ginny and me at the hospital in Holsum had shown up at the funeral.

"Did he only ask you, or did he also ask others who they were?"

"I saw him ask several people. Interestingly enough, he only asked people in our age group. Who ever he was, he was fishing for information. I doubt he got anything. Actually, I don't think he recognized me. The day we went to the hospital, I was still in my old grubby farm clothes and I had my hair all up in a ponytail. I got dressed up for the funeral. Gotta do that every once in a while, or sometimes I don't recognize myself."

I wasn't really listening. I couldn't. The wine, the stars and the slow rocking motion of the boat started to make me feel sleepy. I must have dozed off, because all off a sudden I heard Tom softly calling my name over and over. I opened my eyes and he smiled at me.

"Been a long day for you, hasn't it sweetheart. Come let's go to bed."

He held out his hand, and I gladly let him lead me to our bed for the night. Morning would come soon enough.

Chapter 43

I awoke to the delicious scent of fresh coffee. The sun was peeking into the cabin, and I had to admit that I felt great. Then I remembered that this is the day Sam would have to report Marty missing. It would be very important that our stories were straight. I didn't have time to contemplate that, though.

When I went after my cup of coffee, Sam was talking to two Water Patrol officers. Their boat was tied up at our side. We were a lot closer to the shore than I remembered, and I certainly didn't wake up when they arrived.

Sam seemed genuinely upset, he was pale and he was pacing.

"What's going on?" I asked of no one in particular. Sam turned to me.

"Marty is missing. She went swimming last night, and I fell asleep in one of those lounge chairs. When I woke up, she was nowhere to be found. I went in the water looking for her, and found nothing! So I radioed the Water Patrol."

I didn't know what to say. I just sat down and held on to my cup of coffee. Slowly, one at a time, the kids appeared and Ginny joined us. The officers' uniforms impressed the kids, and the boys were quick to point out the pistol each officer carried. I pulled the kids away from Sam and herded them back into the cabin for breakfast. Let Sam tell his kids what's going on, I thought. Finally the officers left. After making sure each kid wore a life jacket, I turned them loose in the water in front of all the adults, and then joined the group for my second cup of coffee.

"So far so good."

Sam looked tense, pale, and uncomfortable.

"You heard what I told them. They said they would alert the other boats on the lake and the other officials, and get a search party going in the area where we last saw Marty. They asked us to stay in the vicinity and to check in with their station before we headed home. They will search the lake, and they said they pretty much know where a body will drift to in these waters."

215

"They were concerned because the spillways were open for a while last night. The body could have ended up in the river below the dam and then she may never be found. Anyway, they will be searching for her. I've already told them we would be leaving here by noon today."

"Daddy, where is Mommy?"

Sam's little girl had climbed back on board.

"I wanna show her how I swim."

Sam pulled little Samantha closer and held her tightly. With tears running down his face he whispered. "Mommy went swimming last night and didn't come back."

"Mommy drownded?"

His voice failed him and he just hugged her closely, rocking back and forth. Samantha is such a little doll, and she definitely is Daddy's girl. She has Sam's coloring and personality. I haven't made up my mind yet about her brother.

"You're squashing me."

"I'm sorry, baby."

"Daddy, are you crying?"

"Yes, baby, Daddy is very upset."

"It'll be okay, Daddy. Mommy, will be right back, you'll see." Samantha put her arms around Sam's neck, hugging him as only Daddy's little girl could.

I felt myself choking and turned away, not wanting to add to the confusion of the children. Allen stood in the background watching. I went to him and held him to me. He may think he's a man, but to me he will always be my baby. No one spoke for quite some time. What was there to say in a situation such as ours? The adults knew what was really happening, and that did not lessen our grief.

We quietly packed up our belongings and returned to the marina. To our surprise, reporters and others who had heard the missing persons report bombarded us. One of the reporters asked Sam if he realized that his wife was the twenty-first drowning in the state this summer alone. And I watched Sam come unglued. He's really getting into this, I thought.

"No!" he said firmly. "My wife is not a drowning, my wife is my wife. She is the mother of my children and all we know right now is that she is missing. We last saw her swimming. For all we know, she may be in some remote cove, trying to find a phone to call someone, to tell us she is all right. I will believe that my wife drowned when we find her body. And then she will be my dead wife. She will never be just a drowning."

That was the last sentence I heard out of Sam to any reporter. He just did not answer any further questions. We drove home in separate groups. I took all the children in my car, so that Tom, Sam, and Ginny could talk. I'm glad I did. The kids were wonderful. They talked about what happens when people die, and they turned an absolutely tragic moment into something magical. I hope they will keep this magic with them.

At Sam's house, we separated once more. Ginny picked up her car and left. We stayed with Sam for a while longer. He needed the help. The kids needed to get settled in, and he had to make calls to Marty's family. It was a long evening.

After actively searching the lake, the spillway, and sections down river for two days, the Water Patrol notified Sam that they were ending their search. Notices were posted all over the area encouraging the public to be on the look out for Marty's body. After two more weeks without any results, Sam contacted an attorney and had Marty declared dead.

Almost a month to the day after our ill-fated canoe trip Sam was finally able to bury Marty. The memorial service was typical Sam: Brief, simple and understated. It's intent was solely to bring closure to a chapter of Sam's life.

Then we drove out to Ginny's, we let the kids run and play with her assorted animals. While they were busy chasing chickens and little goats, we visited Ginny's garden. Here, underneath the apple and peach trees, the air scented by flowers, we scattered the meager, powdery remains of Marty. The bees buzzed around us as if in homage. Ginny had set an old garden bench under a twisted and bent old apple tree. There we left Sam to his thoughts.

I don't know who wore out first, the kids or the goats. When the kids finally retreated to the shade of the covered front porch, we had cold Kool Aid and cookies waiting for them. And we did not make them wash up. Even Doc Humphrey dropped by, and Sam rejoined the group, smiling and appearing happier than I had seen in a while.

217

When the kids returned to their games, we were able to talk openly and to our relief learned that no one had come around asking questions. Aside from the one little article in Doc's paper, nothing had appeared in the local press.

Ginny said she had driven past the mysterious corporate retreat quite frequently, but noticed no unusual activity.

"You might consider the total lack of activity unusual." She had said.

* * *

The dog days of August came, and with them the activities that lead into the new school year. Tom had to prepare for his lessons, and I was busy coping with Allen's most recent growth spurt. Sam had taken the kids to Marty's parents for a few weeks and used their absence to do some remodeling on the house. He was still undecided if he should keep it or sell it. It was really hard for him to deal with the memories. In the end, the kids made up his mind for him. When he asked, they told him that this was home and this was where all their memories of Mommy were. Sam also spent a lot of time in Ginny's garden. I began to wonder if he went there to visit Marty or if he went there to be with Ginny. Whatever the reason, it was a positive note in Sam's life, and the children thrived with each visit.

We all met once more for Labor Day at Ginny's. The guys cooked on the BBQ, and Ginny and I sat in the shade of the covered front porch watching Samantha chase chickens. One of the many dogs around Ginny's place had a litter of puppies. I don't know who found whom first, but when puppies and kids connected, the laughter did not stop.

The new school year brought an end to our summer frolic. Sam called weekly with progress reports for the kids, and every call also had news of Ginny. I recognized a romance in the making, but Tom thought I was being too much of a romantic.

"Sam's just after Ginny's body" he'd say. Whatever it was, there were sparks, and I liked it. Ginny is good for Sam and for the kids. They are so incredibly compatible. With October came cooler temperatures and nature's changing colors. The guys were planning for

218

deer season, and this would be the year Allen would get to go and shoot.

I suppose that's sort of a rite of passage. It's okay. I love being outdoors too, but I want to be at home in my nice warm bed over night.

One rainy Friday evening, while the kids watched spooky movies and we played cards, Sam quietly asked us what the proper time of mourning would be for him. Needless to say, that question raised at least my eyebrows. Tom, of course, never batted an eye.

"Depends," was all he said. Me, I just asked Sam what he had on his mind? And he shared with us that his relationship with Ginny had really blossomed into something very special and wonderful. That the kids just loved her, that he was tired of being alone. He had been thinking about asking her to marry him.

"So, what are you waiting for?" asked Tom, the great communicator. Me, I just cried, I felt so happy for Sam. Our acceptance opened the floodgates and he talked almost nonstop all evening long. I had not seen Sam this animated since that ill-fated canoe trip in the summer. He planned a whole weekend around the big question, right there in our kitchen, and I must say I felt like cupid helping him plot.

Of course, I did not agree with his choice of weekends. Why would you plan a romantic weekend and propose marriage on Halloween weekend? His only reason was not one of romance, but one of convenience. The kids would be spending the weekend from Friday evening until Sunday afternoon at Marty's parents. He could devote his time 100 % to Ginny.

There is no arguing with that kind of logic.

Chapter 44

October thirty-first is Halloween, and I will now remember it as the day my life changed – again.

This year Halloween was on Saturday, and Tom and Allen were out cutting firewood. I was scheduled to work another twelve-hour shift, from seven a.m. to seven p.m., in the ER. It's not my favorite, but wasn't a real problem since my guys would not be home until late and would have eaten dinner somewhere along the way in some greasy burger joint.

About three o'clock, I finally had my long overdue lunch break. I decided to remote-access our telephone answering service. The system told me that we had two new messages. Worried that something might have happened to my guys, I punched P for PLAY on the number pad of the pay phone.

"Hello, my name is John Saylor, I'm with the Missouri Department of Conservation. Some fishermen recently found two abandoned canoes. I was able to trace one of the serial numbers to a Thomas A. Landly. I have secured the canoe at my station and if it's yours, you can reclaim it at your convenience. Call me at 765-2584, and let me know when you are coming. Oh, and be sure to bring ID with you."

I sat stunned for a moment, I had forgotten about the canoes. After all, it had been a couple of months. I had not been back to that part of the state, and really had no desire to go. I felt overwhelmed by the thoughts racing through my brain. It seemed like just yesterday when Tom and Sandy had pushed those canoes into the brush with plans to retrieve them at a later time. Things being what they are, however, none of us ever did make that return trip. I can only guess that when fall eliminated the foliage, the canoes once again became visible. I felt my throat closing. I could only hope it was just a couple of fishermen who had found those canoes. And did they have to be so damned honest? Couldn't they just have kept them?

I pushed S to save the message and then P to play the next message. With the first words I felt the hair on the back of my neck rise.

"Hello there, Mr. and Mrs. Thomas A. Landly. My name is

Jonathon Brooks and I am with SERPAC. I believe you know who we are. We really should talk. Please, call me so I can arrange everything. I am so looking forward to finally meeting you. Oh, do bring your son along. Bye now."

My hands were shaking as I quickly punched the code to save the message. I felt my heart racing, my throat closing. Oh no, I thought over and over and over. Somehow I made my way back to the ER and into the nurse's lounge. We have a big recliner there, that's where I curled up, trying to hide within myself. Of course my solitude didn't last long. One of my coworkers walked in, took one look at me and said,

"Chris you look like shit. What happened?"

I explained that I just didn't feel well – not a real lie, but not the whole truth, either. She left and returned with the house supervisor, who told me I had been working too hard and really ought to take some time off. Then she sent me home. On jelly-legs, I wobbled out of the building, climbed into my car and headed home. But in the car, the significance of the phone call suddenly hit and I started to cry. I really wanted to stop the tears, but it was as if someone had opened floodgates – the tears just flowed and flowed.

I made it home, but then I sat in the driveway with the engine running and I couldn't leave the car – couldn't walk into the house. I don't know long I sat there and I can't explain why I felt safer in the car than in the house. Tom and Allen's return, and the arrival of little trick-or-treaters, finally brought me out of my stupor.

Later, after Allen was asleep, I told Tom of the calls. I cried, but this time more out of anger and relief. Tom, my wonderful Tom, just hugged me and held me. "We'll be okay," he whispered. "Come on now, honey. Help me think of what to do."

"We could just run away," Was my instant response.

Tom just held me even closer.

"Would that solve anything, running? And where would we run? What about Allen? Our families?"

"Tom, I'm scared to death of these people. Look at what's happened to Marty, to Ralph and Sandy. I don't want to end up that way and I definitely don't want you to end up that way, either. And Allen…" I sobbed.

221

Tom just held me, almost a little too tight.

"Why don't we just wait and see?"

I pulled back and looked at him. "Wait?"

"Well, yes. They didn't leave a phone number. If we call, we admit that we know who the hell they are and that we are the people they are looking for. If we run, we accomplish the same thing. But if we don't do anything, don't react to the call, they may just think that we are the wrong people. You know, something like a wrong number."

I couldn't believe I was hearing him correctly.

"Do you really think this is a good idea? Just think of Sandy? What if they come after us?"

"Let's just be careful and stick close to home for a while. But let's also just wait and see."

Reluctantly I agreed. Tom has never steered me wrong.

Two days later, just before supper, the phone rang. Tom answered it.

"What are you trying to sell me? I have no idea what you're talking about, you've got the wrong number." He hung up shaking his head. The look in his eyes told me it had been them. He just didn't want to talk openly in front of Allen.

Chapter 45

Two days later, we had Sam and Ginny over for pizza. We parked the kids in the den in front of the big TV, with a movie and lots of food, while we gathered in the kitchen.

Bringing Sam and Ginny up to speed didn't take long. Everyone agreed that we needed to maintain our position and continue with "you must have the wrong number."

For the moment, at least, we were up against an unknown enemy. For some reason, I felt no fear. I had replaced fear with anger. Plain, simple, pure anger. How dare these bastards try to invade my world? How dare they threaten me? How dare they?

After Sam and Ginny left, I snuggled into Tom's arms for the night. I felt better. The anger was very therapeutic, and I always feel safe in Tom's arms. I can handle this, I thought, as I drifted off to sleep. I can handle this.

The next morning, I wasn't so sure anymore. As I escorted Allen to the school bus stop, I noticed an unfamiliar white Lincoln Towncar parked across the street from our house. Its dark, tinted windows prohibited a view of the inside. I felt watched and exposed, but I also felt angry again. Angry enough, in fact, that it took every ounce of self-control not to walk over and ask, "What do you want from us?" But I didn't. I told my self over and over to keep cool, act normal. After seeing Allen off, I called Tom.

Tom was home at noon, and within ten minutes our doorbell rang. A rather plain and ordinary looking man, who introduced himself only as Ron, said he was with SERPAC. Tom tried to get rid of him at the door, insisting he had the wrong people, but he was most persistent. We asked him into the kitchen. I even offered him coffee. A really smooth talker he was!

"SERPAC, the company I represent, conducts agricultural research. We recently did some testing and found out afterward that some people were in our test area even though we had sealed it off." He smiled, but I could see the ice in his eyes. "I understand you like the outdoors?"

Tom just nodded his head. I couldn't answer. My stomach was tied in knots; I felt scared of this man.

"Folks," he continued, smiling that phony smile. "We have reason to believe that you were out and about, possibly in that area. And that's okay! It's just that because of the nature of our tests, we'd like to have our medical people look you over. You know, monitor you for a while. Make sure you're all right. Be on the safe side! Of course we'll cover all of your expenses. Whatever it'll take."

"Well, that's interesting." Tom sounded confident and calm. "But I keep telling you, you have the wrong people."

"Chris, Tom!" He spread his arms as if to hug us. "Your canoe was found along Coon River, at a pretty secluded spot. Our testing took place along that river. Come on now, help me out a little. Make it easy on yourselves! After all, I'm only trying to help you!"

Tom spooned some sugar into his coffee mug and stirred almost hard enough to wear out the bottom of the mug. It showed the emotions churning within him. Tom prefers his coffee black. I could sense his anger. I wanted to jump up and scream, but fear held me back.

"Our canoe was stolen some time back." Tom sounded so calm. How did he do that? I admired his strength. "Whoever took it are the people you are looking for. Sorry, we can't help you."

I nodded in agreement and could only hope to look as calm and unruffled as Tom did.

Ron slowly sipped, staring at both of us.

"There is a lot at stake for SERPAC, I hope you understand. The industry being what it is…" He paused. "We have a lot of competition out there. This was a very, very valuable experiment. Of course, SERPAC would reward you handsomely if you would come and live in our corporate compound for a little while. We only want to make sure all is truly well."

"You don't seem to understand." Tom sounded firm and in charge. "We haven't been canoeing this summer because our canoe was stolen. We are not who you want."

"No, YOU don't seem to understand the position you are in. You have information within you that is of extreme value to SERPAC. It is equally valuable to our competitors, regardless of whether you are dead or alive. That puts you into a very precarious position.

"You need to understand that. We want to help you, and at the same time we want to learn from you. That means we need you to spend some time with us. But at the same time, we simply cannot allow any of this to fall into the hands of our competitors. Under any circumstances. If you do not wish to cooperate with us - so be it! But understand there will be consequences. You have a son, don't you?"

That did it for me!

"Now you listen to me!" I was up, my blood was boiling, and I was ready to kill. "My husband has been extremely patient. How dare you come into our home and threaten us? How dare you threaten my son? Get out of my house, you bastard!"

I felt Tom's hand on my forearm. His firm grip was reassuring. But I wanted – I needed – to release my built-up anger.

"I don't know what you're talking about, but let me make this perfectly clear to YOU. Come around me or my family, especially my son, and you will wish for the cops to…"

I did not get to finish my angry outburst. Tom stood up and put his arm around me.

"Ron, it has been entertaining, but you have the wrong people."

We stood up. He tried to shake hands, but neither one of us accepted the extended hand. All I could think of were Marty, Sandy, and Ralph. Oh no, I thought, there is no way I could touch you; I'd rather kiss a rattlesnake.

The doorbell rang. The goddamned doorbell rang!

Sam had two flat pizza boxes in his hands. Ginny was bright as a new penny, but just for a moment.

"We didn't get enough of this stuff last night," Sam grinned, turning toward the kitchen.

"We didn't expect to catch both of you at home…" Ginny stared at Ron's face.

For a mad moment I thought Tom was going to introduce Sam and Ginny. I inhaled sharply. Don't introduce this creep - my mind screamed - oh God please don't! Just kick his ass out of here!

But Tom just held the door open with his left hand and pointed out with his right.

"OUT!" he said in a no nonsense tone.

The son of a bitch left. With shaking hands and a racing heart I slammed the door behind him, hoping it would hit him in the ass.

"My God, Chris!" Sam looked concerned. "Are you alright? What the hell was..."

"Who was that man?" Ginny sounded urgent.

"His name is Ron something. He is with SERPAC..."

"Chris, you're not gonna believe this, but that man was in Ralph's cubical in the ICU just before Ralph died. Don't you remember? You practically had to push your way past him to get out. Think back! The janitor with the expensive cologne and that gorgeous gold watch? That's him!

"I am certain! That man had something to do with Ralph's death and he also must have killed Sandy. To me that means he's behind Marty's death too."

My knees began to buckle. I found a couch and collapsed. Tom sat next to me as I sobbed my brains out.

Chapter 46

Outside, daylight had become darkness and it was much colder than earlier in the day. As he walked toward his car, he could feel the stinging of freezing rain on his face. For five seconds, Ron allowed his thoughts to drift to the warm breeze that had washed over him just days ago as he lay basking in the sun of the Bahamas. The moment passed. He was too focused on the problem at hand to dwell on warm breezes. The big car's engine came to life and warm breezes from the heater soon surrounded him. He drove about a block and a half, out of sight of the house he had left, and stopped again. There he quickly dialed a number on his cell phone.

"We have a problem," he said to man who answered.

"Oh?" The response was short but then he was used to Jonathon Brooks' style of communication.

"Let's sit down and go over this in person."

"I trust your judgment, but if you think that is really necessary..." Jonathon Brooks' voice was void of emotion.

"I do. I could be at the hotel in about fifteen minutes."

"Fine, I'll wait for you in the lobby. Then we can drive over to Smitty's. I understand they have excellent steaks and the best beer in town."

"Sounds like a winner."

They met at the Excelsior Suites Hotel, and in minutes they were on the road.

Jonathon Brooks adjusted his seat to accommodate his large body. "Towncar, nice choice! Is it a local rental?"

"Oh no, from the airport in Kansas City. I like the way it handles, a smooth ride too."

Jonathon Brooks nodded in agreement.

"Where is this Smitty's?"

Jonathon Brooks chuckled, he was known for his ability to find the best food in town, no matter where he went. Today was no exception.

"The clerk at the front desk gave me detailed directions, turn right."

They followed the expressway, made a couple of turns, and were in the downtown area. Smitty's was situated in an alley off a side street, and had convenient parking next to the building. As they turned into the alley, Ron noticed how his rear wheels slid ever so slightly. Getting slick, he thought, and considered checking into the Excelsior Suites himself for the night. There would be time for that after business and dinner.

Jonathon Brooks did, indeed, have a knack for finding a good place to eat. They had cocktails and then dined on steaks and genuinely great beer, taking their time.

"I don't get it," said Jonathon Brooks, finally, between bites. "These are the right people, aren't they? Why aren't they dead? If they were out there, why aren't these assholes dead like those soldiers? If we eliminate the wrong people, we draw attention. If we leave them be and they are the right people – oh what a nightmare! Our futures are in their puny hands. If we eliminate them and they are the right people, we'll never find out why they are still alive. What's your take on this mess?"

"I have considered a couple of scenarios." Ron cleared his throat. "I'm just not so sure these are the real people. Let's hypothesize: They're telling the truth, and their canoe was stolen. Then someone else used it that weekend on that river. That someone else got caught up in our test and has died, somewhere. Our problem is over."

"Yeah, right!" Jonathon's voice had an edge to it.

"No need to be defensive, Jonathon! We're just hypothesizing, after all. Sure, I have seen her in the hospital in Holsum. No doubt about that. But she is a nurse, and appearing in a hospital is not enough to link her to the river. I am certain I have never seen him before."

"So, what are you telling me?"

"I think we need to seriously consider what options we have. If we do nothing, these are the right people, and they talk, they can cause a lot of damage. If we eliminate them, we can control the damage and it won't matter if they are the right or the wrong people. And if we do this correctly, we can get our data from them as well."

Jonathon Brooks just shook his head.

"Can you believe this screwed-up mess? It started out to be so simple and then got completely fouled up. Too many people involved in the planning, that's what I did wrong. Should have kept it simple.

228

Well, we can still salvage everything, but we've gotta be fast."
Jonathon Brooks looked at his dinner companion.
"Can you eliminate these people? Clean, no traces, make it look like an accident?"
"What are we talking about?" Ron shrugged. "Two adults? You wanna include the kid? Is that it? I mean, once they're gone, is that all of them or will there be more popping up?
"Think about it. I really don't think we have a problem here. I think they will keep quiet. They know what's at stake. If we just monitor them, discreetly of course, we'll know what's developing with plenty of time to deal with it if we have to."
"What's with you? Getting cold feet?"
Ron shrugged again.
"Cold feet? No, I 'm just concerned that we will attract attention that we don't want. Keep in mind that this is a small town. A couple of people are dead already. Now some more? They were friends. Someone will make a connection. I don't like it. But if you want me to do this, I'll do it. But it'll be my last job."
"I don't see us as having much of choice, Ron. It's them or us. What guarantees do we have that they won't talk? AMAG is the future, and I am not willing to let that profit slip through my fingers just because a couple of locals decide to frolic on some godforsaken river at the wrong time. That's their own mistake. What business did they have there anyway."
"It won't be cheap."
"It's never been, my friend. What are you thinking off, double the usual?"
"Well..."
"Triple then, I don't care, just get it done. I want to be able to read the paper without worry."
"All right, but like I said, it's my last assignment. I am retiring after this one."
Jonathon Brooks just chuckled.
They finished their dinner, had a fourth beer and talked about anything but business. Football season was well under way and Jonathon Brooks was a diehard Cowboys fan. Ron didn't care. He wanted to return to his favorite island with the powdery white beach,

229

turquoise water and gorgeous women in thong bikinis.

By the time they stepped out of the building, the car's windshield was coated with a layer of ice. The heater quickly defrosted it, and Ron soon had them back on the expressway around the city. Although the hour was late and the weather nasty, there was still quite a bit of traffic; much of it was heavy semis. They traveled in the passing lane at 75, speeding past the slower trucks.

"Slow it down a bit. I don't want to become a statistic."

Ron turned his head and looked at his passenger.

"Don't worry, boss. This car is built for safety."

When his eyes returned to the highway in front of him, he saw red brake lights glaring at him. He saw them and his mind registered them as brake lights, but the recognition did not get translated and relayed to his right foot in time.

The white Lincoln Towncar plowed into the rear end of a flatbed load of steel beams at more than 75 miles per hour.

The crash sent the trailer off to the side. The Towncar skidded sideways and was immediately broadsided by the car behind them.

Neither of the men was wearing a seatbelt. Despite the airbags Ron's head hit the windshield with a sickening thud, knocking him out, as his chest crushed into the steering column.

Jonathon, propelled by his greater weight, went through the windshield. He bounced off the hood and cannonballed into the steel beams on the trailer.

He did not feel his bones braking or the protruding edge of a steel beam that pierced his skull.

As the momentum carried him on, he left behind a trail of blood and brains.

Chapter 47

My phone rang a little after seven. The hospital's house supervisor asked me to come in ASAP. Some of the staff had called off because of the lousy weather. I had wanted to sleep a little longer, but I was scheduled for a night shift anyway and so I agreed to go in. If Tom was concerned, he didn't show it. He just urged me to be careful.

My assignment that night would be as the float nurse. I would go where help was needed. From experience, I knew I would be bouncing all over the little hospital.

I had been on duty for less than ten minutes when my pager went off, summoning me to the ER, STAT.

A crowd had gathered: Paramedics, cops and nurses. The house supervisor, Rosie, pulled me off to the side.

"Thanks for coming. We had a pile-up on the expressway. So far we've received two men who were in a passenger car. Didn't wear seat belts. Pretty bad. You take one, I'll take the other."

"Any ID?"

"The cops and paramedics have all that info. Right now, we need to get them stabilized."

I walked over to my patient. The other nurses had already started an IV and were hooking him up to the monitor. One of the paramedics was filling them in.

"He was driving the car. Nearly went right through the windshield. Wasn't wearing a seat belt. Just another superman. His head must have hit the windshield, lots of blood on the inside. He was pinned by the steering wheel. We had a helluva time getting him out."

It took a few seconds for my mind to register the features of my patient, then it hit me: This was the man who had been at the house earlier, a Ron something or other. My legs felt like Jell-O. I didn't want to be here, I didn't want to help him. I wanted him to die.

I did what needed to be done, anyway. I did the job I was trained for, but I did not like it.

His vital signs stabilized some and I started to clean up the blood that seemed to be everywhere. The paramedics had put a foam brace around his neck. I thought about taking it off and choking this beast to death. But I'm a professional, and professionals just don't choke semiconscious people to death.

As I cleaned dried blood from his face, I noticed that his breathing seemed more labored. I knew I should call the doctor over, but I hesitated. In my mind I went over everything that had happened since that fateful canoe trip and I wanted this beast before me to die. But training took control of me once again and I called the doctor over. We rushed Ron to the CT scanner, and quickly learned why he had trouble breathing. The accident had fractured his cervical spine just below his skull and had damaged his spinal cord.

I didn't have to choke him. He had a broken neck and would be paralyzed for the rest of his life, if he lived.

I said a silent prayer of thanks.

We called Respiratory Therapy to stand by with a ventilator. He would be needing one soon. As we were starting a new IV line, Ron woke up and tried to speak. He could not move his head because of the neck brace. He probably couldn't hear me over the hissing of the oxygen and the beeping of the monitor. I tried very hard to keep out of his field of vision, but I still needed to check his blood pressure and listen to his lungs. That meant he would see me.

Just then someone crashed on the other side of the ER and, when the others rushed out of the cubicle, I took a deep breath and moved into his field of vision.

His eyes widened. He recognized me.

* * *

Ron did not remember hitting anything. He was engulfed in darkness and, although he could hear sirens and voices, he felt strangely detached.

The wet cold cleared his senses. There were bright lights, and he heard a voice ask him if he was all right. He struggled to sit up, angry that the voice told him to stay down. Nuts, he thought, it's cold here; I want to get warm. He didn't hurt, and he didn't feel anything but cold. Then the lights went out.

He regained consciousness in the brightness of the ER, acutely aware of the hissing of oxygen into his nose. He could hear a cacophony of other sounds and voices, but couldn't understand what was being said. He tried to turn his head away from the bright lights, but some awful force kept him from moving. Annoyed, he finally opened his eyes. His vision slowly cleared, and out of the corners of his eyes he could see people moving around him.

"Sir you have been in an accident," a male voice said. "You are in the hospital. You have some injuries and you must lie still. Do you understand?"

He tried to talk, but no sounds would come out. He heard the different voices, and one female voice seemed familiar to him. Where have I heard this voice? he wondered. Why is everyone so frantic? I feel okay. I'm not hurting anywhere. His field of vision was severely limited, and his eyes remained focused on the ceiling tiles and the big water spot directly over his head.

He became bored. He knew he was not alone in this room, but the people moved in and out of his field of vision too fast. Finally a face came into view, a female face. It took him a moment to recognize it.

Oh God! he thought. It's her! She knows everything, and I'm helpless. What is she going to do?

* * *

"Listen to me, you worthless bastard," I said slowly and softly, making sure only he could hear me.

"I know who and what you are and what you have done. We're playing by my rules now. I'll be cool as long as you are. But piss me off and I'll make damn sure that you never forget me. Do you understand?"

He didn't answer. He just blinked a couple of times. I assumed that meant yes.

Then the physician entered the cubicle with bad news for Ron.

"Sir, we have to put a tube down your throat and into your lungs to help you breathe." He was loud and brusque. "You fractured your neck and the broken bones have damaged your spinal cord. This is causing paralysis and is interfering with your breathing."

At the word paralysis Ron blinked rapidly and seemed to mouth

233

something to the physician.

"Yes, you are paralyzed." The physician moved closer to Ron. "From the neck down as far as we can tell at the moment. Right now we have to put a tube down into your lungs and help you breathe. Then we will see what can be done about the paralysis, I have called in a neurosurgeon. But first we need to get that tube in."

Ron stared at me, ignoring the physician. Perhaps he wanted to scare me, perhaps he was scared of me, I don't know and I don't care. I stared back, never blinking, willing my hatred of this man to burn deep into his brain.

The physician injected something into Ron's IV and he closed his eyes. It only took moments to intubate him. The respiratory therapist hooked him up to a ventilator, and another float nurse from ICU took over for me.

I washed up and walked over to the other cubicle. The patient, a huge man named Jonathon Brooks, had just returned from a CT scan. He was intubated and attached to life-support equipment. So this is Jonathon Brooks I thought. Until now he had only been a voice on the phone. The physician came up to me.

"Well," he said with a sigh. "If more people could see this mess, they may actually start using their seat belts."

"How bad is he?" I asked.

"Bad. There's massive head trauma. Part of his brain is gone. I don't really understand what's keeping him alive. And then there are numerous internal injuries. The bleeding is under control for now, but I really don't expect much from this one. Let's move him on up to ICU. The neurosurgeon can see him there, and Social Services can notify the next of kin. I don't even think he can be an organ donor – he's too banged up."

"What about this other fella?" I had to know. The physician shrugged.

"That's another sad story. He's a quadriplegic now, if he lives. His damage is so extensive, I doubt that even neurosurgery can salvage anything. We'll keep him going for a while, but he won't grow old."

I didn't know what to think, let alone what to do. Just a few short hours ago, this Ron had threatened us, and I knew that Brooks man was also involved. Now they were here before me, helpless vegetables.

I grabbed the phone in the utility room and called home. Tom's voice sounded sleepy, but not for long. When I finished my story, all he could say was:
"Wow!"

* * *

Ron heard the hissing of the ventilator and thought he felt his lungs fill with air. He was angry that the doctor had acted so fast and had not given him time to think, time to make his own decision. At the lowest edge of his field of vision he could see the tube that helped him breathe, and above him that ugly brownish water stain. Was this the same stain he saw earlier, or had they moved him? What had that doctor told him? Broken bones in his neck? Damaged spinal cord?

Oh my God! he thought, I'm paralyzed. He frantically tried to move his hands, arms, shoulders, anything. Nothing happened. He could blink his eyes, that's all. He stared at the ceiling stain.

Shit! he thought, I'll spend the rest of my life this way!

He had trouble staying focused and caught himself drifting off to sleep. In his mind he went back to late summer. He saw himself dousing Sandy's truck with gasoline as she hung suspended by her seat belt in the upside-down cab of her truck. He heard her voice begging him to cut the seat belt, begging him to help. He felt the rush, the incredible feeling of power that came over him when heard her screams. Then there was nothing, a void, total emptiness.

She was lucky, he thought. She died quickly. I'll spend the rest of my life here, with a fucking tube in my throat and a machine breathing for me while I stare at the damned ceiling and admire the stains.

Tears filled the corners of his eyes and pooled in his ears.

* * *

It took almost twelve hours to determine the extent of the massive head injuries to Jonathon Brooks. His family chose to have life-support discontinued. Thirty-six hours after the accident, he was dead.

* * *

Ron remained in ICU for almost two weeks. Then SERPAC arranged to have him transferred to a rehab facility in Virginia. He did not enjoy the journey. While his companions were able to marvel at the scenery along the way, he was forced to stare at the ceiling of the ambulance. There were three brown stains and two yellow ones.

The End